IMAGINE

Imagine

a novel

RICHARD A HARRIS

Richard A Harris

For my beautiful wife Tine who lived a life of courage, full of love for her family and filled by a great love for the natural world that she treasured and savoured. Loving mother to our two children Anneliese and Sean who adore their mother with all their hearts. She was taken too soon from us by a disease that she battled with dignity and strength for 18 years. Tine was the sweetest and most supportive partner a man could ever dream to have.

Imagine

Prologue

New York 40 years before I Day

"John, do you think we will ever have a world that is really like your song?"
John picked up his guitar and looked out over the Park and started strumming a few chords randomly.
"I don't rightly know love. I think the way things are going they're gonna go the other way."
His wife, dressed in black leather pants and a soft white cardigan with huge sunglasses wandered over to him and hugged him from behind, seeing, as he did, the children playing on the Alice in Wonderland statue at the edge of the Park.
"I'm serious John, think about it for a minute. Talk to me."
He put the guitar down and swung around to face her, pulling her in and giving her a passionate kiss before gesturing for her to sit down.
"Let's imagine this shall we? A world of intelligent beings, where love was the guiding principle. Let's see a world transformed in a day. Let's call it I Day or Imagine Day, a moment when everything changed and we were free to dance and sing and love one another without fear and restraint."
"That's beautiful John. But how? How could this happen?"
John picked up his guitar again and stared over the trees to the East side towers rising into the blue sky.

"If somehow we could figure out how to be truly intelligent, rational. I have no idea how it could happen but it could happen. I'm not sure I will see it in my lifetime, my love. We can still dream. We can still imagine."

"John, if it's ok, I am going to write that down and put it somewhere safe. Maybe someday will come and we can live just with love."

She couldn't help but notice the tears streaming down his face and she loved him more than ever. She didn't really know if they were happy tears or sad.

He looked over the green that stretched before him and wondered what would happen today in this strange and wonderful city. He imagined he wasn't the only dreamer.

Chapter 1

Afghanistan 5 years after I Day

"So, this is where it starts?" Amanda murmured.

They were staring out from the edge of the town.

"Yes, we travel soon." Gholam replied.

A lone kite flew above the flat-roofed city billowing in the gentle wind and drawing their eyes up to a startling blue sky. The laughter of children could be heard from every direction. The four of them walked through the markets where the men in traditional dress bantered with their customers. The colours in the wide, shallow round baskets were eye-catching with every local grain, fruit and vegetable bursting with freshness and promising deliciousness. Pomegranates, tomatoes on vine, saffron, wild rice, blueberries and wheat. They walked beyond the lentil and pepper sellers and again the laughter of children couldn't be missed. The group passed by the purveyors of meats where the smell of fresh vegetables was overpowered by the pungent variety of goat and sheep cuts; barrows of hoofs and heads not easy to ignore as they made their way through the market. Finally, the odours gave way to that open blue sky, arrayed with duelling kites of every design. The wind was picking up, and the streets were now full of eyes turned upwards. To see the men, women and boys manipulating their kites was like watching a dance of their practised arms. Strings invisible, hands and arms tumbled over each other in loving coordination. Their faces, the picture of concentration and joy.

Finding some shade Gholam organised doogh for the four, and they sat quietly appreciating everything about them. The cool drink finished with a crisp, fresh mint welcome as they sat to discuss their day. Everyone was excited and relieved to finally be here. It was such an eclectic group from all around the globe that had come to experience the culture and beauty of this ancient land. For so long it had been considered too dangerous to even think about travelling to, and now they were here to see as much as they could in the next two weeks. They had been discussing the whole trip for months.

Mark had seemed the loudest online but here he was quiet and considered. Amanda as vivacious in real life as she had been in the discussion forum. She was full with questions and possibilities and looking forward to adventures with her new friends. Gholam was the linchpin, eloquent in his welcome and the realisation of a special time in his land, straining a little in person with emotion, communicating in real life with the group now entrusted to him. Joe was the unknown quantity. No one had really gotten to know him but he was clearly intelligent and curious as well. He intrigued the entire group. Gholam dashed off to acquire a large batch of mantu and as he had promised, his friends devoured the local dumplings filled with beef, finished with the garlic and chickpea sauce. This was an exciting time. Sharing a meal for the first time as real friends and enjoying the cacophony of sounds and sights around them.

"So, what do they do in the mosques these days Gholam?" Joe asked.

They were sitting just below the grand structure. The lively minarets reaching up, intricate layers of tiles placed lovingly 700 years before. Wall upon impressive wall of patterns to fill the landscape with beauty. An imprint of care, design and thought to impose symmetry, asymmetry, colour and grandeur for the people to wonder upon for centuries to come. This was a place that had been the site of worship until very recently. A focal point for disparate groups to battle over. Where rival versions of Islam were debated and fought out. Amazingly, over the last 35 years it had been spared the brutality of the destruction of modern warfare that had wracked the rest of the country. The grounds were complex and they made their way beyond the outer walls and found themselves sitting within the shade of the vaulted garden Iwan, they waited for Gholam to explain what was happening inside.

He walked with them a little way to show them the details of the walls. What appeared from a distance to be intricate vines and flowers painted upon the surfaces became a dizzying array of tiny tiles of different colours carefully crafted together. The very notion of the planning and execution of this on such a massive scale impressed them. They gazed up to the higher domes, a brilliant turquoise against the cloudless sky blue.

"Would you like to come in?" Gholam gestured them inside.

They all nodded enthusiastically as they crossed the baked brick pavers that welcomed them into the inner world of the mosque. Via arched tiled portals where one walkway seemed to escort them into the next few arches they wandered. It was like an endless parade along history's walls as different perspectives of the massive inner sanctum were encountered. The silence of the courtyard was impressive. Sun shone on hedges and water features of exquisite and ancient design. Small trees and palms reminiscent of an Arabic oasis and flower beds of every variety were scattered about the courtyard. Rose bushes lovingly tended were to be seen in every corner.

They were about to enter the inner sanctum when Gholam turned to them and said.

"It's ok for everyone to come in. There are no longer any restrictions based on gender or culture. Please, however, take your shoes off as a sign of respect to our tradition and this special place."

He appeared excited and proud. Gholam could only hint online to the group of what they were about to experience. Now the first exhilarating moment had arrived. As it always did, his skin tingled at the back of his neck, as he entered quietly and reverently.

Amanda turned to Joe. She knew he had been fascinated with the history of this land and wondered what his expression was under that florid beard. His eyes spoke a gentle delighted surprise, and she was strangely drawn to their emotion.

Gholam led them inside. Again, the structure was magnificent, drawing their vision up along swiftly rising arches and complex octagonal structures. One visual cue supporting the other in a myriad of various patterns and shape and ever taking their eyes up to the highest domed structures. The magnificent capping a series of spirals and circles of floral images, inscriptions and a deep blue background rose to the cupola.

What lay before them was surprising and impressive as Gholam led them forward with some pride. On the far wall was an enormous LED screen. On this display was a wizened gentleman talking softly and surely. He was speaking Pashto, but there were English and Chinese translations in text at the base of the screen and a life-size picture within the larger image of a signing interpreter who was enthusiastically trying to keep up with the speaker.

They sat together within the main forum, cross legged on the floor. It was a very relaxed atmosphere with many smiles welcoming them into this ancient space. It became apparent that every nook and cranny of the building was now a hive of meeting places and discussion. The main talk was quite philosophical. The leading speaker was meandering about topics from preservation of local languages in a world that was increasingly becoming globalised to educational opportunities for locals in nearby districts and even overseas. It was heartening to hear that not only was there a chance for people now to come and see the beauty of this country but that they also were reaching out across the globe to teach, build connections and stimulate learning and to progress this place that had until very recently been so battered.

Joe decided to wander around the discussion groups and was delighted to be able to understand the trains of thought as the translational technology was so well set up. He sat in on a group discussing love and the nature of loving. He was surprised at the openness of the discussion. People were willing to lay their hearts on the table. Old men were giving their perspective on what love had meant for them. Young women were describing their confusions about the balance between completely giving their hearts away and the difficulty they had in understanding how men could commit to their love. It was beautiful to see the respect between the speakers and listeners. There was an intensity and commitment to try and understand each other. One man said that he only felt really fulfilled in his life when he was prepared to be generous with his love and give it away. It seemed to Joe that everyone here was doing precisely that. They were giving their thoughts, dreams and love away to each other in order to understand better and in doing so, making them whole again. So strange, he thought to see a culture turned around so quickly. No more was there a question of women being inferior or beholden to the men. The obvious confidence and expectations of the females was exhilarating, and the men had thrown their cultural barbarity into the fire and had learnt that now an equal footing, total respect and a listening heart created much better relationships and partnerships in life. This meant that their children would be brought up in a house of discussion, compromise, negotiation and equal rights. Joe could not have imagined a more enlightening conversation than this. He was able to shed tears of joy.

Mark and Amanda found themselves involved in an exploration of traditional tribal dance. Before long they were wheeling each other about in a mad frenzy of twirls and steps trying to copy the locals. Amanda was more skilled in keeping up with the syncopated drumming while Mark couldn't stop laughing as exhaustion started to overcome his initial enthusiasm. They formed a circle with their new friends, and a gentler, sensual dance began. They were given colourful scarves and slowly started with arms behind their backs, circling each other and swaying gently. Gradually the rhythm picked up, and arms became the lead for their bodies as first scarves, and then torsos started swirling and spinning. The broad skirts and scarves and hair almost became one organism. The group's frenzy increased, and it was impossible to not feel part of the energy and joy of the dance as the music's pace steadily grew. It was a blur of faces and smiles. They would never forget that moment as the music reached its crescendo and their eyes locked.

As the days' activities in the ancient building concluded and the enthusiastic crowd poured out into the warm evening the murmur of excitement mingled with the happiness of the townspeople as the streets came alive with the business of the evening meal. Huge pots were apparent outside and aromas were calling to the crowds for attention. It had been a somewhat draining day, but the group was keen to try the foods as Gholam suggested they try this and that. He also made sure everyone had an ice-cold beer to wash the flavoursome biryan, tandooris and chapli kebabs down. They sat on the steps of the market area as the far horizon ahead, and the mountains behind were suffused in the violets and pinks of sunset.

There was not a soldier or a gun to see.

The kites flew into the darkening skies, and the conversation turned to tomorrow's plans to explore the countryside. It seemed natural that Mark sat by Amanda's side as the evening closed about them, but Joe was closely following events and had become a little lost in the curl of Amanda's lips and the light that played with her eyes. Amanda was not quite aware of his eyes on her. She was busy talking to Mark and Gholam about the mistakes she had made during the dance of the scarves when it dawned on her that he was mesmerised. She broke his stare with a nod and a flick of her long ginger hair, brushing it back over her forehead and catching his gaze again.

Joe came to his senses for a minute.

"Have any of you ever met before?"

Gholam and Amanda looked at each other sheepishly.

Amanda replied. "A long time ago I met our host in a faraway land riding upon a tall white horse. We sat in the sun and we became instant friends. We have not seen each other since that day."

Gholam looked at Joe.

"Everybody fell in love with Amanda didn't they? She has been too busy these years shaping the world to ever see me in real life again. I also, as you know, have been engrossed in things that have taken me all over the world and back here to home. I cannot tell you how excited I am to have you with me now."

Amanda looked at Gholam as if for the first time and realized that she had been deeply in love with him all these years. He had a very odd way of talking and looking at the world through those dark brown eyes. He was strong and lithe of body and mind. She knew that she had arrived finally.

Their first morning of travelling had arrived and they headed to the two brand new Land Cruisers and the adventure to come.

"It doesn't matter how big your house is. It matters how big your heart is." Gholam said quizzically.

Everyone was so excited to be finally on the road, and they were going to the centre and the south. The skiing gear was already packed away and dreams of trekking the famous National Park, and lakes were on everyone's mind.

The road was excellent, and they quickly scooted along a combination of motorway and picturesque country road as they headed into the heart of the country. Gholam had instructed the drivers to mix up the route so that there was a taste of the once tortuous 8-hour trip. However, even the winding mountain roads were now fully sealed and engineered to move people across the unique landscape without the risk of sailing over the once narrow track into the green river valleys below. Looking up they were engrossed in the numerous old fortifications dotted along the mountain passes. These were elaborate constructions within such a barren and rugged environment. Gholam explained that these structures had histories going back to times even before Alexander the Great had briefly ruled this land. The villages they travelled through in the morning were full of happy smiling people, and they stopped at one or two to check out the food and the markets. The light brown stone of the housing and shops a perfect reflection of the escarpment's colour behind them. With the speed that they had managed Gholam had directed the drivers to head south via the spectacular Salang pass. Since the reconstruction, the road blistered through 16km of mountain tunnel and yet still provided spectacular views of the lower Hindu Kush mountains. This was a road where previously more than 40 people lost their lives every year, not counting the military deaths. Avalanche, collision and simply sliding off the mountain was commonplace. Now the journey passed with the fascination of the endless ridges of snow-covered mountains which reminded people of the Rockies in Colorado with their relentless height and shape.

Back down out of the mountains they headed west now to Bamiyan, the landscape became once again a little dusty with small streams cutting through granite beds as the road followed beside. It had been a long and memorable day of driving and the evening settled about them as they came to the first overnight stop of their adventure. In the tight river valleys, they were astonished at the number of dwellings that were cut into the side of the mountains.

As they pulled into Bamiyan, they were taken by their local hosts to one of these intricate structures. From what seemed to be so simple looking from the road, the dark arch lead into an impressive lobby. They immediately noticed how the relative cool of the outside was buffered once they were into the cave system. They were given a chai and sat in the lounge briefly admiring the reality of being in a space roughly hewn into the solid rock of the mountain. As they were led by a local with candlelight into the cave's interior, light flickering from the candles and the old kerosene lamps along the way, the rugged walls were naturally dramatic. On the way Joe couldn't help but take Amanda's hand for the briefest of moments. She looked up and gave him a smile in that light which he would take with him for the rest of his life. Taken to their rooms, they were all entranced with the artwork and comfort of their surroundings. Inside, alone, they were served by welcoming and courteous staff a simple and delicious meal and the absolute quiet of the caves was very calming.

Over a hearty breakfast they heard the harrowing tale of the local Hazara people and the way they had been so harshly treated just recently. They were told how in 2001 some of the men had been lifted by ropes placed round their waists with the threat of death if they were to refuse and told to drill into their sacred monuments. Forced to place explosives along the wondrous curves and artistry of these massive structures built around 1500 years ago. They were then forced to watch as their Buddhas were blown to rubble.

The morning was crisp as they gathered in the lobby in their hiking gear then headed to the cars. It was still so strange for them to hear nothing from the engines as the cars raced up the hill and on to Band-e Amir National Park. It had only been the last 12 months since electrification of the entire transport system worldwide had become compulsory. The roar of the petrol engine was becoming a dim memory, even in the most isolated territories.

The four of them felt that their welcome to this area had been extraordinary. It was almost as if they had all come home. The valley was stunning. Greener than they could have imagined right up to the dusty, rugged sandstone cliff face that could not be ignored, as they drove through the village. The cliff was almost entirely punctuated by the cave openings along its lower levels, but quickly the focus shifted fully to the near-finished restoration of the great buddhas. The fortuitous discovery by archaeologists and the recent successful erection of the giant sleeping buddha was a stunning engineering feat they couldn't miss as they motored past. This was the one stone buddha that the Taliban had not destroyed. It had lain hidden in the earth below a massive Buddhist monastery designed to protect this great statue. Legend had it that when it was erected the world would finally be at peace with itself. It now towered as high as the cliffs themselves some 300 metres into the blue, blue sky. On either side of the great buddha were the restored buddhas within their cave shelters. They were now completely gilded, the niches protecting them, decorated in bright and daring oil paints on the stucco of the inner sanctums. They were absolutely awe inspiring, shimmering in their colourful spaces. It was not the time to explore the restoration work today. They were on to the deep, blue lakes of Amir but this journey through here today would never be forgotten.

The trucks motored along the edges of the series of splendid lakes and waterfalls of Band-e Amir. It was too cold right now for wading or boating, and apart from the odd trekker there wasn't any activity on the lakes. The air was pristine as they hopped out for a better look. The way that the reeds gave way to various shades of aqua were simply stunning. The group stood high on ancient igneous rock formations with the view stretching across the deep blue lakes and beyond to higher waters, falling across untouched travertine marble spillways, into the lower reaches of the system. The slopes rising high above the water with the snow line low providing a stunning contrast to the water. This simply whet their appetites for the main business of the day, the powder snow of Bamiyan.

They packed back into the trucks and turned up the car heater to maximum and headed back along the road they had just come from. Past the giant Buddhas which once again stunned them and onto Jawzari. The infrastructure that had been placed here in the last five years was impressive. While some chose to live in the traditional mountain huts of the Hazari people most had adopted the modern lifestyle that went with a developing ski resort. But this was a very different ski resort. The first thing to notice was the wind turbines but not because they stuck out like a sore thumb, but rather they stood on the ridgeline like a thousand colourful Afghan kites. Somehow the engineering gave this illusion, and it was stunning. Every single roof of every unusual shape and design was a solar panel, and all were subtly changing their form to catch the shifting mountain sun from dawn to dusk. It was interesting watching their subtle movements as the shadow lines of the housing shifted over minutes. It reminded Joe of his days as a boy sailing and catching the shifting breezes on the harbour. They learnt that the lake before them that was now frozen formed part of a chain of an enormous hydro-electric system that not only powered Bamyan but contributed significantly to Afghanistan's total power needs. Every lift, every light in Jawzari, was powered by sustainable energies. More than 80 percent of the resort's waste was recycled including treated wastewater into the snow making system. The slopes looked colourful and challenging. Boarders and skiers were crisscrossing the mountain valley slopes and they couldn't wait to join them.

Chapter 2

California 3 years before I Day

"Pete, check this out!" Mike was excited.

The guys had been noticing some odd behaviour amongst the animals in the lab now for quite a while, but this was something else. They had been experimenting initially with a combination of ultrasound and radiofrequency wave transmissions but had added in a microwave component, and now the results were quite different.

With just the two initial wave sources they had found that behaviours could be significantly affected, appetites controlled, sleep patterns altered, and interactive response slightly modified. Now with the addition of the microwave, Mike quickly turned and physically hauled Pete up to the pens.

"Man, can you believe this?"

Pete's eyes were wide as he surveyed the activity. He'd never seen animals behave like this either in the wild or in the laboratory setting. There suddenly wasn't the jealous fighting for food, there was, in fact, an absolute absence of aggression. If anything, it appeared to the scientists that the animals were cooperating in gathering food for the group and even more astonishingly distributing it in what seemed a democratic and generous manner.

Pete turned the microwave element off, and within seconds behaviour reverted to normal. The typical staring contests, pushes, hisses and squawks were back. Fighting at the food pump resumed, and a bite recorded. Back on with the additional microwave component and the remarkable behaviour and cooperation returned. The colleagues stood and looked at each other, hardly comprehending what they were witnessing. Strangely, for the first time in their long days in the lab together, they found themselves hugging each other for quite some time. Perhaps, the two of them had noticed that the hug had lingered more than they would have anticipated but hug they did and then they hugged again.

They set to monitoring and recording every nuance of the new behaviours. Meticulously noting each animal and how they responded to the new signals.

"Do you think we should tell Lorenz about all of this?" Mike asked.

Professor Lorenz had worked with the combination of waves with Pete and Michael these last three years. It was Lorenz who had suggested adding in the microwave component, but it was late, and the guys decided against ringing him. Nobody in the lab really liked Lorenz. He was brilliant but completely deceptive and an exceptional practitioner of academic passive-aggressiveness. His work on the effects of electromagnetic radiation on human health was world renowned, but he carried his record as something of a tool for intimidation rather than as an inspiring learning model. He would mock the younger scientists' ideas for innovation and experimentation and then later adopt the work as his own. Almost like clockwork, his colleagues had begun to predict his behaviours. He had never crossed into academic fraud, but his bullying around ideas was all too familiar.

They had never seen Rattus Norwegicus behave like this. The albino version of the brown rat was now the standard template when studying almost every behavioural and medical question pertinent to the animal genome. With over 85 percent of its DNA identical to human's, it was a tried and truly reliable vehicle for answering almost every question about biological effects that could be imagined.

They spent the next 48 hours fine tuning the frequencies and responses of the animals. There was no doubt in their mind that they had stumbled on something quite remarkable. No one had ever demonstrated significant behavioural changes with environmental radiofrequency or microwave sources. It seemed that they had found a harmonic between the three sources that could, in fact, alter interaction, cooperation and possibly intelligence parameters. They set to meticulously lay out the theoretical, practical and statistics related to these new findings. Oddly they worked without complaint late into the evenings and into the weekend with a cheery manner that hadn't been seen in the lab for a very long time.

Once the maximal harmonics had been discovered and deployed, Pete and Mike turned their attention to devising experiments that could demonstrate the effects of the waveforms. Maze experiments were fascinating. The rats seemed to relay routes back to the following group. No longer was there an individual scramble for food. The leading animals returned to convey the correct path to followers, and they trusted the leaders. Even more remarkable was what happened when the food source was finally found. Not only was the time to discovery significantly decreased, but it was clear that the animals were organising and distributing the food in a cooperative manner. No longer was the smallest and slowest rat receiving nothing of the reward. Every animal received a fair share of the food as the orderly placement and distribution took place.

Experiments with the rats that had previously demonstrated causal responses between particular lights and tones emitted within a chamber and successful food lever activation were also very different under the influence of the waveforms. Prior to the harmonics, rats would continue pressing for food on the prompting of the signals of either green light or audible clicks, the rats now seemed to hold back on activation once they had been delivered a certain number of food distributions. The number correlated inversely with the number of animals in the experiment. The more animals present in the experiment the less the animals were inclined to press for extra quantities of food despite the established Pavlovian responses.

The colleagues pressed deep into the evening, coffee aromas mixing with animal and feed smells. Somehow, they had stumbled onto something quite remarkable, and they were busy and happy documenting it.

"Imagine if this could apply to humans!" Pete said.

Mike reached across to pat Pete on the shoulder. "This will keep us in research grants for the rest of our lives Pete. We are going to be famous."

"This is some kind of day Mike, Lorenz is going to be impressed with this. I'm getting him in tomorrow to assess our preliminary results."

They turned the lights off and headed out into the cool of the fall evening. As soon as they left the building, not a word was exchanged.

Next day dawned bright and full, and Lorenz drove his Volvo slowly and carefully along the shore drive taking in the snaking views of ocean and sky, cliff and road. His radio was on full blast, and The Beatles were playing which filled his head with harmonies and bass lines which he knew well and made him smile broadly. The Professor had sensed from his conversation with Mike earlier in the morning that something odd had been happening in the animal lab over these last few days. He wondered how this would impact on his academic standing at the University.

He parked his car, locked it and whistled his way to the lab. He swiped his card and made his way in to be greeted by a tired but happy Pete and Mike.

"So, what's all the excitement then?"

Pete nodded good morning and took Lorenz over to the animal house. What he saw he really couldn't believe.

"Why have you rearranged the platforms in the house?"

The blocks within the cage had been set up as a series of steps to the main food containers. "That's the thing Prof, we didn't do it. The animals did."

They spent the next few hours poring over the statistics and behavioural experiments. Lorenz thought there must have been some errors in recording the findings. Lorenz was gruff and dismissive. He wasn't focussing on what they were saying. It was then that Mike thought it best to live demonstrate the effect. He set up the microwave, Wi-Fi and ultrasound signals to the appropriate frequencies and intensities and waited for Lorenz to assess the changes for himself.

Within seconds Lorenz became chatty and enthusiastic. He looked intently at his colleagues and their results. He marvelled at the behaviour of the animals and how they were clearly cooperating on a whole new level. He proposed that Mike and Pete should take lead authorship on the slew of papers that were sure to follow from these unique findings. It was this strange transformation of the Professor that the boys were now becoming conscious of. The bellicose and shifty academic had disappeared, and they were presented with the team leader and confidante that they had so desperately needed earlier. He was effusive in his praise and enthusiastic for the project to come.

Pete turned the microwave transmission off and Lorenz's demeanour immediately changed. Suddenly, the room became the icy space of distrust and disillusion that it had been for years. Lorenz looked sullen as he walked out into the greying morning and quietly slipped home to ponder the day's events. Michael and Pete were confused and alarmed by what they had witnessed this morning. The Professor, a brilliant scholar with a brutal reputation, was not himself that day. Their keen eye at once recognised the correlation between the Professor's remarkable attitude transformations and the presence of the harmonics. It was dawning on them that this combination of transmissions was capable of profoundly altering human behaviour as well.

When they met again the next day, Michael and Pete were utterly taken aback by Professor Lorenz's thoughts and proposal. Lorenz admitted that he had seen the transformation of his personality in yesterday's events and broke down as he described the joy and angst he had felt as he recognised within himself the young, eloquent and idealistic scientist of years before in that hour. James Lorenz had had the opportunity of thinking clearly about the application of the findings to the world. He spent the next few hours outlining his thinking to Mike and Pete.

"Lads, this is going to change the world! Imagine if this was deployed across the planet?"

The two junior scientists stared at Lorenz. This was a bizarre thought, but it clearly resonated with them at the same time. They had noticed that their level of cooperation, positivity and cognition was definitely improved during the harmonic transmissions. Both had quietly considered the effect that the waveforms may have been having on them, but with the events of yesterday and the Professor's transformation it was all too clear.

Lorenz went on... "We are going to have to think this through very carefully and thoroughly. We must work out who to talk to about this, how it will be enabled and deployed, and what will happen as it is deployed. Have you got any thoughts?"

Pete and Mick stared at each other. These were towering questions. Now it was their turn to fall inward on their thoughts. They both agreed with the Prof that these were scientific findings with huge potential implications for the world. They told him they needed some time to work through how they saw it all going forward. Pete thought they should simply publish the results and leave it to governments and corporations to utilise the findings. Mick's initial reaction was much more guarded.

Overnight they stirred in their thoughts. Sleep was difficult as the implications of their discovery were just starting to dawn on them. Strangely, they all came to the same conclusion. They had somehow stumbled upon one of the most significant, and potentially the greatest discovery that man had ever made. Whilst they had not formally tested the effects on a group of humans, nor assessed the side effects or safety it seemed clear that the combination of these waveform harmonics had profound positive behavioural effects not only on the rats but also on themselves.

They got together finally after a tense 48-hour period and initially sat quietly, looking at each other across the lab bench. Eyes searching for understanding while the body language spoke of tension and animation.

Pete asked. "Should we turn the wave transmissions on prior to the meeting?"

"I think it would be helpful." Mick remarked.

"Let's just have a sensible discussion before we have any potential distorting effects of the harmonics." Lorenz wisely and aggressively suggested.

"OK, where do we start then? What do you make of it Prof?"

"Boys, I think this is bigger than we can possibly imagine. We have been given an opportunity to assess and potentially provide the world with a system to take us forward finally as a cooperative and peaceful people. I cannot deny the remarkable effect it had on myself. I know I am a crusty, cynical and cantankerous academic, but I liked the way I felt and thought when I was subject to those waves. What do you brilliant young men make of all this? For me, we should proceed with great caution because if this gets into the wrong hands it would either be suppressed or used to subjugate people. We need to do this right."

"Prof, I couldn't agree more. I've been racking my brain for ways forward on this. I thought long and hard about Pete's approach to just publish and maybe perish, but I know that perish would be the outcome."

Pete turned to each of them laser eyed with such intent. "I have changed my mind. That was my initial naive reaction. It was completely stupid, this is our chance to change history for the better, for the best. It's rare that an inventor can see the implications and potential rewards of their innovation straight away, but we need to have vision for this and act carefully, and then I can see such enormous changes ahead for us all."

"Pete, I'm so pleased to hear this! I was wondering how we were going to convince you of the implications of all of this. I'm sure you have thought through some of the practicalities and how the hell we are going to pull this off. I mean the ethics, the politics, the secrecy and ultimately the deployment are all massive issues. What are your thoughts?"

"Pete, before you answer that. Guys, I think we should turn the harmonics on as we proceed in this discussion. We are all in favour of a widespread application of the technology but let's use the technology itself to garner ideas for moving forward. Everyone agree?"

Michael and Pete nodded.

As soon as the waveforms were engaged, the mood lightened, and the conversation flowed brilliantly. It seemed as though their brains were acting in concert as they were feeding off each other's cues and listening so very intently.

"We are going to need some very clever engineers. If I am assuming correctly, we all agree that a wide deployment of this technology could transform the world. Has anyone got any feelings about how we might do that?" The Professor asked.

Mike commented. "Our biggest weakness is going to be the microwave signal, to get the correct harmonics across a vast swathe of the population is going to be tricky with the current set-up internationally. Ultrasound and radiofrequency are relatively easy. So, I agree we need some genius engineering to get this technology off the ground."

Professor Lorenz smiled and looked intently at his two charges.

"I'm so grateful that we are all seeing this for the unusual and important opportunity it is. Of course, an engineer only, would be able to facilitate the deployment of the technology, and that may be all we need to do to ensure some truly positive changes on this planet, but I think there is no doubt we are going to have to involve an ethicist, a political scholar and a futurist. I think we should also consider bringing in a historian both to understand the changes and to record the history from our perspective as it happens. Marketing may also be an area we need to consider as there is a small chance that the changes will bewilder some so much that they at least need pointing in the right direction as their lives change."

"Prof, I agree with everything you just said. Do you think we need to look far and wide for these people? Have you anyone in mind?" Peter asked.

"No, not at all. This university has some of the most brilliant minds in the country, and despite my cranky disposition over the years I have had the opportunity of getting to befriend some intrinsically caring and forthright people who just happen to be geniuses. With your permission, I would like to put forward some people. Have you guys got any other ideas on people or ways forward from here?"

Mick was looking a little nervous for a moment. "The thing is my gut feeling is that we are going to have to be incredibly patient with this. I'm no engineer, but I think the only way we are going to be able to reliably deploy all three signals to the entire world population is going to be with hybrid technologies. One of the basic requirements will be the instalment of an amplification device into existing systems and then to be able to coordinate the turning on of the technology simultaneously across the world so that everyone can be brought under the positive effects straight away."

"My first thought is somehow incorporating an amplification chip into other common technologies. For example, smartphones. There is a brilliant and sympathetic silicon chip engineer that now works across many company platforms in Chinese manufacturing whom I know from my undergraduate years that might have some ideas about this. I know it is sensitive, but I completely trust him. Can we call him in at this stage?"

Lorenz and Pete looked at each other then at Michael again. The Professor spoke.

"Yes Mick. Bring him on board. I have a feeling he is going to be the lynchpin to any success here. It's all very well getting the history and ethics right but no good if the deployment is poor. Let's go through these names I have and see what you think? These men and women for me are going to become the pioneers of a world that our imaginations can only begin to fathom."

Chapter 3

Chicago 3 years after I Day

The afternoon sun shone across the lake, and the reeds on the shore were lazily leaning and standing in the gentle breeze. The famous boathouse was resplendent in the background. It was a gentle walk on a perfect day.

"Do you remember that time before the great migrations? When we lived in separate communities, and there were gun deaths every weekend? It seems so strange looking back just these few years with all that has happened."

Mac loved these afternoons with his old mates and was looking forward to their beer.

"Of course I do Jordan. Haven't we moved on! I don't believe we would have become friends, let alone family if it wasn't for the migrations. I ended up in Nairobi teaching philosophy, and you were there gathering data on medical needs in the African populations and setting up the tertiary hospitals in the cities. They were exciting days, establishing those institutions that have now become world leaders in new medicines, tropical diseases and virtual health care. You must be so proud?"

"You are so right Mac, fascinating days and still very exciting. The integration of the emigres was quite spectacular. Almost half a million Canadians, Americans, Australians, Brits, Russian and Chinese within the first few months. They were determined, enthusiastic, empathic and skilled, and the locals embraced their influence and care with such grace. The thing I found most curious of all was the profound effect the students had on their mentors and how that translated into positive actions back home."

The bird life on the lake bustled and squawked as they made their way along the shore.

"...and here we are now, back in Chicago, probably more changes here than in Africa almost."

"True, the mixed marriages just like our two kids have is now just commonplace. Guns, not an issue anymore. 400 percent increase in school resources and college enrolment up to over 80 percent, military expenditure not even talked about anymore."

"Would you want to go back to Africa Mac?"

"You know what Jordan, I kinda like it here now. Walking through Humboldt Park with you on this September afternoon, life couldn't be much better. There are still plenty of challenges, but life here is good."

Their walking pace was slow and they stopped to look out over the water many times on the way to the bar.

"Mac, to be able to see the changes in my community, the one I had tried so hard to escape from as a young man is mind-boggling. Who knew that within months the South Side of Chicago would be transformed into a district for the fine arts? That people from all races and walks of life would be drawn there for cultural enrichment and that it would become a huge tourist mecca as the arts thrived and the drugs disappeared? I'm so incredibly proud of my city now, to feel free to walk any street. To know that diversity, peace and goodwill has arrived in my neighbourhood. And that anywhere in this great city I will find interesting shops, museums, great ethnic food. I just love this place now. It's great!"

"Yeah, remember when you locked your car door and looked straight ahead driving through 'the black neighbourhoods'? Thankful those days are over. Remember the despair on the faces, the shuttered shops, a land of lost hope, filled with anger and revenge."

The park was quiet apart from their quiet thoughts and the stirring of goldfinches, woodpeckers and herons.

"The gangs used to rule in those days. Filling the place that family should have been playing. Young guys preyed upon by mob rule, boredom, poverty and criminality. How we lived with it and were frustrated by the submission to poverty and illiteracy that was passed from generation to generation, I will always struggle to understand. Why couldn't we do anything for those neighbourhoods until I day? I still hang my head in shame a little even though I was teaching in those areas for years."

"Let's go get that beer!"

"Let's!"

They walked to the edge of the park and headed to the monorail. The silent vehicle approached as they made their way up to the platform, and they swiped their phones as they boarded. Within four minutes they were in the heart of Englewood. They took the stairs up to the converted train line which was awash with people and colour. No longer the dilapidated and abandoned rail corridor, it was now a conduit for smiles, walkers, bikers and lovers just going for a wander between suburbs. The redevelopment was near complete, and the boxed plants and art pieces were being installed as they walked along.

"Apparently they are having parties up here now. People can hire out the old railway yards at the terminus and a section of the corridor. Terrific place for a 21st or even a 60th, you old man."

"They really have done great things restoring the Mall, haven't they? Let's go find Fang."

They walked along the cobblestone street as the evening descended, and their appetites increased. Almost every shop they passed now was something that drew their interest. Antique books, local fashions, cafes promising world class coffees and every type of traditional food, electronic gadget stores, artist supplies, galleries. Fang had finished his day and was sitting at his usual spot on the Mall in the French styled bar. Chatting away with Lisa over a glass or three of chardonnay from Napa Valley or Australia, which was their favourite poison. Most people at the bar were black, but there was a good smattering of people of Caucasian, and Asian ethnicity. It was heartening to see the young, mixed couples who were now so familiar. The public displays of affection so good for the heart of this part of town which had been renewed wholly in such a short time.

"Hey! Mac, Jordo... You guys made it. Come take a pew."

Jordan sat down and immediately accessed his smartphone and ordered the beers. The bars interface was fairly primitive, but the selection was wide with over 200 ales alone to consider. Jordan had initially struggled with the Internet of Things but gradually he found that the service was usually better and the choice much broader and he became a happy adopter. He settled for a Northern English pale ale, and the waitress had it out to them in moments.

"Ahhh that is good Mac, you can choose the next round. Reminds me of those English beers we shared in Nairobi at the end of those long hot African days. Delicious!"

"Oh, yes this is good Jordan. Well picked my friend. So, Fang, what have you been doing apart from regaling the lovely Lisa this afternoon? Have you been saving the teeth of South Chicago as per your purpose in life?"

"Mac, as you know, I have been drinking quietly and serving the good people of Englewood for over 25 years now. Things are a lot easier these days, I actually get to charge most people for fixing their mouths. I mean everybody has a job or is in a programme these days. So, no more evening demands for my daily earnings or for my technician's body has left more time for a quiet chat with my beautiful wife in this charming establishment."

"Ha, you're a classic Fang. Mac laughed.

"Fang, why don't you ever call me beautiful to my face?"

"I come from esteemed Chinese family tradition, much more subtle than that my darling Lisa."

She always managed such a gorgeous smile when Fang was charming. Mac and Jordan would look out for it as well. It was like a tradition of their get-togethers. To make Lisa smile that smile as often as they could.

Fang turned to Jordan "What's new Jordo, how's the family?"

"All good Fang, Dan is in Texas, his last year studying International Diplomacy. Lou is doing an intern year with one of the new corporates, one of the biggest in novel sustainable energy technologies. He's down in New Zealand working on tidal harvesting at the moment, and Janeka is following her old man into surgery. She's doing a series of resident exchange programmes these coming two years. She has some time in Eastern Europe, Africa and China. She is really looking forward to the teaching and the subtle differences in training."

"The two love birds coping with being apart for now? It just seems like yesterday that we were at their wedding."

"They seem to be doing ok. The whole holographic experience has made it so realistic. Once they get the tactile parts right, there will be no need to ever meet in a bar again. But seriously, yeah I do think they miss each other terribly. Another six months and they can work together anywhere in the world they choose to. No doubt it will be somewhere exotic."

As the afternoon sun cut across the deck, they took a couple of virtual reality calls with Jordo complaining that his phone wasn't up to projecting the hologram in the bright afternoon light. He was fed up and thinking of going android again. They caught up with Fred from Australia who was holidaying in remote country doing some Barramundi fishing. They always knew they would catch Fred somewhere exotic and he gave them a tour of the wetlands where his tinny was anchored. The morning sun of his today glistened off the crocodile-infested waters and sparkled into the air between them.

"There's one of the mean buggers."

He said, directing his gaze and hence theirs at the ancient creature gliding across the surface of the lake, snout distinct, two eyes cold and menacing with her body unseen until she came to the reedy bank and quickly ran out of sight.

"Fred, it's Fang. How are you going, my friend? Isn't it about time you came back to Chicago for your teeth checkup? That New Zealand childhood of yours didn't do you any favours. Hope you have been flossing!"

"Ha, Fang. I'm trying to concentrate on not getting eaten by a crocodile here. Nearly fell out of the boat laughing with that one. Yeah, you are right. I'll be in the States for a conference in the next couple of months. Will try and drop in and have a beer with you guys."

They noticed the cacophony of bird song on the billabong and signed off to ring a couple of the kids before winding up over another beer or three.

Chapter 4

California 18 months before I Day

Lorenz was in the Chair. The lab had been improved and significantly extended after Lorenz hinted to the Vice-Chancellor that something major was in the pipeline. He gave no significant details, but it was enough for the well-endowed University to accede to the hints of their esteemed Professor. All of the people that Michael, Pete and Lorenz had wanted were gathered together in the new meeting room which was an annexe to the lab itself. They had had little trouble in assembling the group, again on hints of something extraordinary in the wind. The very nature of the people was marked by intense curiosity, a passion for learning, renowned honesty and discretion. Lorenz knew that trust was key here and was confident that he could persuade them to act as a cohesive force in the investigation and hopefully deployment of their discovery.

"Welcome, ladies and gentlemen. I appreciate your presence here today. It marks a significant step in the assessment and possible introduction of a new technology that may have significant implications for the progress of mankind in the very near future. You have been selected because you are brilliant minds in your fields and also for your ability to remain absolutely discrete with regard to what we shall be presenting and discussing. You have all signed the confidentiality clauses, and I can only emphasise that it is essential that nothing goes out from this room until we have decided the pathway for this technology and how it can and whether it should be deployed. Can we go around the room,

I know many of you are familiar with each other but please tell us who you are and a little bit about yourself. Let's start to my left."

"Hello everyone, and welcome to our humble lab. My name is Michael Malone, I have been working here with Professor Lorenz and Pete Hamelin as a post-doctorate fellow researching the behavioural effects of electromagnetic radiation on rats, and as it turns out also on humans."

"I am Pete Hamelin, I also am a research fellow here at the lab and we have some fascinating things to show you this afternoon."

They both were very evidently nervous, and it showed in the stiffness of their welcome and their postures. Both were literally shaking the podium as they talked to this elite gathering of minds.

"Good afternoon everyone, my name is Evelyn Finfer I am currently Professor of Ethics at this fine institution, I'm intrigued to be here."

Evelyn spoke with a calm voice; she was no stranger to innovation and bold ideas.

"Cesar Alexander, Associate professor, History here at UCLA."

Cesar was a wiry, dark gentleman with an enormous forehead.

"Petra Schwartz, Media and Journalism Analyst. I'm currently working in the publicly funded Think Tank, Pacific Council, based here also at the University."

Petra had been a model in a former life. Her dress sense remained acute, and it was impossible to ignore her intense stare when anyone else held the floor.

"Hello all, thank you for having me here. My name is Thomas Maddison. Currently unemployed, I have been working at Google for the last 15 years in marketing, my expertise is around corporate internet exposure and Digital Marketing optimisation."

Thomas was marked by his staccato vocal gymnastics. He used tone and pauses to emphasise his main points.

"Good afternoon all, Professor Anthony Wells, Dean, Faculty of Medicine. I do paediatrics in my spare time."

Professor Wells was rotund and jolly looking but had a fierce reputation for academic rigour in his faculty.

"Rebecca Warren, Faculty of Commerce. Specialty, International finance."

It was hard to make out any facial expressions from Ms Warren as her extremely thick rimmed glasses dominated her face.

"What a group! Hello, I am Sati Persaud. I've spent a lifetime organising unions, currently Professor of Political Science here in LA."

Sati was an extremely handsome man. He was as engaging as he was mischievous. His face literally danced as he spoke.

"My name is Cong Ming. I am a doctoral graduate of this fine University in Computer Sciences and currently spending my time building smartphones in China these days."

Cong was quiet and assured.

"Once again, thank you all so very much for coming today. We are excited to be able to present to you our findings on the Harmonic Behavioural Effects of electromagnetic radiation on human and animal behaviour. I think you will find the results astounding or at the very least novel. You have been selected for your individual skills to consider taking this project further. Without taking away any of your skills of judgement, it is my and my team's conclusions that this discovery has the potential to change the course of history and may be one of the most important discoveries of science to date.

"I am not saying this to boost our own egos, but rather we have seen the implications of the data into the real world. We need you good people to temper our thoughts or to join our team in bringing its deployment forward as rapidly as possible."

There was a general murmur of astonishment and genuine surprise. Almost everyone was quite familiar with the surly and intense Professor Lorenz and to hear him talk along these lines left them all quite incredulous. Something big was about to be revealed.

The team spent the next hour presenting the extensive animal data and the early human trials that they had conducted. The room was stunned, as the implications of this discovery dawned on all of them. Each seeing the findings from their own specialist perspectives but with the kind of universal wonder that such a finding would be expected to elicit. The close attention and quietness in the room was palpable as the group tried to get their heads around such unusual and very profound positive effects virtually across the board in every ingenious test that the researchers had devised. There was an immediate and close to 100 percent positive behavioural, cognitive and cooperative response to the harmonics within the test setting. They were starting to imagine the possibilities, and this was where the second part of the forum was heading. The practicalities, ethics and implications of a comprehensive implementation programme.

The buzz about the room at the end of the presentation was palpable. Nervous laughter and glances were exchanged, and Lorenz set about hearing the first impressions formally.

Anthony Wells rose to speak first: "Gentlemen, this is outstanding work and definitely groundbreaking. It is clearly so powerful that it will never be able to be released to the public in any significant way as it would alter behaviour so much that choices would be distorted, and the subsequent effects just could not be predicted. The longer-term health effects would also need to be taken into consideration. This is brilliant on paper, but it will never get government or corporate approval."

There was a general murmur after this comment and several people immediately put their hands up to speak to it.

Thomas Madison was next. "I have to disagree with the learned Professor. This is the most easily marketable social revolution I have ever seen in the making. If these effects are real, then getting people to change for the better and adopt cooperative practices worldwide would be extremely easy. I think the most difficult thing we will be contemplating is not whether we should deploy it but rather how and when.

"I see no ethical issues here at all as the effects of the waveforms in all testing so far detects only positive cognitive and behavioural effects. If these results are accurate, we should be contemplating deployment as soon as practicable. Imagine how easy it will be to promote a world of intelligence, cooperation, non-aggression. I think I have just found my next job."

Sati Persaud was keen to speak.

"The political ramifications of this discovery are absolutely mind boggling. Actually, every ramification of this discovery is mind boggling. If these early human trials tell us anything, it is that politics as we know it are dead. This has implications for culture but in a gentle and integrative way.

"In terms of politics, it could be completely revolutionary without a gun ever being fired. The combination of positive cooperative traits with loss of innate behavioural aggression is what the world has been lacking to make it a peaceful and fearless place to be. Courage and willpower can be directed to inventiveness and sustainable progress. There will no longer be the need for nation states as such and government will be so much more streamlined and smaller."

Evelyn piped up. "Wait, wait!" "We are getting ahead of ourselves here. The ethical consequences of brainwashing every single human on the planet in order to act on what amounts currently to little more than a hunch are considerable."

Cesar quickly saw that whichever way this discussion progressed it would be a momentous one. He had been furiously writing down everything that everyone had said and now chimed in; "Evelyn, Evelyn, I totally agree. Let's not get too far ahead of ourselves, but I do see this as an important opportunity and responsibility that we now carry forward from this day. We have been thrust into an awkward conundrum and puzzle of decision making and planning for a phenomenon that may well dramatically alter the course of history. This is a fork in the road that we must manage as best we can. My first instinct is that we have in this discovery the makings of a vastly better future for mankind."

Evelyn responded "Cesar, we cannot afford to go on gut feelings here. There is too much at stake if we get this wrong. If we impose this on society and take away certain choices. I hate to think."

Petra Schwartz stood to speak; she was excited. Her animation at what she had just heard palpable. "As a journalist, this is the biggest story in the world today and one that I am a little sad I won't be breaking on prime time news tonight. To be frank, I really think we are way ahead of ourselves. I mean, Professor Lorenz was not able to outline any practical way for this to be deployed across the world simultaneously in the foreseeable future."

Cong Ming finally spoke. "Actually, ladies and gentlemen, it is ever so easy to deploy this technology. So, please, back to the ethics and the future. If you want to deploy it, I can explain that to you a little later."

Everybody stared at Cong. He had just brazenly given the green light to the actual widespread deployment of the technology. Petra turned to him and gave him a hug; she knew she had an even bigger story to tell now.

Lorenz replied. "Cong, I kind of knew that you would say that. Perhaps it's time to hear from our futurists because ultimately it is in the risks to benefits analysis of this that our ethics will be decided I am sure." He turned to the group and deliberately caught every individual gaze. "I know what I am about to say may disturb some of you. I propose that the rest of the meeting be conducted under the influence of the harmonics. If the majority of you disagree then this will of course not proceed, but if you are happy, I propose we turn it on now. If any individual objects, then that person may, of course, excuse themselves."

Professor Wells did look very concerned about the proposal, but he was also an inquisitive man and the animal and human data so far had not indicated any health effects of the waves.

"Ok then. Michael, would you do the honours?" The Professor said.

As soon as Michael turned the harmonics on the group's dynamics were altered entirely. Ideas flowed so rapidly and fluidly that Cesar was struggling to write down even the essence of what was being said. Complicated algorithms in finance, politics and the day to day living of the world that was to come were being forged in an intense and incredibly fruitful discussion. The ethics of the deployment were dealt within the first few minutes of the discussion as the reality of enhanced cognition and cooperation were understood personally by the group. They quickly moved on to health issues and the practicalities of transforming society. Professor Well's concerns and cynicism evaporated when he was able to promptly integrate all the health data that had already been performed. He somehow recalled in quite astounding detail all he had ever read about the effects of wave harmonics on the human brain and seemed confident in that knowledge that here the risks were completely outweighed by the enormous benefits that the technology would produce.

They spoke into the early hours of the morning with the schema for future meetings and emerging details on the hows and whys of deployment. The consequences for mankind was frankly and earnestly debated in a display of interfaculty cooperation and support that none of them had ever witnessed before. I Day was now more than an idea.

One thing that was very apparent was that they had quite some time to discuss every possibility of going forward. Cong Ming had outlined his strategy for practical deployment. Most of the waveforms could be delivered in adequate amounts via existing infrastructures, but the microwave signals would have to be boosted to become reliable. His plan was to begin installing an appropriate chip into every smartphone in production from the next few weeks. All future Androids, Apple 17s, Microsoft and Google phones would be manufactured with the same chip installed. When I Day came, it would be a simple matter of activating that chip universally, setting the harmonics correctly and a synchronous deployment across the globe could be completed.

Chapter 5

Afghanistan 5 years after I Day

Gholam was by far the best skier. Everyone admired his perfect parallel skis and the way his body was at one with the slope be it gentle or savage. He seemed to have absolutely no fear as he plunged off the edges of sharp ridges and plummeted across the soft powder with the group trailing behind the symmetrical grooves of his ski tracks. Everyone enjoyed the terrain and as they stood upon the highest point before the last run and took some photos the stark beauty of the surrounding valleys and stunning peaks stretching to the horizons dawned upon them. Each breath up there was exhilarating, and they could not help but feel absolutely alive as the sun commenced its descent to the west as they pointed their skis downward and flew across the mountainside.

The food in the resort was delicious. All the flavours that they had come to love from that first day in the markets and from the small towns along their journey were being put together by talented chefs with the freshest of produce. The chef's fusion style blended Asian, French and modern cuisine with the best of local techniques. They sat in groups of three and four in the dining room which was spacious and modern and featured a huge fireplace. The copper hood and chimney were suspended from the ceiling by heavy metal chains. The fireplace had a large slate base below and plenty of clear glass to display the burning logs. The view to the valley was magnificent with the wall wholly composed of glass panels that stretched 10 metres to the steep roofline above and offered a view that showed off the evening light display of the ski instructors as they made their way in a giant snake down the mountain. Shouting and echoes from across the Valley added to the flavour of the night and fireworks lit up the peaks and tree lines. The wine flowed, matching the exquisite food in elegance and the conversation was animated and loud. At the end of the meal, the group gravitated to the long bar and mingled with locals and other tourists who had their own marvellous tales of travelling in this very new and very ancient land.

They ended up in the lounge, forming a great circle, some sitting on the comfortable, giant cushions scattered about, some standing and chatting with a glass of something delicious in their hands. Joe and Mark were discussing the past few days with a couple from Australia who had been following the Alexandrian trail. To their great surprise, they saw Gholam sit next to Amanda; his arms were reaching about her shoulders and she reached to him. As he cupped her smiling face and with his other hand brushed away the fringe of hair from her eyes, they leant in for a soft but very loving kiss that lasted until the boys had trotted off to their respective rooms.

The next few days of skiing were very relaxing for everyone. The romance between Gholam and Amanda was a little surprising at first, but it was now known that there had been significant communication and attraction between them before this trip and it became a source of joy for them all. Rather than jealousy, it was clear to everyone that a very genuine affection had grown between the two in the real world.

As they became more familiar with the local people and had the opportunity to hear their stories, they began to understand the enormity of fear that people had lived under for so long. Particularly in this area where the ethnic diversity was strong and the intolerant Taliban had made life nearly impossible for so many years. On the lifts and in the bars people would describe how a cousin had been killed here, a sister raped, houses burned down. Then suddenly everyone laid their arms down and for the first time in 4000 years, peace had reigned in this ancient and proud place. The skiers spoke about a subtle, strong hope that had welled up from that first day. There was a sense of certainty and pride that peace had finally come between them all. How the American soldiers were stunned and overjoyed as their call to go home or to stay and wander came within 48 hours of I Day. Suddenly, they felt very welcome in this land that had been so much trouble for them. The stories of how immediately, all arms were surrendered by every side, and vast stocks of weapons were brought to central collecting agencies and destroyed quickly. The war machine was disassembled within a month, and then the influx of scholars, medics, educators, builders and engineers came. The transition was sudden but incredibly positive, and the spirit was one of cooperation and innovation, coupled with a drive and confidence that this was not about to be reversed, that this was the reality and the future. A future to be filled with smiles, construction and learning.

The mood in the group was for more adventure. The exhilaration and adaptation to the high altitude was complete. They were ready to see the rest of this country that promised so much but had been off limits due to terror, war and oppression for many years. Gholam promised them so much more and so they set off back down the mountain highway saying goodbye to the joys that they had experienced there and were looking forward to making more great memories.

They had a couple of hours to explore the great Buddhas up close, and as they stared upwards toward the sky and across the sheer sandstone cliff face that contained the intricate man-made statues, they were utterly awestruck. The reconstruction of the Buddhas in their niches was stunning, but the resurrection of the sleeping Buddha towering straight into that endless blue was the most impressive. Buried for centuries, it now stood as a sentinel for peace across this remarkable land.

Their next stop was 700km away, and everyone was very excited to be going. Gholam hinted at another cultural treat as they headed south-west to Helmand Province and to the town of Lashkar Gah. This was previously known as the poppy capital of Afghanistan; now known by its more ancient name of Bost. On the new roads that Afghanistan boasted this would have taken just six hours, but they stopped for lunch for a couple of hours in Khaz Uruzgan, a sleepy oasis in a high river valley. It had been the site of much bitter fighting, retribution and revenge just a few years earlier. A town occupied by a mixture of Hazaras and Pashtuns who had lived an uneasy tolerance for many centuries and who were thrown into deadly conflicts largely on opposite sides.

The tourists chatted quietly with them over an Okra dish that made their taste buds swim with joy. They were told how both peoples had been unwilling to take positions and actions as they simply tried to survive the lust for power and the consequences of personalities driven by skewed ideologies. For as long as many in this now peaceful village could remember this place had been one where just to survive was the main goal in life.

It was so special to be able to share and enjoy each other's company, delicious food and this green, quietude and serenity that stretched up to the impressive mountains about them.

Joe couldn't help musing on all of this. He was taken back to his days of travelling through Europe and especially Greece and Italy. The landscape was eerily familiar and the feeling that they were now sitting where so much blood had been spilt and for absolutely nothing really. Just as in those ancient battlefields of the warm Mediterranean countries, this land was settling down hopefully to centuries of peace. It was transforming into a place of warmth and welcome.

It was hard to conceive that half of the people they were now sitting down with had either been Taliban or had been on both sides of the conflict as it had progressed and changed over many years. Here, they were breaking bread and conversing with tolerance, friendliness and real interest with people who had been the very opposite of those ideals in the past. These were people with expertise in manufacturing Improvised Explosive Devices, some were crack snipers. Some were tunnellers who had burrowed under the local opposition commander's home to plant a bomb to unseat another oppressor while killing his entire family doing that.

While they did talk about how much everything had changed, especially their perspectives on cultural differences, their position in the world, their history, they were more focused on how lovely the day was, how fresh the fruit and what their hopes for the future were. The focus now was on the present and the immediate future, their dreams for their country, their hopes for travelling and seeing the world. It was so refreshing that the lunch extended seamlessly into the early afternoon. The shadows of the giant mountains started playing with the deep valley below as they grew to know and like each other.

Gholam finally signalled that it was time to resume their adventure, so fond farewells were taken after such a brief but meaningful visit.

As they came within 50 km of Bost, they started to notice the transformation of the landscape. The narrow strip of green of about 1 km that had been present along the river valley was now extended to the horizon on both sides. Initially, there were demarcated villages and farms, but eventually, they coalesced to a vast farming plain with a diversity of animal life and every crop that they could imagine. Gholam was visibly disturbed as he remembered coming along this route when it was a dusty and simultaneously muddy dirt road with hardly a tree to be seen.

"This used to be a barren, soulless area until the city of Bost was in sight when in the old days poppy fields could be seen everywhere in the Helmand River delta."

They turned off the main road about 20 km out of the town and headed through glades of gorgeous and colourful orchards bearing apples, pomegranates, lemons and limes. They noticed the sophisticated drip irrigation systems as the cars negotiated the gentle, winding lanes uphill and down dale. They came to the farther valley which was a riot of healthy grapevines stretching out in the sun over rich, red soils for as far as they could see. They noticed the spacing, order and ornamentation of the vines as every row began with either an olive tree or a rose bush. Upon the final rise they passed the sign welcoming them to Naparosa Vineyard and Hotel. They caught a glimpse of the imposing structure at the top of the drive and knew they were in for a treat of a stay. As they approached the buildings, the road diverted to become a final circular route. The car slowed, and they observed at least a dozen kids of every imaginable ethnicity racing around the elegant gravel driveway on their small bikes. The joy was palpable as they followed and chased and raced each other about the simple course. The lawns and gardens on either side of the driveway were meticulous. Whoever had conceived, designed and built this haven had an eye for detail as corridors of trees and flowers drew one's eye to features in the middle and far distance of great interest. Natural rock formations, snow covered mountain tops, sculptures and fountains were to be found in the gaps between the carefully manicured vegetation. As the cars rolled slowly around to the entryway, everyone was stunned by the beauty of this place. Mark noticed some of the adults riding off down a gently sloping laneway, the late afternoon sun cutting across the fully-grown poplars which cast a zebra pattern on the shell-pink gravel. It immediately took him back to his childhood and the simple joys of riding in the countryside.

The welcome was swift as they exited the cars. Staff greeted them at the base of the steps to the lobby of this fabulous vineyard hotel with a choice of a glass of the local Sauvignon blanc or a Rose that proved surprisingly palatable. They slowly made their way up to the Tuscan style balcony that was generous in its views across the gardens and vines. They soaked up the afternoon sun and were brought a selection of local cheeses and delicacies that complemented the wine and the magnificent scenery.

With the second glass served the manager of the hotel came out to greet them. Abe Baumann introduced his wife Ebele, a stunning dark woman with an accent that was very hard to place and who was incredibly welcoming in her very graceful way. Abe talked in great detail about how the property had been transformed over the last few years essentially from a desert to this oasis of which he was very proud.

They sat at one of the umbrella-covered tables on the broad verandah.

Abe was a good talker. "The community had come together, the scientists and engineers, the latest technology that was produced locally and imported from my home country of Israel to achieve all that you see. Irrigation and recycling systems, solar, hydro and water channelling systems had been installed in very little time at all as the design expertise and coordination was so straightforward. Local farmers and their families were involved in a cooperative ownership and development of their land and now get to enjoy a legal and diversified income from their orchards, vineyards and tourism."

Abe talked about the environment before the change as juxtaposed desert and poppy fields and how the local population was now so very proud and astounded at their newfound haven. Their homes were not uprooted in the design at all but rather modified to fit the transformation and to become aesthetically pleasing giving guests the ability to wander among the villages and get to know the people. This had greatly enhanced the development of arts and crafts and cultural events as the economy changed rapidly.

"The project allowed for the children to finally attend the newly created schools at both primary and high school level. Menial tasks that used to take up the children's time like water carriage were eliminated as services modernised and the importance of education was finally recognised."

Joe asked Ebele what her story was. She beamed an incandescent smile that instantly warmed everyone to her.

She started speaking "Ahhhhhh, I am a geek! I came here four years ago shortly after the first big wave of migrations. When I Day came, I first went to the States from my native Senegal to learn all about computers. My English skills were good and my brain not so stupid and so I was very fortunate to get into MIT where I studied quantum physics, engineering modelling and applications development. I was about to go on to Harvard to do a doctorate in public policy when I read of this exciting project here in Afghanistan.

"The rest is history, as originally, I started off as a teacher and then met and fell in love with this very strange Israeli, right here. He had me planning the engineering works for the whole project within months and we also developed the mobile apps that coordinate the community effort for our guests. At any time, villagers and guests can tap into the app that can advertise, book and develop events of a cultural, educational, artistic or just for fun for people to do while they are here. It allows the locals to explore our guests' knowledge and interests and vice versa. It has been so much fun developing it and I hope you all use it while you are here with us for this short visit."

Amanda asked Abe what his charming secrets were? "As you can see, Ebele is an awesome and stunning creature. She is a gifted teacher, communicator, engineer but mostly she is just a lovely person. So, I eked out every ounce of charm I could muster to procure her attention. Maybe I got lucky? Maybe, it was meant to be. On my side, I think you would agree it was very easy to fall in love with this elegant lady. You may have to ask Ebele exactly why it was that I succeeded."

Again, Ebele produced one of those unforgettable smiles, looked at Abe and gracefully swept her arm across the escarpment.

"You see all this? This is Abe. He is a very, very passionate man and it was his vision, determination, negotiating skills and sense of humour that ultimately produced what you see right now. He brought together the technologies and the people behind them, he convinced his friends from Israel to drop what they were doing and help him achieve this dream. He answered the job application I sent to become a teacher here, and he was relentless in his charm until I also knew that here was the man I loved, in the place that I love."

"So, what do you fancy this fine evening?" Amanda said as she opened up her Naparosa app. There were three hours of sunlight available to them. "I've booked it guys. We are all going on a helicopter ride. We leave in 10 minutes."

Ebele beamed. "Oh, that is wonderful. Quite the experience, we shall see you back here after dinner then. Enjoy."

The garden and house were fabulous to see from the air and as they climbed the view over the valley was splendid. The vines stretched to each horizon, and they could make out the clusters of houses, all draped with solar panels of every shape and conformation but balanced with village vegetable plots, pretty gardens and difficult to spot communication hubs. The extent of the orchards was also enormous, and again little communities were seen in areas shaded by copses of trees. They even saw some swimming pools and sporting fields on the complex and the helicopter pilot was very proud to point out the newly opened schools, he described how proud he was that his two children were attending. It was clear that this wasn't the only similar project as the chopper swept across the landscape, which was definitely a mixture of old and new. Areas of parched land were being swallowed up by the renewal process almost all the way into town. Clearly, Abe's example and success were being replicated on a huge scale.

Suddenly the chopper turned rapidly and lifted up across the rugged escarpment. Amanda hadn't told the rest of the group, but the main attraction for her was to come at the top of this mountain range. Their ears popped as the valley, river and vineyards disappeared below them and they found themselves looking at dense scrublands, dense forests and proud granite outcrops. They reached the range line and dipped into a small clearing surrounded by tall conifers. Almost as soon as they were clear of the chopper around 15 men appeared in the long dark tunics and knitted hats of the salwar kameez style, they were Taliban. They were a little taken aback before they were quickly bundled off down a dark track into the forest before they were abruptly stopped and warmly hugged by their hosts and told that their photo opportunity had arrived. They posed for the official photographer who wore, strangely, some very cool Ray-Ban sunglasses and took their own selfies at liberty. Soon they were once again marched off down the path to the former stronghold of these mountain men now turned Afghan cooking lesson site.

They found themselves in a small clearing and the entire community now came out to greet them warmly. Their language skills were remarkable, especially from the younger people who were full of questions for the group about their travels and backgrounds. It seemed that this was as much a cultural exchange as a gourmet Afghan cooking experience, and they spent the first half an hour exploring the housing and facilities. They were surprised to find high definition, high-speed communication resources in every dwelling and happy to see the children playing joyfully without a care in the world and the teenagers doing what teenagers do everywhere. Listening to music, looking on curiously at strangers and rather reassuringly gaining confidence and asking everything and anything of their guests.

It was almost overwhelming, but the group were as curious as the villagers, and before the meal was to be prepared, they mingled and tried to understand the changes that had happened over the last few years. They discovered that the girls were now leading and pushing the boys in their achievements and excellence in education. They learnt that several of the elder children and many adults from the village had gone overseas for further improvement of tertiary education skills. What was impressive was the high rate of return of these people and the fact that they had brought back friends and mentors that they knew could help enhance their community. That is how there had been such remarkable developments in language skills and how they had been able to integrate with the very active community in the valley to develop their tourist initiatives.

Discussing the dark days of conflict and repression and death was surprisingly easy. The day that they were released from such a narrow cultural path was now warmly celebrated. Their suspicion of foreign involvement in their land dissipated immediately and they could see the positive impact the gentler aspects of their culture would have on others. When they travelled, it was the sense of community, the waft of genuine cuisine and the depth of curiosity that charmed people around the world. They knew from that time that they had so much to offer the world and they had since pursued it vigorously and with confidence. The reception had been both financially rewarding as they secured a comfortable existence in their native land but also emotionally as they had finally felt able to embrace change and all that the world had to offer.

They looked back on the dark days as a history of ignorance and lack of opportunity. They welcomed the new standards of law and ethics that were now a worldwide standard and in retrospect only too happy to abandon the strictures of Sharia law. Sharia had contributed in its positive aspects to the universal standard that now all had adopted as the basis for mankind's new rule of law.

As the conversation delved deeper and the language skills perpetually stretched, they returned to the clearing in the woods. The tourists were in the inner circle, and the Taliban surrounded them as the chief gourmand started explaining his wizardry.

This particular villager was most impressive. He had a beard that stretched to his tummy and a woollen hat of a size that they had never witnessed before. He beckoned and directed his minions back and forth to bring and do. Soon his pot was produced, the stove fired up, and he explained his genius. The pot was enormous, and he had several people chopping and preparing the fresh ingredients that were to be used.

His voice was voluptuous and intriguing. He waved his arms around like a magician and placed a layer of lamb fat cuts into the base of his pot. From the back of the circle, a string quartet and drums began a tune that had some of the villagers immediately up to dance. As they started to invite their guests up for a spin, the chef glared briefly and then nodded. Some danced, and some watched the chef as he added choice lamb cuts, lots of salt, whole potatoes and tomatoes and a handful of green chillies. He made a show of his lemons and squeezed away for five minutes. He sealed the pot with flour dough and settled it over the fire. He then grandly dismissed everyone as he had work to do to prepare the rice, condiments and dessert.

Gholam and Amanda took a small group with them to the edge of the escarpment. They found a rocky outcrop and watched as the sun set over that ancient valley. The smell of the food being prepared and the light playing upon the ranges and the green valley below was entirely intoxicating.

Chapter 6

San Francisco 60 years after I Day

The Professor stood there in his black jeans, black shirt, slightly balding but looking rakishly handsome as he was about to deliver his opening lecture of the year. The students looked younger every year with their baseball caps invariably pointing backwards and the girls all wearing various shades of grey as was the fashion that year. He stared at the crowd, and there was something about him which commanded instant respect and attention. Of course, his reputation was immense, but it was here in the flesh that they were to gain insights into the history and development of the world since I Day. Professor Johnson was a world respected historian and analyst of the postmodern world, and the students were salivating for his address.

"On the day after I Day there was not so much a vacuum of power as a clamour for the multitude of sensible voices with a million ideas to take the world forward positively. Some things were very clear and obvious to everyone. All weapons were surrendered immediately in countries that were at war and also those enjoying peace. Vast depots and factories for repurposing weaponry systems for civilian uses were constructed. Myriad alternate purposes were invented using the high-tech systems that had been previously closed off to civilian use. The cross-seeding of ideas from ex-military engineers and strategists exploded into vast global networks of support for ways to take the technology further in a peaceful manner."

"If you have any questions during this lecture please simply raise your hand, and I will get to you. It is often in the jumble of understanding that the greater truths are uncovered."

Immediately five people put their hands up. Johnson ignored them momentarily and went on.

"The clamour to be organised and heard as a cooperative and sensible talisman of ideas was ultimately coordinated by the donation of and linkage of corporate computer networks to allow high speed communications on a mass civil scale and so a true democracy was finally heard and came to power. Some thought it ironic that the Baldwin organisation and Baldwin Towers in New York and Chicago became facilitators of this global network. They became places where the new global leaders could come together personally and discuss the best ways to take the world forward in this vastly different atmosphere of world cooperation, peace and invention.

"Baldwin himself was terrific and his quick ability to recognise his own humility in those days was much appreciated and remembered by the people. He opened the doors of his hotels, networks and properties and quietly retired to a humble family life and never further contributed to public affairs unless it involved some of the innovative members of his family who went on to contribute generously to the common good in the years that came."

"Yes, you, in the baseball cap. What do you want to know?"

"Did the inventors of the waves predict that they would be able to overcome the massive narcissism and egos of those in power? What did they anticipate?"

"Excellent question. I refer you to the online course bibliography. Many of the people on the feasibility committee, including all three founding scientists, have written fascinating books on this subject. They knew they had a very powerful tool in their hands. They predicted almost all of the changes remarkably well. All except that one instance of madness that was a case of the serendipity of both electromagnetic isolation, pure paranoia and a powerful weapon. We shall come to that later in the course.

"Professor Lorenz's group had anticipated much of the events of those first few weeks and much of the direction and steps toward a global imagination had been expected. Many in the group did become prominent leaders as the new world emerged. Some thought it was due to their inside knowledge, some thought it was Lorenz's genius in selecting them in the first place for their skills. In a world where massive profit and economic advantage was no longer an expectation or goal, the individuals that emerged did so out of sheer determination, intellect and skill. What they had not anticipated was the relatively smooth roll-out of the technology and how quickly it was recognised as both revolutionary and totally practical.

"Within a few weeks, the global democracy was taking shape. Almost everybody on the planet had access to the collective wisdom, and people were inventing systems to make the most of both the cerebral knowledge and physical skills that people possessed. Obvious needs for education, farming, irrigation and food distribution were rapidly reformed. The real work was in organising the best minds to come together to provide leadership on a global scale. The systems were designed to allow both the introvert and extrovert to contribute equally to the system. Weightings were assigned by both Artificial Intelligence methods and mass human assessment of proposals.

"People put forward ideas and problems in terms of the organisation of territories, traditional lands and former countries and where critical needs were and how best to address them. Discussion forums of every type; face to face, academic, social, medical, in online chat discussions, in blogs and tweets, in news reports and journal pieces were gathered, noted, assessed and collated. With the combination of advanced AI and dedicated human determination and hard work, the very best ideas and policies that people agreed could and should be implemented were quickly implemented.

"From these practical outcomes and from the analysis of who had the abilities to coordinate, shape and achieve outcomes, the leaders of the new world emerged. Weightings toward not only academic and technical knowledge were factored into the progression of the leaders but also proven compassion and empathy."

"Yes, you in the grey, what would you like to say?"

"Professor, what would you have done if I Day had not happened? I mean how would you have been different?"

"Another good question. I have studied the span of history just before I Day and obviously since. The path of a man like me was one of cynicism and dry academia. This course that I'm teaching will allow us all I hope, and has given me in particular, a view of learning that encourages emotional input and seeks to answer deeper questions. That has been the biggest impact across all of the sciences and learning. The push to bring together humanity, spirit and learning and not to disrupt and separate them."

"The day after I Day was one of momentous relief for many of the governments of the world. Never had cynicism been as great. Never had the foment for revolution and disrespect for leaders been so high. Never had the rule of law and the threat of terrorism been so difficult to combat. Wars were spinning out of control and threatening to become the holocaust that people anticipated as World War Three. The threats to utilise nuclear weaponry were almost nonchalant and certainly more specific and strident than the Cold War days.

"Proxy wars between the pseudo empires were becoming increasingly belligerent, and it was difficult at times to understand in the least what the overarching strategy of the superpowers was. Apart from the local destruction of areas chosen to test out their latest weaponry, there seemed little point in trying to dominate another nuclear superpower. In a world tired, battered and fearful it was a great relief to hear of one government after another resigning or putting in to effect plans to resign imminently. The very notion of being at war or even being a nation became more and more absurd. With no weapons or military that were aiming to kill others, the great task of the existing organisations was to morph into something cohesive, useful and practical in the new reality."

Professor Johnson pointed to the second row. "Baseball cap?"

"Sir, do you think the world will ever be ready to turn off the harmonics again?"

"You young people are really asking some good questions on day one. The answer as far as I can tell is no. When there have been outages over the last few decades, while the general behaviour was quite good, the particular behaviour in some cases quickly returned to pre I Day norms. Murder, rape, stealing returned but it would seem that statistically we are evolving positively and maybe one day I can reverse that answer.

"Untold billions had been put into educating the personnel of the military, and their structures were such that under the new systems the demobilisation of troops and officers were not to meaningless tasks but rather to areas of need within their skill sets. Some indeed were essentially just trained killers, but once the instinct for destruction had been obliterated the physical and survival skills of these people were fairly easily deployed to useful survival skills to build the new world. Others carried immense technical knowledge that was now easily shared across the globe to utilise the technologies previously aimed at surveillance, penetration and destruction to coordination, invention and building."

Johnson had so much command of attention in the lecture hall. His nonchalance was well practiced and the students anticipated how he would unleash his next pearls of wisdom. There was utter silence in the auditorium. "The early democratisation efforts were quite primitive compared to what would eventually come, but the leaders had anticipated that there would be a willingness to utilise existing social networks of every type to understand the will of the people.

"As governments started to slowly pull back from many of their usual roles Facebook and Twitter and their Asian equivalents were sewn together electronically to allow collation and expression of views that meant something on a global scale.

"Despite the primitive nature of the collective expression at that time, several sentinel decisions were quickly made. The basic wage determinations were immediately installed. This constituted that across the globe, no person could earn more than five times any other person on the planet. The early Democratic Councils decided that there should definitely be an ongoing incentive to work hard and be successful, but there was no situation where an executive of a company could earn 2000 times his fellow worker at his own company. Investment income rules were also made outlining excess earnings distributions to the workers themselves. Beyond those distributable profits, other amounts were released to those projects that demanded the most emergent attention across the globe."

Another few hands shot up, and the Professor went to the very back of the hall.

"Yes Miss, firstly explain why you are sitting at the back of this hall. Then ask your question."

"Professor, I am long-sighted and relatively shy. Sir, why did religion melt away so rapidly?"

"Religions were not outlawed but following I Day just a few people remained for a relatively short time within a formal religious designation as the pursuit of universal spiritual goals and the understanding of the true nature of the universe became the principal concern of the people. Religion no longer formed a nidus for the incoherent discrimination between humans and no one valued one spiritual belief above another with tolerance and curiosity being the main focus."

He paused, and the simplicity and accuracy of his answer was able to sink in for a moment or two.

"The other very significant early decision was to abandon the notion of countries. A world passport was issued quite quickly to everyone, and the freedom to visit, explore, enjoy, contribute to and learn from one territory of the world to another was enjoyed by all. This led quickly to the mass migrations and enormous cultural and educational revolutions both in the established areas and those that needed catching up. What really surprised was how much the counter migrations helped spread the joys and benefits of culinary expertise, artistic diversity, language skills and even medical techniques to the First World."

"Slowly the story of the development of the technology by Lorenz's group became general knowledge. The discussions around that centred about the heroism of making the decision to go forward versus the ethics and any downside to the technology. It seemed that initially there was little opposition to their approach, but as time went on, debate and discussion continued as to their decision."

Johnson went over to the blackboard and started chalking iconic symbols. A smiley face, a peace symbol, yin and yang.

"The people, in general, seemed comfortable and determined to enjoy their new lives. So much richer in the rapid ongoing introduction of further useful, entertaining and productive technologies. So much more peaceful without the threat of local and global war or terrorism. Guns were no longer seen in any community. No one felt the need to protect themselves because all were confident that there was no violent threat at all anymore. People simply didn't think that way anymore.

"People were keen to be able to speak out and have their ideas listened to seriously. They became confident with the feedback and that action would be taken if the idea had support as it was assessed. Patents were no longer a negative issue because companies wanted desperately to share new ideas and techniques so they could improve their products and services to the people. So, it was in their interests to publish and collaborate with others, so efficiency, innovation and reward were delivered."

"Red baseball cap?"

"Sir, why did it take this technology to change the nature of man to one of cooperation and tolerance? Why if it was recognised before I Day was it not adopted universally?"

"There were heroes before, lone voices, artists, musicians, prophets who imagined such a world. Their voices were drowned in the petty distractions that cursed mankind up until I Day. From then, it was easier for all of mankind to remain in the present moment and to savour it more easily. From there, everything else fell into place.

"Another decision that was brought in very quickly was global universal access to health care. Significant improvements in transportation methods and the sharing of vastly superior techniques of communication meant that wherever you were in the world, you could now get access to the very best medical advice within minutes. If appropriate care and advice via instruction over video link or holography were not able to be conveyed to the local health practitioners for a patient with a medical condition, then a retrieval team or rapid transport of the patient to an appropriate facility was immediately facilitated.

"People quickly lost their fear of hospitals as the level of care across the globe quite soon evened out, and the training of doctors, nurses and paramedical teams became standardised. With vast exchanges of personnel in those early years to facilitate all of that the transition was fast. It has since become normal practice for both medical students and established practitioners to spend quite some time away from their territory of usual practice to take in the nuances and skills of practices all over the globe."

"After a tumultuous but ultimately very successful initial twelve months, the form of world governance started to emerge into the institution that has proven so successful up to this time. It was agreed that while the vast majority of world issues could be decided by an informed plebiscite, quite a few issues benefited from face to face discussion and debate and then feedback to the people.

"From this realisation, the United Nations Building in New York was refitted completely to accommodate multiple forums throughout the year where people could present and network face to face and come to a consensus on difficult and contentious issues. Sometimes, an individual due to his skill and brilliance might appear as a leader at several summit conferences a year, but the flux of expertise was vast, and government was truly seen to be by and for the people. The process of selecting people for these meetings was based on known skill areas, communication abilities and a willingness to lead."

Several arms shot up again after Johnson outlined the evolution of the governing systems.

"Sir, have we reached the perfect form of government yet?"

"No, absolutely not. That is the whole point of me explaining the background to you. You will become the next government. The thinkers, the youth. Government is all about effective and practical ideas, implementation of technology and growth of democracy. In other words, get involved. Become a leader and a thinker. The world is just begun."

"The rapid decline in formal religious allegiance led to a whole raft of social tensions being released. Rather than being known as a Muslim or a Coptic in Egypt, people just became people. Objections to same-sex marriage melted overnight as people realised there was absolutely no reason to deny to any loving couple the same institutions within which they could declare and commit their love to one another. Religious law gave way to universal laws that all the peoples of the earth had carefully considered and deemed appropriate for everyone to live by. The proscription of knowledge regarding the science of the earth was lifted. All children were given an education not based fundamentally on scripts written out of context in ancient books but rather incorporating the importance of myth and story and the strength of truth."

"As it became clear that from a very early age that learning had become much easier and brains were working so much more efficiently, the entire education syllabus was altered dramatically. Unstructured and problem-based learning was the model not just at tertiary level but at all levels of education. The rate that information was acquired was high, but it was the way that it was shared between tutor and pupil and very importantly peer to peer and pupil to tutor that was striking. No longer were there systematic barriers to learning and utilising that knowledge to further society. It was relatively easy to pass on ideas for the communal good from the school system. As the ability to conquer simple knowledge tasks in science and maths and reading skills was so much better, there was much more time in the school week to explore esoteric subjects like philosophy, psychology, art and ethics. Kids were learning how to learn to help them become positive contributors to society as they progressed.

"There was an explosion in post-graduate and mature age studies. Every topic from ancient history to mathematics was revisited from fresh perspectives and energies. Synthesis of previous doctoral theses was found to be a whole new branch of academia with minor individual discoveries put together in ways that became a practical and useful whole. People with commerce backgrounds were doing Masters in Fine Arts, and painters and sculptors were doing Mathematics and Music degrees part-time to round out their knowledge base. Religious studies were by no means abandoned, but the best parts of each religion were dissected and analysed and amalgamated into practical moral arguments that went before society for debate with recognition or rejection. Mythology and story once again became vast industries with movies, books, plays, street theatre and performance exploding in every city and town. Rather than some kind of dull grey conforming society the performing arts flourished and appreciation for the abstract, surreal, impressionist and realist interpretations through art gave the creative souls much work and much scope for expression."

"Criminology and Law enforcement became a minor field quite rapidly. The security industry collapsed, and the physical and technical skills of the workforce were redeployed across the new employment areas. Crime was limited to areas where the harmonic waves were marginal but as time went on virtually the whole earth was reliably covered by the waves and there was positive motivation to study how the system could be improved and made more stable. There was little serious debate that it should never have been deployed. The standard of living had improved over fivefold on average across the world and multiplied more than that in what were the 3rd world countries. Poverty had been completely eradicated. The elimination of war was something that was celebrated the most on the anniversary of I Day. Crime was limited to confusion about democratic decisions and was generally dealt with by a process of education and never by incarceration. "Interestingly, in times where there was a system failure, there was not a mass return to poor human behaviour. It seemed that the years of positivity had rewired the basic thinking processes so as to be able to conceive of a workable non-violent solution to most conflict. Mental retardation, brain trauma and mental illnesses were not eliminated but were lesser problems in the new cooperative and supportive society. The ability to connect and the understanding of the pathophysiology of brain disease allowed for immediate familial and societal as well as medicinal needs to be catered for. Accurate diagnosis, improved living conditions and rapid sharing of pharmaceutical breakthroughs meant early delivery of better care and a big difference in negative social outcomes.

"And that my dear scholars would be that for my introductory lecture were it not of course that I had to mention our friend General Freddie Horowitz. The disaster he unleashed after I Day will haunt us forever. So, I will urge you to study up on the whole sad affair and be back with more questions, answers, commentary and conclusions at our next meeting.

"Finally, I would like to welcome to our campus two of the earliest pioneers of our almost fully imagined world. I am sure you know them simply as Gholam and Amanda." The pair humbly stood and beamed up at the students in the lecture hall, gave each other a kiss and a hug and acknowledged the warm welcome. At the back of the hall, in dark sunglasses, in the finest of Armani suits, a tall old man of Italian origin, stood, as Gholam and Amanda stood. As they acknowledged the crowd, both Gholam and Amanda had a friendly wave for Giovanni as he slipped from the lecture hall.

Chapter 7

Nevada 4 days after I Day

"General, there are some bizarre reports coming out of Central Command tonight and I'm not sure how to tell you this, but we have been ordered to stand down and begin to demobilise 95 percent of our staff by next Tuesday."

Horowitz growled and barely looked up from his briefing papers as the Major went on.

"It seems Washington is ordering all Army units to be withdrawn across the globe and all nuclear submarines have returned to base. It seems sir that peace has broken out across the world. There are some rumours that some kind of mind-altering is involved in this, but I do not have specific intelligence as to what the nature of that may be."

Horowitz stood up and walked around the desk. He was an enormous man with thick eyebrows and thinning hair with a very, very large forehead. The General had no neck to speak of, and he seemed to need to turn his whole body to manhandle his face to where he wished to focus his attention. His fingers were sinewy and hands barnacled as he had spent many of his active years sun-exposed in the Philippines and the Pacific. His face was distorted by multiple surgeries for skin cancers. He whizzed about to face Major Falinski, eyeballing him with asymmetrical eyelids as if the man had lost all his senses overnight.

"Major Falinksi, we ignore this for now. This is nonsense. We are the US Air Force. We are not giving away one man from this facility until I know exactly what is happening out there. We haven't just been inventing every Stealth unit since 1949. Area 51 is not going to sell out to some liberal madness going on out there. Seal the computer systems, close down all movement in and out of the facility and get me those crazy politicians on the line as soon as possible."

"Yes sir, and I will see what I can find out about what's happening out there."

"Good Falinski, get out of here."

Falinksi wandered out to the chow hall and sat in his usual spot. He produced his thermos of diluted poor-quality brewed coffee and sat there thinking how he should approach the General who had seemed even stranger in his behaviour lately than usual. No one ever sat with Falinksi while he had his coffee. He didn't quite understand why, but he was oddly grateful for it. He sat contemplating his three years mostly underground at the complex and how he missed seeing his family back in New Jersey. His position was so secret that he rarely spoke to his sister and mother. When he was recruited to Area 51, he had visions that his duties as personal assistant to the General would give him access to the fabled Alien investigations that were rumoured to be conducted here in the isolation of the Nevada desert. Two months into the job and he realised the task was much more prosaic and less conspiratorial. Unless you considered developing weapons that were beyond the abilities of any other nation to defend against as conspiratorial. Every possible way to deliver knockout blows to a perceived enemy were conceived, built and tested in the complex. Stealth aeroplanes, nuclear devices that could be delivered by air, sea and land, robotic soldiers were near to perfection. All in a day's work here in Area 51 with the madness and genius of General Horowitz guiding the facility. The General had been considered a little of a maverick for many years by various other services, and the politicians had tried to have him removed many times, but his achievements could not be denied, and the US military strength owed much to the direction of this unusual man. Falinski, however, had seen a subtle deterioration in the General's behaviour over the last 12 months and it weighed on his conscience heavily. He asked himself every day how he could go about reporting his observations which were quite vague and he sat with his dreadful coffee every day and couldn't come up with the answer. Complicating all of this was the incredible news from the outside. So hard to get a feel for what was actually going on. The press appeared confused, and it seemed unable to keep up with the rapidity of change that was happening. The air force itself apparently was engaging in the process of giving itself away and in the confines of this special place that didn't quite make sense. Falinski knew what the General's reaction would be. Beyond disbelief, he could imagine him actively opposing what was happening outside, and it scared the bejesus out of him.

Such was the isolation of Area 51 that no one apart from food suppliers who came to the very rim of the complex had been within the outer perimeter for two years. Such was the carefulness of Horowitz that all personnel had been signed up to a non-disclosure and permanent residence agreement for three years. Essentially, the facility was closed, and all genius and trouble had to be dealt with within the electronically isolated and hermetically sealed environment. The biggest problem that was fairly regularly faced was stress and anxiety attacks related to isolation. Bullying was an issue and the higher echelons of the organisation if anything seemed to encourage it as some kind of loyalty test. Falinski was appalled at the official memos he had to distribute which he felt reflected Horowitz's increasing anxiety. The medical personnel at the facility had been handpicked by Horowitz and most had been there for more than a decade. They were burnt out and cynical when it came to dealing with yet another case of 'isolation fear syndrome' and usually prescribed sedatives of the oldest variety that were both addictive and decreased clarity significantly. More than a dozen people had applied to leave the facility but Horowitz stamped refusal on every single claim. He thought that the work and the secrets were too important to risk with some rogue spilling the beans on the outside.

Over the next couple of days, rumours of what was happening in the outside world were spreading like wildfire about the complex. From the cooks to the pilots, there was a buzz. Most were thoroughly patriotic and nationalistic in political orientation. They were from good southern families and elite northern Academies and wholeheartedly supported Horowitz's vision for an apocalyptic solution to any threat to the United States, but there were a few as in any military establishment that came from very different perspectives and were just there to do a job. Some of these characters had always had access to news and communication with the outside world despite the constant efforts of the administration to limit this. So, when I Day came and went, it was to the astonishment of all that not one thing changed within Area 51. If anything, there was a push to accelerate the research, engineering and deployment of these world-beating weapons. It was as if Horowitz had them on the threshold of a war alert. The loyalists were indefatigable when the call came to push the work harder and faster. The more rebellious among them were absolutely confused as the stories of massive changes in the very structure and thinking in the outside world became better understood. Despite the gymnasium, movie theatre and baseball diamond the tension as the rumours gathered pace was palpable. It seemed from the news reports that things were rapidly being organised in a very efficient and sensible manner. The world was literally changing on their doorstep and more and more of them wanted to be part of it and couldn't understand why the facility was being ramped up and they were made to work twice as hard on weapons of seriously sinister mass destructive capability.

After three days of this, Falinski confronted Horowitz. He had confided in some of the known 'troublemakers' that he had concerns about Horowitz's mental state. He cited evidence of increasingly belligerent decision making and broke the General's confidence regarding the orders from Washington to abandon the facility immediately. They were horrified, but in the locked-down environment they were in, any outright confrontation or insubordination could be treated as treason and court martial was always the path Horowitz threatened when he was openly attacked. Falinski noticed Horowitz was even more tense than usual, it looked like he hadn't shaved for a few days and his tic like right eyelid twitch was much more pronounced and disturbing than he remembered. Horowitz stood over him and demanded to know what he knew.

"General, things seem to be moving very rapidly in the outside world now. More than 80 national governments have resigned, and the US government is working to dissolve congress by the end of next week. Power is shifting rapidly to an ideas led worldwide democracy with leaders being identified and flown in from all over the world to begin to establish what appears to be a completely new world order."

"That's ridiculous Falinski, just preposterous. The idea that the United States would surrender its world domination and sovereignty to foreigners is unimaginable and will not be happening on my watch. This is why we developed Area 51. For this very type of occurrence. When the world has gone mad, then we will prevail. You haven't put me in touch with any politicians Falinksi. Who do we talk to in order to get these bastards to see sense?"

Falinski's sense of panic began to rise. It was clear to him that Horowitz was on a path that could potentially be disastrous for the facility and the outside world. He became more and more determined to see this to a good outcome but wondered how he could achieve this. Falinski organised for Horowitz to speak with some of the emerging leaders of the new world order. Some of the team that had steered the technology to the world were aware of the potential for problems in Nevada. Planning for deployment of the harmonic waves had been meticulous, but Area 51 had always been an electronic blackspot. It was thought that the best strategy would be negotiation as the leadership in the Area would be exposed to the facts on the outside and be persuaded to join in. When finally, Professor Lorenz and his chief deployment engineer Cong Ming began their teleconference with General Horowitz it wasn't long before their joy and incredulity of their vision was replaced with trepidation and fear for the planet.

"General, what a delight to be talking with you this evening. I am Professor James Lorenz, and this is my colleague Mr Cong Ming who is here to facilitate the deployment of our harmonic waves into the last of the areas around the world that have not been covered. I presume you are familiar with the profound changes that have been occurring around the world since I Day."

"Professor, cut with the bullshit. I'm not buying any of this crap. This is the United States of America, and it is my duty to preserve the state of the union. You people are in my way as far as I can tell."

Cong Ming was acutely alerted to the General's attitude and rapidly scanned the room that the General was occupying for clues as to how the harmonics could be deployed deep within Area 51. It became clear very soon that it was the only hope to turn this situation around.

"General, my name is Cong. I have been involved in deploying the..."

"Ming, I have intelligence on you. You have spent the past seven years in China. Don't say another word. Listen gentlemen, this is a complete waste of time. I need to speak to who is in charge out there. Where is the President? I need answers, and I need them now."

"General, the President has been magnificent throughout all of this process. He has offered up all his network of offices, intranets and hotel complexes to facilitate the new form of world governance. He has retired quietly to his family home and acknowledges the tranquil and democratic processes that are unfolding."

"I can't believe that bastard has given up the country. What the fuck is happening out there? What have you done to everyone? This is treason. You people are going to be put away forever. Fucking Baldwin, never trusted that guy."

"General, I'm not sure what you understand to be happening out here. You're aware that 84 governments have now officially resigned. The world is rapidly being transformed into a cooperative venture. General, we have forwarded the directive from the World Council to you. Your compliance is appreciated."

"My duty is to my nation. You can tell those imbeciles that there will be consequences to this nonsense. Good evening gentlemen."

Ming and Lorenz looked at each other in stunned silence for a moment as the screen went blank. Ming was quickly on the phone to his team, having observed the General's quarters as best as he could in the limited time that they had. It was time to act and act very fast.

Ming was animated. "This guy is nuts, and we will need to get to him as soon as possible. Intelligence so far has got him in charge of several means of creating absolute havoc so the quicker he is part of the solution, the better.

"Professor, perimeter teams are in place and are steadily deploying the harmonics as they proceed. We haven't had any ugly incidents yet, but it won't be long before the General starts to become aware of the incursions. So far, the team inside has been able to keep that information suppressed. We are going to have to find a man close enough to the General to successfully avoid complete disaster. From what I can see, this man is threatening the current world order with old-world weaponry."

The rebel group inside Area 51 were being steadily pressured and concerned by the feedback from the meeting between Lorenz and Horowitz. It really was coming down to crunch time. Horowitz was threatening to use the power at his disposal to turn around everything that was happening in the world. They clearly saw that if they could get the harmonics to the General, then the crisis could probably be averted. The call came from the outside for them to find someone who they could trust in the higher echelons. Someone who could get to Horowitz. Falinski was their man.

Falinski sat there looking as forlorn and sad as usual, obsessively flipping the spout on his thermos and repeatedly sipping the awful watery concoction. He was astonished to see two of his colleagues join him at the breakfast table.

"Sir, sorry to disturb your delicious breakfast, but we need to talk urgently."

Falinksi looked sadder than ever and just stared at them for longer than an awkward pause.

"I know, Horowitz is not sleeping, he's pacing his office like a caged tiger and he's lost his sense of reality. He has asked the weapons team to deploy and have ready by tonight three nuclear warheads. One aimed for Paris, one Moscow and the other New York. I have no idea if this is bluff or real, but it seems to me that we are sinking into the mire right now. I have no idea what to do. Caruthers, I can't calm him. Nothing anyone has said is having any impact. He seems determined to hold the world to ransom."

It was Major Caruthers turn to pause.

"Major Falinski, we have a plan, and you are the key. We need to slow down this whole process while the deployment team burrows in from the outside. As we are speaking the tunnel has progressed to within 200 yards of central command. We need time and the element of surprise."

Falinski was mortified that day by Horowitz's demeanour. He was focused and repeatedly asked for briefing papers on events around the world, and he seemed to crave an understanding of the scientific discoveries and the personnel involved in the development toward I Day. There were no mad ravings that day. Just studied and deliberate gathering of information as if he were coming to the realisation that this was an inevitable and positive progression in human interaction. There was calm, there was fine food, and he was charming to his junior officers and the personnel interacting with him. Falinksi drew a huge sigh of relief and was happy to keep the information flowing to his boss. He went to bed early that evening, exhausted, knowing that having set up the General's worldwide press conference for the next day that sanity would surely be preserved, and Horowitz would announce his retirement and the Area's demobilisation. There was only one current puzzling issue. Why was there ongoing activity in the research and deployment facilities? If this were all coming to an end in the morning, why the harried look on the men and women in the weapons areas? What really was going on?

As prearranged, Falinksi met Major Caruthers and Colonel Lennon, his surprise breakfast visitors in the map room at midnight and explained his relief at the General's attitude today. Lennon looked at him intensely.

"Major Falinski, we have reason to believe the General will attempt to derail I Day within the next 24 hours. Stay aware, you may be the only one who can thwart his plans. Don't believe for one minute that he has seen the light. Our tunnellers are within 100 yards. Hopefully, we can deploy the harmonics within this time frame."

Horowitz sat in his bunker, looking at the traitors all over his facility. His personal quarters were a mass of CCTV screens and zooming mechanisms. His echolocation and ultrasound perimeters had been breached. He knew he had limited time to turn back the disaster that his political masters had been unable to do. He knew he was the only one who could save America.

The General was due in for his press conference at 0900 hours. Falinski had never seen the General looking so impressive. His combover was perfect, he was wearing medals that Falinksi was unaware existed, and a few for outstanding valour that Falinksi had not realised the General had won. His buttons were polished, his boots immaculate and his neck and face as menacing as usual as they tracked each other about the room as the General prepared himself.

As the production team settled him behind his desk, he refused any makeup touches and this special broadcast, which was the first to be carried on every single television station worldwide simultaneously since the Beatles live version of "All you need is love", was about to be broadcast. The world was aware that within this speech, the victory of peace would be finally achieved. This was a moment that held the world mesmerised.

"My fellow Americans and any foreign friends that may be watching this broadcast today. Welcome to Area 51 for the first time in history. You are inside the bastion of America's power. Be aware that we here have been developing the means to keep America safe for nearly three-quarters of a century now. It is my task to back the will and support the constitution of the United States of America, and I have been doing that since I was a 19-year-old recruit into the finest armed services in the world.

"I have done much research into the events that have happened around the globe over the last six days. It seems to me that a group of maverick scientists and academics have imposed their own ideals and polemic on the rest of the world, including my own beloved country without the consent of the people. It is, therefore, my duty to inform you that I intend that those changes should be reversed, and I am determined that this will happen within the 12 hours from the end of this broadcast. It would appear an easy task to reverse the means by which the world has found itself in this madness. If it is not clear that the reversal has taken place and that the national governments have begun to resume their responsibilities, I will have no choice but to use the power at my disposal to force those changes.

"In that respect, I have instructed my weapons teams to deploy four nuclear weapons, each set to launch three hours apart if the changes have not been made by 2100 hours. These weapons are designed to target four cities, Moscow, New York, Paris and Beijing. As a result of the madness that has existed over the week, I am aware that there is no power, domestic or foreign that can threaten us here in Area 51. I need assurances that the changes have taken place, or a random city will be targeted overnight. I certainly hope that your new democracy is flexible enough to make its first sensible decision."

With that, the screens around the world ran blank, and a small digital clock was visible as a reminder of what they were facing.

Chapter 8

Nova Scotia 8 days after I Day

Nancy and Robert had gotten up very early to avoid the tourists; They knew that the cliffs of Cape Breton still attracted large numbers of hikers even during the cooler months of the year. This time they had made it back here in the Summer. Even though they had walked the Skyline trail before, the lure of finally spotting a moose and revisiting the sensations that the wide blue horizon and impossibly steep coast could provide was too tempting. While they were vaguely aware of the enormous changes that were taking place around the world it didn't seem that much had changed in this quiet corner. The people were just as friendly, the pine trees just as numerous and the peace and quiet of the fishing villages and rugged forests made for a timelessness that they craved. Nancy and Robert couldn't wait to get back out on that famous trail.

The last time that they had travelled there was in an April where the warmth of the greetings at the Bed and Breakfasts contrasted with the crispness of the mornings and even the occasional snowstorm. Today, it was bright andwarm, there was just a light sea breeze as they made their way to the diner on the wharf. They came to very much enjoy watching the fishing vessels pulling in and offloading their various catches. The summer fare, however, was not much more appetising than the spring offerings of stodgy scrambled egg, overdone bacon rashers and ruined tomato. Sitting outside with the sun pouring through and the seabirds concentrating on the trawlers was a true pleasure. The light on the water took on a different character as well. Across the bay, a million shimmering wavelets drew their eyes slowly to the headland of the peninsula now flush in a deep green. The fields were dotted by the brown and blacks of the dairy cows relishing their summer feast.

Their fellow breakfast companions were an eclectic mix of locals, fishermen, lobster catchers, small business owners and tourists. The most obvious difference being the confident and friendly chatter of the locals through rugged and wild beards versus the inevitable North Face jackets and enormous camera lenses and quieter conversation of the tourists. So many languages were able to be discerned. An interesting mix of French and English from the locals and the drawl of the American hikers, various European enthusiasms and the odd Australian accent. Lovers of the great outdoors all and enthralled with what they knew of this place and knowing how much more beauty was to be taken in.

As they had driven into the village last evening rounding the Cape, they had made sure to stop regularly to take in the seascapes especially as it was closing in toward sunset. Here the sun dropped variously over rugged outcrops or endless horizons of water depending on the whims of park rangers from earlier in the previous century plotting the viewing points. All were worthy of time and exploration as the dying sun across the waters seemingly shifted the breezes, creating pockets of pure stillness and others of some disturbance where the pinks and purples played, retreated, merged with deeper tints until the still darkness and hunger called them back to their car and on to town.

Others sitting with them on the rough-hewn wooden benches and tables of the diner had travelled from the South. Nancy and Robert began talking to a couple from Jersey who had just come up from Halifax and the coast beyond. Describing the wild rock outcrops and sensual fishing villages crawling with summer crowds of photographers keen to take that unique angle with the lobster pots in the foreground along with the sheltered bay lined by gorgeous cottages beyond. The trinket and souvenir shops atop restaurants with alluring views across blue and white lighthouses perched on black volcanic rock. Noting how that enticing mix of man and nature was impossible to capture without the intrusion of posing teenagers unless you were the first there at dawn which in summer was well before 5 am. The couple spoke about looking out over marooned anchors of long-lost ships and a coastline alive and wildly rugged, a sea dotted with pleasure craft and swimmers. They told Nancy and Robert how they had learnt it was a coast haunted by the downing of a passenger aeroplane. Tragically, some years before all 229 souls had been lost into the sea and how it had hung over the area as a reminder of the fragility of life.

As they shared tales of exploring this wild and rich landscape, the talkative two from Jersey turned to their experiences in the far south.

Nancy looked at Robert with knowing eyes. She had a personality that drew people in naturally. Robert would think it inevitable whenever they travelled that they would soon be surrounded by children or chatting to an old man from whom Nancy would manage to secure his whole life story. Their relationship had been very strained now for some years. He, much younger than her but utterly besotted by her ability to reach people, to reach him in his very soul. She, not wanting to hold him back but wanting to be completely adored and loved in life by a good man as well. So, they had come here, once again just as friends but once again drawn to each other physically. The past six days had been like the old days. Her smile always caught his attention. His courtesy and the sheer relaxation that the journey had created, the forests and walks and the little touches not missing her attention. The knowing look they exchanged acknowledging the potency and sweetness with which they had made love in the early hours of the morning. With abandon, with no consideration for their platonic intent. They had surrendered to pleasure, and so he returned her look with equal intensity.

They sauntered back to their car and turned the air conditioning on. It was warming up already, and they donned their baseball caps as the sun started creeping over the escarpment. All was bright, and the road was relatively free as they pulled out of Cheticamp and up through the winding ocean road to their trailhead. They were waved through at the gates of the Cape Breton National Park having already secured their season pass. The road never failed to fill them with awe as it hugged the edge of the mountain calling them to frequent stops to take in the views along the way. Giant bluffs of twisted granite plunged at unnatural angles into the surf. Small picnic grounds were dotted along the road taking in mountain vistas and ocean sounds. The smell of the sea on the light breeze was intoxicating as they hugged each other for the sheer beauty they were experiencing together. Finally, they found the turn off for the car park for the Skyline Trail. Only two other cars. They were in luck.

The day was perfect. They retrieved their backpacks, made sure they had plenty of water and headed along the wide flat, dirt road which took them to the trail start proper. This time they decided to take the longer route around as they had never done that before. The terrain was familiar and they were into a good stride; enjoying the sounds of summer birds, the scurrying of red squirrels in amongst the trees and wild turkeys in the long grasses. Rob told Nancy to stand stock still and about 10 metres from where they stood, they finally had a glimpse of the moose they had never caught sight of in the wild before. It was as if it all was coming together for them this morning. Alone, perfect weather, old feelings revived and now this special moment for them both.

They knew not to disturb the large animal which could inflict serious damage if one did not pay respect and stay out of its way. Nancy captured some candid shots as the moose warily watched her every move before heading back into the hinterland. The trail now beckoned them on for they knew they would be rewarded with near endless vision on such a clear day. The wider loop surprised them by its additional length, and they both felt their calves were well worked by the time they started to approach the coast.

The landscape suddenly opened up, the salt once again strong on the breeze and the gulls swept across their path and off down the steep slope to the blue ocean far, far below them now. They came to the wooden platforms and seating, one set of well-groomed stairs taking them to the next platform where they could not help but pause and wonder at the awesome beauty before them. There was just one other couple there and they were heading back now, they nodded an enthusiastic greeting to them. As they explored each level it gave them a different perspective on the massive cliff they stood upon. Their view was the entire coast back to Cheticamp and beyond. The blue, blue sea was far below them and the waves appeared as slow moving lines out to the horizon that peaked to white as they came close to shore. The drop was sheer, nearly 500 metres high and it was impossible not to imagine how a tumble could only lead to one tragic outcome. This part of the trail was well signposted warning to stay on the structured path as the environment was fragile underfoot, but one suspected this included an implicit warning to not fall to one's early death. At the end of the viewing area for the Skyline trail they paused to take in the very earth itself as the sea breeze scuttled up the sheer cliff face and their eyes scanned a blue horizon that curved gently but persistently across their vision.

Their eyes took in the sumptuous view out to sea and along the coast, they turned to each other, held each other tightly and kissed softly. Finally, they turned and headed up the steep slope for the return trip. Halfway up, they saw the sky above the ridge flash a brilliant white. It was like looking into the sun for a little too long, and temporarily they struggled to see clearly. There was no idea about what it could mean, but it was otherworldly. Nancy suggested they head quickly back to the car, and so they walked with great urgency and purpose. Then over the ridge on the high trail they saw the Mushroom Cloud form to the East. It pushed up and up into the brilliant blueness of the sky expanding rapidly with each passing second. Initially, it was yellow, then red was pouring straight up into the atmosphere. It lightened to a typical white cloud colour and ballooned out.

Nancy and Robert stood stock still on the trail not knowing what to make of it all. Four minutes later, they were hit by a persistent and odd gust of warm wind, a breeze from the direction of the cloud like a wall of tepid, stale breath. It stayed with them as an eerie reminder of the sudden oddness of this day as the cloud arched and spread across that formerly perfect sky. At one point they weren't sure if the very massive basalt cliff edge upon which they were walking was becoming unstable. The very earth rumbled below them for several seconds then it did the same a minute later. The cloud was lifting, spreading and dispersing and the atmosphere became suddenly much darker as the sky swallowed up the sparkling morning sun. From the clarity of a perfect morning, they now found themselves struggling to make out the trail ahead in the dark and they felt their way forward back to the trailhead and the car. The dry wind made them very thirsty, and fortunately they had brought plenty of bottled water in their packs. Large, black rain droplets started to fall from the sky. They were pleased to be able to get back into their car and pleased to see the strange rain end very shortly after it had begun. The road was deserted as they headed back into town and turned their radio on to find out what was going on. The radio was stubbornly silent. They looked at each other and gave each other a huge hug at a pullover section of the road as they tried to get their emotions under some control. Something terrible had happened. What was the safe and sensible thing to do? Nancy asked Robert to calmly and slowly drive back to Cheticamp. They felt that was away from the general direction of the massive cloud and flash that they had seen. The rain returned for a few seconds at a time, and the windscreen wipers struggled to get the window clean. They said little, save assuring the other that all would be ok, and it was good to be alive. In their hearts they realised that something enormous was happening out there in their non-holiday world, something potentially very ugly and very deadly. Slowly, they drove past the park entrance. Not a soul in the picnic grounds, no one at the ticket booth. No one on the beaches as they wound about the coast and into town. There was no one on the street, no one having a meal at any of the wharf diners, fishing boats abandoned, shops closed, quiet and shut down. They came to the centre of the village where a police car with double flashing lights was parked in the middle of the road. Pulling up to it, they saw no one inside. There was a note on the windshield that they could barely make out:

> "Head south on the coast road, we are not sure at this point what is happening, but it would appear that Canada has been attacked with a nuclear warhead. Do not attempt to drive inland. Stay calm and head south to the evacuation point which will be established at Port Hawkesbury."

While fear was gripping them both, they knew it would be best to try and follow the instructions to the letter. The road was surreal driving from the town. It was in their interests to keep each other's spirits up, but there was little to say. Robert drove on, and Nancy attempted to tune the radio where every now and then a brief signal would come through. This gave them some hope as they headed away from that erstwhile incredibly peaceful fishing town.

The first 20 or so miles out of Cheticamp was unremarkable apart from the stillness and desolation. No one was to be seen, and it was as if the world had abandoned them to a silent coast to contemplate the unknown disaster together. The ocean lay to their right, dark, quiet and vast. They hardly spoke to each other as the winding coastal road took them from village to village, over quaint bridges and by wooded lakes. The sky remained an eerie hue, and a gritty electrical smell was ever present.

By the time they got to Margaree Harbour, they were starting to catch up with the cavalcade before them. The lines of cars on both sides of the road heading south was at a virtual standstill. As far as they could see, there were cars with hazard lights blinking and people walking out of them and shouting and yelling at anyone and anything. They decided to go off the coast road and planned to make their way down to the South via a more direct and less used way. A few had also chosen to go via this route, and they made their way across Cape Breton with relative ease. They had driven this way before in a snowstorm; they had managed to slowly pick their way through small towns and vast white forests of pines. In some ways this was more difficult. The cars driving this way were incredibly cautious, and there was still no information on the radio. The strident and somewhat terrifying air was, if anything, worsening as they travelled south-east. When Nancy and Robert finally found their voice, they briefly pulled over to the side of the road and simply hugged each other out of the car. Crying with relief and anxiety, both happy that so far they had survived what appeared to be an apocalyptic day. They told one another how much they felt, how much their love over the years had really meant and reassured each other that they would get through this day.

They had no phone signal as they made their way across Cape Breton and approached Hunter's Mountain expecting to be heading south toward Port Hawkesbury and the bridge to the main island of Nova Scotia and hopefully to an understanding of what was happening. The dark clouds had given way to bluer skies but the smell of burning forests became stronger and they were on the lookout for forest fire. The pines here seemed inordinately still as did the many scores of small lakes that they passed. It was as if the whole world was standing still waiting for answers as they crawled behind the cautious vehicles ahead of them. Finally, they made it to the broad intersection of the Cabot Trail and Trans-Canada Highway. It looked vaguely familiar to them, the huge red barn on the left that sold souvenirs and awful coffee, a Canadian flag flying high above, but the scene was in fact very different to the quiet turn off that they remembered. Before them were hundreds of cars heading south, jam-packed and inching along the highway with tempers flaring and car horns blaring. Emergency service vehicles and police were everywhere trying to sort things as best they could.

As the cars streamed through and Nancy and Robert waited at the intersection for direction, they noticed that the vehicles were all packed. Some were filled with people that looked barely alive. Bandaged, anguished, crying, staring out of windows as if they had returned from hell. As more cars passed, it was apparent that many were in agony, some with faces burnt and barely recognisable, some close to death. There were children screaming in pain and many people hurriedly getting out of slow-moving cars to vomit by the side of the road. Nancy and Robert suddenly felt the acrid air as even more sinister than they could have imagined as the steady stream of injured and desperate people made their way south.

They pulled over by the big red barn and surveyed the chaotic scene. A large burly policeman was trying to direct traffic around the intersection with little success.

"Is there anything we can do?" said Nancy.

The policeman kept waving cars through and didn't seem to notice them. He had a strange look in his eyes as if he had looked into hell itself and was detached as his arms flapped wildly above his head.

"Sir, can we help in any way?" Nancy tried again.

The policeman finally looked at them directly. He then just walked to the side of the road, sat in the gutter and started bawling into the palms of his hands. He was inconsolable for about a minute as Nancy and Robert sat beside him, placing their hands on his shoulders.

The police officer finally spoke "I've come from the North. It's awful. I brought a wagon full of sick kids down, and hopefully, they are getting care somewhere, but I had to leave their parents and all the other adults. There is total destruction in some parts, the dead have been left where they were burnt alive. There was panic and terror. We need transport up there, but the Cape's ambulances are already beyond capacity. We just need to get people out of there and to hospitals and care. I feel useless here, but someone has to get the road organised. Help me back out there and thank you for asking how you can help. You just did."

With that the officer rose and walked with resolve back to the centre of the intersection and with purpose resumed his traffic duties.

Nancy looked at Robert, and they both knew what the other was thinking. They hopped back in their car and headed North, straight toward the greyest sky that they could remember and to where the disaster at its core surely lay. There was no roadblock, and no authority was present to tell them to turn back. They spent the next four miles in and out of the verge as the cars heading South occupied at times all the lanes of the road. Mostly, the vehicles were three across on a two-lane road. Again, every car filled with anguished and injured people, some in the cars imploring them to turn back. Mostly, people were just focussed on the injured in their vehicles and many of the drivers' faces had the same listless look that the policeman had back at the turn-off. It started to thin out as the physical environment began to change about them. Nancy turned to Robert and asked him.

"Rob, why are we going up here again? We know there's been a nuclear bomb, we have no idea why. We don't know how big it was or where it has hit, and yet we are driving on a road that seems to lead to oblivion. Why are we doing this again my friend?"

"Nance, what do you know about nuclear bombs? I figure that it must have hit over the sea because if it were over the land all of these people would be dead? Why on earth would anyone want to bomb Sydney, Nova Scotia?"

"I think we know I know why we are here Rob. We have survived something extraordinary. We know many people are suffering and trying to get help. There is something, someone to help here. Even if we can get one family out of there safely."

"Nance, we have to protect ourselves as well if we are going to be of any use to anyone. We need to stay out of this fallout as much as we can and we will have to get these clothes off when we get a chance. There's a gentle southerly wind outside, that is going to help, but we need to get in and out of there as quickly as possible."

The traffic started to thin out and the effects of the blast became more obvious. Spot fires could be seen on the ridges ahead. There was little to say now, they held hands as they came closer to towns that they knew had substantial populations. North Sydney was very quiet at the busiest of times but driving along the shore of Sydney Harbour on this day was surreal. Every boat along the shoreline was driven at an almost identical angle into the shallow banks and crab inhabited rocks. Large holes were visible along the bows and starboard sides of the craft. The tidy wooden houses with their cute shutters along the harbourside were badly damaged. Not one had escaped some destruction from the blast, but none were totally ruined. They turned up one of the side streets and noticed very little disturbance at all. It seemed that all the impact here was along the shore. They headed back and toward the East and drove into the sleepy town of Sydney. Overhead, a helicopter of the ambulance service hovered briefly above them and then headed swiftly

East. The Western side of Sydney was relatively unscathed, even the main dock and giant violin were intact although two strings were laying across the dockside still connected to the large tailpiece of the massive upright structure. The totally deserted dock looked out to the near peninsula where it was clear that significant damage had been suffered, but again no one was to be seen. They mostly stayed in the car as they were aware that the wind could change at any time and they were considering how to limit their radiation exposure so that they could help people. They were questioning why they were there at all and yet they were drawn on. There was somewhere they belonged that day. Robert said to Nancy that they should continue to head east, he pulled up to a convenience store, and came back with two arms full with bottled water which he placed in the trunk and headed back in for more. Nancy had never seen Robert with that expression before, it was a savage kindness he bore, and she thought at once that she would love him forever and never be with him again.

As they drove north and east, the devastation grew by the mile. Spot fires dotted the road ahead, and the salty brush of the coast was blackened and flattened. They stopped briefly, looked out across the sea, turned to each other and embraced. They wove past debris on the small coastal road and stopped to check if anyone needed help in the wooden cottages that were barely standing. Some were ablaze, and it was impossible to know if the quiet, tough families of this far flung part of the Cape had managed to escape. They found no one in any of the cottages, and their instinct took them further east. As they drove, it was extraordinary how far ahead they could see. As they climbed a small ridge, across from them, the pines were gone, and the rolling landscape was stark. The entire Eastern Cape was a charred nightmare. Dotted with half depleted lakes and very few existing structures. They warily drove on. No further cars passed by them going to the safer zones.

Nancy had tears streaming down her face and Robert wondered when he had last seen her cry. She was a very emotional woman but also very good at expression and so it was rare that she openly cried about sad things but rather those that warmed her heart. He remembered her on previous vacations in tears as she hugged a small child that she had connected with. Her open heart was so engaging to those she met as she emanated a welcome and invited trust even with her body language and so people of all ages responded. He remembered her sitting in a park outside an ancient fortress in India with some small bracelets and within a few minutes she would have a flock of youngsters touching her hair and face and asking her questions in their own language. It was impossible not to recognise in her the deep empathy she had for her fellow man. Robert saw that she was overwhelmed by the view ahead of them and simply held her hand as they drove on.

As they were heading out from what remained of Glace Bay, they thought they saw something moving along the side of the road as the Marconi Trail Road crossed the water near the Bird Sanctuary. For some reason, Nancy told Robert to stop, and she got out of the car to see if it was someone who needed some help. She jumped the rail and headed down into the marshy ground by the old road bridge. Robert could see her kneeling down and embracing something. In Nancy's arms was a dishevelled and beautiful brown and white patched Border Collie. The dog seemed awfully happy to have found someone and gave Nancy an enthusiastic welcome. Nancy could tell straight away how intelligent and well trained the dog was. She fell in love with him immediately, and they were swift friends. He was dirty but not obviously injured. Fergie was now part of the family and followed Nancy back to the car. The dog jumped into the backseat, his head shot out the window which was wound down for him a few inches, and his tongue hung out to catch the wind. Nancy fixed him some water which he greedily drunk down. Then he resumed his position on the back seat, lurching out the window as they took off again to the South and East.

They followed the Marconi trail along the coast and found a path of destruction that they could barely navigate. The destructive power of the explosion seemed to be worse as they drove East with large swathes of the coastal pines burnt and about half the houses destroyed. Some were flattened by the physical force of what they understood could only have been a nuclear bomb. Many had been burnt to the ground as a result of the fires that had swept very rapidly through the area. The bridge over Mira gut was intact to their surprise, and they passed over it and found they could not follow the coast any longer. They headed south and east via Brickyard Road where intermittently the forest returned them to the peaceful quietude that they had been used to in Cape Breton and then a little further on the landscape again reminded them of the terror that had been unleashed on this once peaceful haven. The dog mostly hung its intelligent looking face out of the window but occasionally popped back in to reassess his new friends. He had that understanding and loving look and Nancy related to him immediately. She had never fallen in love this fast before.

They came to the junction with the Louisbourg Highway, and the dog barked gently. Robert was about to turn to the right to go back to Sydney and the road south, but something made him turn left toward Louisbourg itself. He had no idea why he did it but felt utterly compelled. It was as if the look on Fergie's face convinced him that their day was far from over. As soon as they headed down the highway Fergus placed his mug back out the window and into the wind and stopped barking. Nancy had long stopped crying, and she placed her hand lovingly on Robert's lap.

They did not pass a car coming up from Louisbourg, and the miles went by through scattered pristine pine forest and apocalyptic fields of ash. They wondered what had become of the people living in the tiny cottages beside the highway and were hoping they were the same people that they had passed on the way up to the top of the island. After about 10 miles Robert slowed and they looked at each other, he pulled the car to the side and did a slow U-turn. They headed back toward Sydney.

As soon as they crossed the turnoff to Brickyard Road and continued to head west, they found Fergus to be agitated. He barked excitedly at the air and constantly turned about on the back seat, seeking the attention of his new human friends. Nancy and Robert were puzzled as to what he wanted. Fergie was barking ferociously out of the window as they passed through the small hamlet of Alfred Bridge and over the bridge itself.

Here the ground was razed, the forest no more and the small towns and single dwellings were taken by what must have been a furious fire. Just an ashen highway and the lonely telegraph wires between burnt and collapsed poles. They slowed to make sure they didn't get tangled in debris. Robert turned yet again perhaps sensing Fergus' animation even more heightened. He slowly drove off to the North. Nancy also somehow felt this was something they were compelled to follow, and she simultaneously tried to calm Fergus and to watch Robert as his face stared forward determinedly. A second turn to the left found them along a short, narrow road that opened to a large car park. As he slowed even more at this stage, they watched Fergus leap through the small space he had at his window and race away across the car park. Nancy and Robert stopped and got out and raced after him.

They could make out a large red, part timber and part brick building which was largely collapsed. Some of it was lost to fire and some from impact. The surrounding pine forest was a smouldering grey and they struggled to keep up with Fergus as he tore around to the back part of the building barking furiously. As they approached, they realised that what they were standing in front of was what remained of a small school. From what was left of the front edifice they made out that it was an Elementary School.

Fergus seemed to know what he was heading toward and bolted for a badly damaged area at the back of the school. As they approached him, they could see he was pawing at a particular part of the flattened building at the rear of the main building. The dog was clawing and digging and yelping excitedly and inviting Nancy and Robert to help him, turning enthusiastically to them repeatedly begging them to join him. He was so successfully insistent that both Nancy and Robert did soon join him. Nancy was on all fours, as she followed Fergus' lead in digging; Robert scoured the surroundings and was able to find a half plank that he could use as a shovel. Fergus was absolutely single-minded and much quieter now as if he had led his friends precisely to the task at hand. His energy was inexhaustible, as he quickly dug under the debris of the collapsed building. As they started to form an opening at this point, they heard some very strange noises. Certainly, there was the creaking of the building as it leaned to under its own destruction, but there were other sounds that raised their curiosity. Fergus's odd bark seemed to be met by these high pitched far away sounds, and as they dug further under the structure, the more curious, they became. Once they had got under the first layer of debris, they realised they were above some kind of patio, presumably on the outside of a classroom. Much of the upper stories had collapsed across the area, and they carefully made their way across this space toward the entrance. Fergus started panting and pawing as they got closer to the door. Nancy and Robert had to rely on odd shafts of light coming down little areas between the heavily damaged structure ahead of them and the collapsed building around them. As Fergus tried to dodge metal beams and half-burnt wooden structures to make a beeline to the entrance, Nancy and Robert were more careful and wary, picking their way through the entanglement. They still could hear the strange noises ahead and the creaking and cracking sounds of imminent possible further collapse about them. Something drove them on, the crazy enthusiasm of the dog or their own instincts.

When they finally got to the door, they thumped as loudly as they could. There was no response. There was no access as the door seemed to be jammed or blocked from behind. They pounded again. This time Robert heard the high-pitched sounds coming from what seemed deep within what was left of the building ahead of them. They looked at each other as Fergus raced excitedly to what was left of a small ledge to the side of the door. They removed all the debris and found that it was a window. All three of them peered inside and there they saw around 10 little faces looking up at them, waving. They must have been kindergarten or first-graders, and some were crying and some sitting but as the news spread of the kind faces staring at them from outside and the friendly dog there were even a few relieved smiles upon their faces. Nancy told them by expressions to stand away, and Robert smashed the glass as carefully as he could. Fergus immediately jumped through and was cheered and hugged by the kids. Robert managed to slide through as well and realised that there were in fact about 20 children down there and they were very happy to see each other. One by one they were lifted up to the window and out to Nancy and led outside. Just as they were nearly all out the fire department truck pulled up, and to their astonishment they had 20 little faces, two adults and a dog to rescue. The crew had been told that all the children that could have survived the fire and collapse had already been taken away to safety. They didn't dream that they would be returning with these kids thought lost to the senseless actions of the General in the Nevada desert. The Firemen, sick with exhaustion and exposure themselves briefly let their emotions go and hugged and cried with Nancy and Robert and the kids. Fergus was calm and playful never leaving Nancy's side. Before long, they were all back and being monitored in the main hospital in Halifax.

It took Robert months to recover from his radiation exposure sickness and to get back to some semblance of a normal life. Nancy continued to travel the world, finding ways to bring Fergus along with her at every opportunity. Her love for Robert never left her heart, but she knew from that day on that she would never be able to love him as a lover again. Her instinct was to draw back from the madness and the heroism she had seen that day. Nancy never stopped giving of herself in empathy to strangers, family and friends but felt that she only had the very deepest of friendship to give to her former lover. They met occasionally and rarely talked about that day. There was some talk of going back to the Cape on some distant future trip, but neither was sure that it would ever happen. Years and years passed, and Fergus was now too old to travel beyond his backyard. It took 9 years for them to return to the Cape. They were astonished to find the same far flung accents, the same endless vistas on their walks and they were happy to find a completely recovered and beckoning forest. The lakes and cottages restored, their hearts recovered and their friendship like no other.

Chapter 9

Area 51 8 days after I Day

Horowitz slept very well and was woken at 5 am by his trusty Disney alarm clock. His wild eyes surveyed the sterile chamber that he called home. The uniforms hanging in his open wardrobe all perfectly pressed and covered in plastic. His medals arranged in chronological order on top of his grey metal drawers. From the bottom to the top, each drawer was arranged with respect to the physical height of his body. His socks, then his underpants and finally his ties at chest level. All were arranged in what the General declared as correct and consistent spacing. He had just one small mirror in the room within the tiny toilet and shower area which was open to his room. In the corner, Horowitz had a small table, beside which stood a harsh metallic, simple tray chair made with a cheap chrome that had lost its lustre many years before. On the table was a copy of the Bible which he had not read since he had joined the Air Force and a scrapbook of family photos from his childhood days which he would flip through every night before he went to bed. It had grainy pictures of his forefathers, most of whom had fought in wars that were to define the nature of the world and his country. Their peculiar jawline and determined expressions would inspire him to renew his cause every night. His favourite picture was of his mother, black and white, pitchfork in hand working the tough soil of his childhood home. Her hair in the photo was in the beehive fashion of the day. In the background of that photo was the black woman who had spent so much time trying to discipline the young Horowitz as his mother had shown him very little attention. It was to the black woman that his eyes fell when he studied that picture every night.

Bell had seven children of her own, and her family had been on the Horowitz land for over a century. She had felt for the strange little boy who spent his days alone playing with and blowing up toy soldiers with his endless supply of firecrackers and air rifle ammunition. Bell had tried so hard to reach him. Every now and then he would stretch out for a hug, but inevitably before the embrace had been completed, he would scurry away back to his isolation. She could see that his older brothers had been brutal to him. Bell was terribly saddened by the loss of her old boss, his father, who had been a kindly figure; she was also very troubled by his mother who used her social status as a war widow in that small farming community as an excuse to wreak havoc in the local bars and disrupt the moral code of the small town they all tried to survive in. Mary Lou Horowitz felt the glare of Bell and detested herself even more. She drank and whored herself to every travelling salesman or lonely husband in the endless quest to quench her grief at the loss of her husband. Tragically, he had been drowned as a prisoner of war in a Vietnamese swamp. All she had were his gleaming medals that had eventually been returned with his dog tag. They sat atop her mahogany drawer to remind her of her abject misery.

Horowitz sat on the edge of his bed, already he was a minute over schedule. 5.06 am, and he had not yet opened his leather briefcase which lay under his bed to look at the day ahead. Nevertheless, he knew exactly what lay ahead this day without looking at the papers. This was the day he was going to save his world. To restore the Constitution and end the madness that had gripped the outside. This was his day to make his mark on history.

In his mind, he imagined the destruction he was about to impose upon the world in order to bring that very world back to some order. He realised that the four cities he was targeting were densely populated. He knew that given the profound enhancements that had been made to nuclear weapons since they were last utilised in Japan that their killing capacity was exponentially bigger. He knew he was condemning about

1.5 million people to instant death and at least three times that number to slower destruction with burns, blindness, and radiation effects. He knew well the art and architecture that he was condemning to eternal loss. He was well aware of the physical and emotional impact his decision would unleash. He sat calmly, now swiping his few stray locks of hair out of his face and back across his balding pate and prepared himself for the morning. In exactly five minutes, he would expect Falinski to appear at his door, to lead him through to the control room and hand him the codes for the bombs. He glanced over at the scrapbook on the little table.

Falinski was relieved when the deployment team had completed their tunnelling and had made their way into the main complex. He had ordered a security detail sympathetic to the authentic outside orders to abandon the complex be placed in the sector where the team were due to come through. Over a 20 minute period, the breach systems were disarmed, and the team quickly set up the harmonics that swept through Area 51 domain by domain. Once Falinski himself had been exposed suddenly everything made utter sense. His mission was to ensure a peaceable transition to the new order as he could, but Horowitz's chambers were buried deep into the protective infrastructure of the base, and the Control room was adjacent. Falinski was suddenly able to integrate all of the events of the past week and consider how he would go about trying to make for a calm and peaceful transition. He understood the General's position, could see his reasoning and method for achieving his aims and fully grasped the complete insanity of it as he comprehended the positive change that was happening outside. As the team went from pod to pod and exposed the personnel, the atmosphere in Area 51 changed dramatically. Within minutes of deployment smiles and hope had filled the base. Everyone knew that getting Horowitz exposed to the harmonics was the aim. How that was to be done was much more difficult to imagine.

Falinksi was two minutes late, and the General was furious. As soon as Falinski entered the deeper chamber, he felt the clarity slip. He was back to trying to expose the General to the waves without raising suspicion. Whilst he saw that the General was about to commit mass murder, he couldn't afford to directly contravene an order from his superior officer. He was no mutineer, simply seeing himself as an engineer to a happier outcome for all. He understood that some sacrifice had to be made but he would not be the man to shoot his commanding officer to achieve this despite the exhortations of many of his colleagues.

"Falinski, what is the meaning of this? Man, you have never entered these chambers more than 15 seconds before or after you were due to arrive. This, the most important date in the proud history of Area 51 and you are 125 seconds late! What the hell Falinski?"

"Sir, there has been some difficulties in programming the codes for the cities you have chosen to destroy. Some of the senior programmers have families in New York and London and just couldn't bring themselves to code them into oblivion."

"What are you talking about Falinski? I gave a direct order for that weaponry to be deployed and ready for non-executive use this morning. How is this to look in our negotiations with these clowns out there? What have we got prepared? What can I take to them?"

Falinksi quietly placed the iPhone 17 under the Bible and turned to face the General.

"Sir, our options practically are limited at this point. Would you be able to come out into the conference area to discuss it with the senior staff?"

"Falinski, I haven't got time for discussion now. Get on to a solution and come back to me within the half-hour. I will be on air three minutes after that with my finger on a button. Is that clear?"

"Yes sir."

Horowitz paced his small sterile room not once picking up the bible but rather flicking obsessively through his scrapbook and mumbling incoherent messages at his forefathers about how they would be so proud of him right now.

Falinksi felt defeated, there was no way he could think of to get a team past the inner cores' alarm system which he knew Horowitz would be monitoring intermittently.

He returned with a heavy heart as he knew he would have to deliver a live nuclear weapon to Horowitz within minutes. Exposed to the harmonics again, he came up with a plan he thought may work.

"Falinksi, you are damn late again! What has gotten into you today? Do you realise how important our work is? I understand you think our measures are harsh, I have had my eye on you for the last four days, but I know you are my loyal deputy. Now hand me the codes. Which city are we destroying first? Beijing or Moscow?"

"Sir, in terms of deploying quickly a nuclear bomb that would create the most havoc, we have chosen a different city for you. This city is western, cosmopolitan, English speaking and cultured. We feel it will provide the easiest target and be a warning shot for the other cities you have pinpointed for destruction. The senior team feels that this city is our best option."

Falinksi handed him the Top-Secret document with the name of the city and the codes for launch.

Horowitz looked at him at first puzzled but then with a broad grin.

"Sydney! Of course. The world could do without those pretentious Aussies. Let's do it Falinksi."

Falinksi nodded without saying a word. He needed the General out of his bunker, comfortable, and he needed 20 minutes to get the harmonics deployment team through to the control room.

Falinski escorted the General to the launch and control area without a word. Horowitz had a wide, satisfied grin on his face as he recalled his brief dispatches to the Harbour City which he was about to destroy. He had never appreciated the brash disrespect the Australians had given the then Sergeant as he marched the streets alone in full military dress and decoration. He couldn't stand it when he had a quiet whiskey in a Sydney bar and a local would come up to him, spill half his beer over his jacket, and spit out some incoherent insult. He remembered a man approaching him and brazenly calling him a "cobber". The man had the temerity to say he wanted to "Shout him" before leaving him with a beer and shaking his head. Unbelievably rude.

As he settled into the broadcast position, he wasn't aware that every cable company and every independent broadcaster was about to put his face across to an audience of over seven billion people. There was nothing else discussed in the early hours of that morning in the democracy that had formed other than the impending destruction of several major cities of the world. There had been a calm evacuation of all four named cities, and they were all virtually ghost towns. Then the General spoke, and the world once again shuddered at the madness he was proposing if his demands were not met.

"People of the world... "

He trailed off, leaving everyone wondering exactly how mad he really was.

"People of the world, we have a few minutes for you and your leaders to come to your senses. On behalf of the constitution of the United States and the power invested in me as I was sworn in 42 years ago to protect that very document I demand that any technologies that alter brain function, that lead to brainwashing, that leads to the disintegration of my country be terminated immediately. You have two minutes to accede to my demands or a nuclear warhead will be deployed and will destroy Sydney, Australia. You have two minutes to confirm that the technology has been destroyed or Sydney will be."

"General, we appreciate your position. We understand that you are about to destroy the lives of close to a million people within the next three minutes and condemn a further million to a slow death from radiation burns and cancers over the next few days and months. We would like to propose a compromise, sir."

The face beamed to billions across the world and whose gentle tone seemed so reasonable to the entire world was no more than 15 years old. Paul Tyson had been chosen by the interim world governing council to talk to the General. To find a middle way, to delay activation of the order so that the Harmonics team could gain access to the man that was threatening the world so violently.

The split screen showed the General steely faced but every now and then mopping the copious sweat from his forehead as he listened to the young man.

Finally, he said. "Enough with this nonsense. I expected at least the President of my country to address me on this issue today. You have 40 seconds."

Paul calmly looked straight at the camera.

"General, you don't recognise me, do you? I am Bell's youngest child. I still live on the very farm you grew up on. The corn is coming up for harvesting, and the cows are producing just fine. The town is going grand, and I am looking to go to University next year on Exchange in Sydney. You remember me now General, from your last visit to the farm?"

Horowitz's eyes narrowed. He seemed to be trying to focus and then he appeared to be adopting a softer face.

"Paul, that is you. Yes, I remember. And I remember promising you that I would help get you to College. What will you be studying?"

"International relations, Sir. I want to be a diplomat. General, can I ask you one thing?"

"Yes Paul, go on?"

The world held its breath as the strange interaction continued and the General was now two minutes over his scheduled destruction of Sydney.

"General, I know you loved my mother Bell, dearly."

"Yes, I did Paul."

"General, she loved you very much as well sir. She used to talk to me about you quite a lot. How she felt that if only she had had the time to give you the love you deserved as a child that you would not only have been a great war hero but a great hero in her life. She so wanted to be proud of you...

"She's dying General."

Horowitz turned away from the camera. His bald patch the focus of the world. He turned slowly back again, tears in his eyes.

"Paul, I am so sorry to hear this. I think she would understand what it is I have to do now to save the world from this madness."

In his hands, he held firmly, a bright, red-tipped plunger button on a black console. In the other, he had punched in the coordinates and codes that Falinski had supplied him with.

"I'm sorry Paul, but this is for the good of the world."

And he plunged his arthritic left index finger down upon the red button.

The world's eyes fell to a new scene. The trajectory and timing of the destruction of Sydney. Within a minute, the General started roaring.

"Falinski, Falinski. You fool, you idiot, you traitor."

The trajectory of the rocket with the megaton nuclear weapon was headed for Sydney, Nova Scotia. As the ICBM was tracked across the sky, it was heading across the continental USA to the North and East. The estimated time to impact was just over seven minutes. The flight path took it over Utah, across the Great Lakes, whistled over the Catskills, and Maine and was seen to impact 30 km to the Northeast of Sydney where it exploded at the edge of a rugged, near abandoned coastline killing 45 people in the first moments after impact.

Horowitz was roaring incoherently, and Falinski could see that he was serious about sending the other nukes on their way. He was screaming.

"It's the only way Falinksi, It's the only way." He raged on and on blustering about the control room incandescent with rage.

Falinsksi gambled, he raced across the control room at his fastest clip, he smashed into Horowitz with all the fury and determination that he could muster, knocking him to the ground. He dived on top of him and used his arms and legs and head to try to slow the enormous, powerful, raging General down. Horowitz gave everything back in his mad scramble to save the planet from its own lunacy. He fought off Falinski calling him a traitor and swearing to have him court martialled as they rolled about the floor together arms and legs flailing in a battle resembling a very poor quality UFC fight. Just as Horowitz was working his way free and heading for the command console, Falinksi tackled him from behind, and as the General hit the floor for the second time, the deployment team had made it into the control room.

Mid-sentence, mid punch, mid reaching for the red button the harmonic waves hit him. He sat down, his arms now relaxed by his side, a thoughtful look upon his somewhat scratched face. His expression softened, and he said.

"I was being rather ridiculous, wasn't I? Anyone for a drink?"

Falinski dusted himself off the floor, readjusted his tie and tucked his shirt back into his pants. He stared at the General, not believing what he had just seen. He sat down beside Horowitz and turned off all the command equipment. They hugged each other and Falinski went to grab the best bottle of Cognac he could find.

They sat there quietly sipping the strong liqueur.

"Falinski, imagine this! A world without countries, a world at one with itself. Imagine."

Chapter 10

Syria I Day

They had travelled this dusty and hazardous road many times over the last four years. Twice their driver had been taken and once they had been successful in having him returned intact by paying a heavy ransom and calling on some connections within the execution wing of the Caliphate. The other time their driver was featured headless in the monthly webzine of the Daesh. Apparently, he had been seen as too aligned with the Western dogs. Today, the driver, Ahmed, looked especially nervous as there had been reports of IEDs and ambushing already that morning. The blue ambulance van, nervously covered in some plates of battle-ready armour coating but largely exposed, jolted over and around pit holes and debris left from last night's brutal conflict. Bodies were still to be seen scattered about the main road and smaller streets, guts hanging from contorted torsos, brains blown out, expressions of agony retained and no one to collect them for the next few days.

On every panel, the white of the UN symbols and letters were to be seen, but sometimes it just made them feel more of a target than heroes. Targets in a vehicle bringing aid, medical supplies and comfort to those torn by this cruel place. This stupid war. Today was different though, their 'aid' on this day was something really very unusual for them. It wasn't bags of saline to keep a man alive whilst they tied tourniquets around his spurting femoral artery and rushed him back to the mobile field hospital. It wasn't rice and a couple of blankets to keep the starving, freezing children surviving in the rubble from worsening malnutrition. It was electronics, the like of which they had never seen before and for which they had been given a very brief description of how and where they were to place the 20 or so devices throughout the ravaged city and how to turn them on. They were no more than a small black box with a conventional power supply, but most came with a solar power generator and panel. They were to drop them off at the specified locations without attracting attention, turn them on and disappear as quickly as possible. On that day some 300 such missions were carried out throughout Syria. Ahmed drove on confused as to his directions that day. He was used to heading to the heart of the site of battle and laying his hopes aside until he drove back into the compound that night. Today, with the multiple destinations, he thought his chances of returning were minimal.

Many of the targets were odd, placed in between communities, at known areas of conflict and in public markets or what was left of them. They'd placed more than 15 of the devices before afternoon tea where they took out their thermoses and sat in the back of the van parked in a gully off the main road hoping not to be seen. They talked about their families and dreams. They were three men in their early 20s who had joined the UN for the adventure, the pay and the good they thought they could do in a world ripping itself apart. Always, in the background, there was the clatter and thud of bullets being fired off and hitting slabs of twisted concrete and smashed residences. The flyover of helicopters and jets was another constant. They had almost forgotten the sound of birds and the sounds of people going about their normal business. After eight years of bloody conflict, constant anxiety, wariness and expectation of loss was the norm.

All of the immediate families of the three men deploying strange black boxes across the beleaguered city were abroad. In general, most families had not been so lucky with many enduring daily horrors from the rubble of their own homes. Some in filthy tent encampments on the edges of the cities or roaming aimlessly for a safer harbour. All three of them had stories of unquenchable tragedy that had affected theirs and their family's lives forever. Nephews shot in crossfire, Aunts lost to suicide bombers in crowded marketplaces along with their neighbours and friends. Cousins dying fighting for one faction or another and the hard decision about where and how the body could be honoured. The constancy of the dreaded noise of the barrel bombs sometimes falling for 12 hours at a time. Filled with propane fuel and nails and dropped from helicopters over rebel territories.

For the war had split people arbitrarily. No one knew exactly how this friend or that brother had ended up fighting on Assad's side, why this one went across to ISIS or had they been forced to cooperate. Many were joining militias simply to try and protect their own families and to earn a wage. The war had ruined the usual ways life could be lived. The war had taken over and become all of their lives. The politics of it all was discussed endlessly over coffee sessions that lasted as long as the bombs did not arrive to herald yet another move if they survived. That black, bitter, thick coffee sipped slowly and deliberately that brought focus and ceremony and a reminder of some of the old ways. You could almost eat it toward the bottom of the elegant pewter cup, and then you were reminded that it was time to top it up and change the subject. No one quite understood how it was that the war had so quickly engulfed them in such horror and why it had not been dealt with at a political level. But the intrigue, the power games and the ideologies dominated everyone's thoughts as some sense was required just to go on living. They needed to talk it out so that they could carry on with a vestige of hope that one day it would end. One day they could have peace back in their lives.

They found a house that they had been able to shelter in before and took yerba matè with the old woman who was there while her two little grandchildren played on the floor. The kids looked up curiously every few seconds at the three unfamiliar men in their house. The herbal infusion perked them up immediately as the caffeine hit them, and they prepared to deploy the remainder of the devices.

Adnan turned to Sayid and Jack and said.

"Let's go, we don't want to be placing these things as the sun is coming down. People will mistake us for soldiers."

Jack agreed.

"We still have seven devices to place and into some of the most dangerous areas. Let's go my friends, and we can get home in one piece, God willing."

The whirling sounds of far off bombardment and the utter silence of the street otherwise struck them as they left the house and into the ruin of their old city. In every direction utter devastation spoke of a war that had been waged purely for political purpose and had wrought so much material and personal destruction.

They knew of some of the other teams that had volunteered to take the devices even further into rebel and ISIS territories. Some were planted the night before in the dead of the night. All they were told was that this was likely to be the most important and significant thing they would do as aid workers in their entire lives. That it was essential to place the devices exactly as planned and that their reward for success would become very apparent. So, with some cautious enthusiasm and trepidation, the three continued the unusual mission into the late afternoon. Managing to avoid all but the most unenthusiastic of sniper fire.

In the relative safety of their compound at precisely 7.00 pm they were sitting about eating when suddenly the conversation was cut by the oddest thing. Silence. This was the time of the heaviest fighting, the mortar exchange, the street battles engaged. Across the city was the hubbub of destruction. This silence was odd, the three friends looked at each other and wondered if another useless ceasefire had been agreed to, but there had been no talk of that. All sides had remained locked into the senseless cycle of attrition and misery that had become their lives. Everybody got up from their tables, those who had finished and were playing some pool in the lounge, those watching the news on the television. All stopped and gathered together to listen to the sound. The sound of peace.

How did they know it was peace? How could they tell that the war was over? They felt it and knew it in their hearts and minds. They all knew as a group of humans that there was no longer any need for guns or hatred, machines of destruction were pointless and absurd. They all suddenly felt it. It was a moment of joy that they would never, ever forget in their lives. A moment where not only their hearts but their brains were transformed to new ways of thinking. Where suddenly, the concept of an enemy became ridiculous. That harm should or could be brought to another human being was beyond any comprehension. They knew that if they drove to the war-torn Eastern part of their city that they would find like-minded people. There was no longer an imperative for hate.

On the battle hardened streets of Aleppo, the soldiers of all the main three factions and more laid down their arms and walked across the known passageways of death to embrace their brothers. Families knew instinctively where to go to reunite. The joy was boundless as mothers embraced their sons who had been ensnared on the other side of the battle lines and survived. The news was full with the resignation of Assad and the complete withdrawal of all foreign military powers within the next week. A cooperative assembly had been formed in Damascus with all the people to have input into the future rebuilding of the country. Indeed, on that very night, the first steps were taken to remove the rubble as it became believable that there was a future ahead without the need for any further bloodshed.

Somehow, the long beards of the ISIS fighters, the military uniforms of the Assad soldiers and the Western street gear of the rebel faction really meant nothing anymore. As people walked through the tangled concrete and steel that had been the Old City, they embraced and laughed and talked of hope and a future for their country together. They hugged, gossiped and drank coffee together deep into the night. The sweet kiss and embrace of the families and lovers they had left behind were now to be looked forward to with great hope and promise. The Old City came alive with music and dancing, kissing and embracing again; no one would ever forget I Day in this place.

Dawn broke, and the party was still happening across every street, in every village in that ancient nation that had been brought to its knees by modern politics. There was not a hint of aggression, only the intense relief at everybody's situation and people gathering with purpose to re-unite, to plan and to start rebuilding. The temporary devices that had been implanted in every populated corner of the country were quickly replaced by communication towers and other more reliable infrastructure. The architects of I Day breathed a heavy sigh of gratitude for the bravery and reliability of the teams that deployed the mobile ultrasound and wireless transmitters. Harmonics had come to Syria the very day that it had been able to be deployed around the world in more conventional ways, but perhaps no place on earth had needed those waves like this country had so desperately.

Adnan knew where to go if he were to reunite with his brother, his secret these past six years was Suske, his oldest brother, at first volunteering to help the Islamic cause as a humanitarian effort and later radicalised was a liability for Adnan's career in the UN. Somehow, they had not been traced together, and Suske had kept a low enough profile as a doctor working to save all of the victims of the war but on the enemy side of the lines. Adnan loved his brother throughout these dark days, but he did not dare attempt to contact him and rarely had he heard of his whereabouts and how he was doing. He understood how he had come to be on that other side but was very angry that his brother had remained there as the evil of the people he worked for became more and more apparent. So, to the old house on the outskirts of the ancient part of the city he went.

He sat in the early morning sun as the silence of the street surrounded him, reminding him of his childhood days. Yet he was surrounded by utter destruction. Not a single house had survived intact on their street. Their own home was just recognisable by the thick, strong lintel that had kept their front door standing. The only other feature that had survived somehow was the neat limestone rock wall that had formed their front fence. This was the border of their soccer field and the wall they battled for marbles up against. It was where they sat as kids to watch the passing parade of merchants and customers in and out of the marketplace and where they waited for their father to come home from his long day in the city administering the heritage museum. Adnan sat there recalling all of this as his barely recognisable and long-bearded brother sauntered up to him and gave him the biggest hug he had received since they had said their goodbyes all those years ago.

There was no need to speak of the atrocities that both had witnessed. There was no going over crazy philosophies and a world of domination by religion. It was not a time for recrimination. It was a time for planning, reminiscing on the best of times, for finding something traditional to eat and some good coffee to drink and to hug each other very often. To the brothers' surprise, already some three or four families had set up stalls in the old market place and were selling clothes and food. Suske ordered some kata skewers and bought a large bowl of tabouleh. Adnan couldn't resist the smells of the kibbeh and the pots steaming with the stuffed zucchini in their tomato broth. It was wonderful to look into each other's eyes again and enjoy the delicious food that they had not been able to share all these years. It was a morning of smiles, full bellies and the sense of a city quickly remembering how to be productive and peaceable.

Adnan actually found it remarkable that Suske did not mention the dogma that had seemed to dominate his talk before he had left. His words were full of promise for his country, but in fact, he was most focussed on where he felt he could do the most good. He told Adnan that he knew he must go to Gaza and Israel as he was called inside to understand the outside world in a much more comprehensive way. He would be travelling in the next few days and wondered if Adnan could help him with a few dollars.

Adnan had no hesitation in telling Suske that he would be happy to help him. "My brother, you know you always have my love. Wherever you are in this world, you are my beloved blood."

"Adnan, I know I have let you down all this time. I see now how foolish I have been. You will be happy to learn that this beard will be gone before the day is out. Such an odd night last night, what magic has brought this peace to our land? The hospital was busier than at any time. We were taking in 200 dead and 300 injured every day. The toll on the staff in the hospital was almost unbearable, and yet we carried on. Many of the injuries were self-inflicted. I could never have approved of it, and yet I put my head down and stitched up the arms that had been summarily amputated. The mutilations were abominable, but to stay alive, I simply had to be the surgeon, the robot that fixed things. And then 7 pm last night, everything changed. The yelling and ranting of the elect were over, their voices quiet and contrite, even sensible. Everyone immediately sensing the war was over. It was such elation, such relief, such joy. To see you here today, alive and well, sitting on our front rock wall was like a dream. Is it a dream, Adnan?"

"Suske, is it you? I think it is real. I think we are sitting here stuffing ourselves with this deliciousness and contemplating a world with hope. Yes, I am fairly sure it is real."

"I can remember the beheadings and the tortures. I saw where the elite would randomly select civilians for brutal torture and execution just because they had some vague connections to the outside world. It was madness Adnan, and I supported it because I believed that the word of Allah was being spread from these harsh hands. Then suddenly, last evening as if a veil had been taken from my eyes, all of the horrors became horror again. All of the beatings and hatred was senseless, all of the dogma meant little in a world of people that just wanted to get on with their lives in peace. A world where love for everyone made total sense again. I became instantly aware again of the deep love I have for you and all of the family and immediately knew I would seek you out and be with you today. To me, even more remarkable was the change that occurred in those that had so fervently sought to bring about the Caliphate. From that moment last night, the weapons were immediately dismantled and laid aside. The prisoners were freed, and the talk was of universal brotherhood and understanding. The men with the longest beards wept as they spoke of their mothers in faraway lands and how they could not wait to be back in the loving arms of their families."

Adnan started to weep and hugged his brother until they were both sobbing with laughter and emotion.

"My brother, I do not understand what happened last night, but it is so great to see you. Go, get that beard shaved off, it's way too hot to be wearing that where you will be going. Come, stay with me tonight at the compound and we will have you adventuring, where you must, shortly."

They embraced again and wandered off together through the familiar but largely destroyed streets of their childhood. They looked at each other, and both were quiet for a little while as they noticed the songs of the birds that had returned to their beloved city.

They awoke to a new day somewhat disoriented. They had not slept in the same room together since they were teenagers and Adnan struggled to recognise the cleanly shaven young man who emerged from their small bathroom and sat at the end of the bed.

"Suske, you look like my brother. It's so good to have you back. Here is $500 and you know you also take with you my love and best wishes. Tell me why you need to go to Gaza?"

"Brother, I need to ride somewhere. I need to know the world. I need to help and explore and know that my hands can work their miracles in that ancient place of so much past trouble. I am called, I cannot really explain beyond that."

The morning was eerily quiet, but it wasn't long before Suske had found his perfect ride and supplies for a few days. Adnan knew in his heart that Suske had fundamentally changed. He hugged him with all the joy and sadness that a brother could give as he had no real idea when he would see him again. Suske fired up the Kawasaki and lowered his visor. He looped back and headed towards the East waving to his brother as the bike roared down the dusty road.

Chapter 11

Syria and Lebanon 2 days after I Day

The bike felt good and strong beneath Suske as he pushed its power along the quieter stretches of straight roads south of the city. He immediately noticed the trickle of people travelling in the opposite direction he was taking and carrying what seemed to be their whole world upon their shoulders. He saw a family or two and they all looked tired but were smiling broadly. Heading further south and intending to visit some friends in Lebanon he began to see more and more people heading back along the stretches he passed through. They were coming back toward where they knew their home to be. Strangely, they also all carried somewhere upon them, in a shirt pocket, a tiny hand, sticking out from their large burdens, a single white flower. Every single person carried this instrument from nature to announce their peaceful arrival home.

As Suske made his way, the road filled with the joyful hum of more and more people coming from the North and East. There were few heading in his direction and yet he still felt called to his new home. It gave his heart great pleasure to see his people returning, and the slow progress was still very much a procession of joy. At one point, the whole road was so choked with people that the potent fragrance of the small flowers dominated the senses. The happy faces, the order in the disorder of such a crowd with single peaceful purpose, the smell of the lilies were images and sensations he would never forget.

And then she was there, a beautiful little girl who was wearing a red skirt that was way too big for her and dragging along on the ground behind her. They caught each other's gaze. As he slowly rode through the crowd, she made her way over to him. She held up her white flower for him and gave it to him with such a beautiful smile that he would never forget. He touched her gently on her forehead and then she was gone back to her family and her trek home.

Suske, riding now without a helmet headed steadily for the south and west. Already farmlands were being worked again, and piles of debris were appearing. Construction teams, engineers and architects were mobilising in every town and village he passed. Men and women in earnest discussion, hard hats and colourful vests with notebooks and laptops in hand. It was a hive of hopeful activity, and he felt great excitement as he left village after village for the open road and a countryside being restored by the hour. There was still much tumult, but it was clear that order and reconstruction were both being rapidly and actively pursued. In every location, the overwhelming sense was one of hope and joy; he was greeted with smiles and conversation everywhere he paused. There was the feeling that all were part of a great step into a brave new world of practicality, cooperation and peace. It was so different to the atmosphere in his country just a week ago. Then, destruction, suspicion, fear and violence reigned. It was remarkable what a new week had brought to his beloved home.

He had a simple tent, and it was easy to find a quiet, soft field of grass amidst a shady copse of cedar trees at the northern edge of Rableh. He found some dry twigs and some larger bits of wood and lit a fire. The scent of the cedar as it popped and burned was intoxicating, it gave a fierce heat as he lay back and looked up at the myriad stars above. Suske climbed into his tent to sleep and dreamt. In his dreams Suske found himself looking out from a high clifftop across a seaside village and people relaxing and playing on a fine beach. The clouds drifting past the headland on to the far horizon, the sea an emerald blue.

He awoke to the usual calls to prayer and crawled out from his tent to greet the morning and the town from his campsite on the highest hill to the north of the town. He then realised the familiar verses and calls were odd in this town of crosses and churches. When he listened more carefully, it wasn't the usual Adhan and wasn't a Christian greeting. The call was an ancient Arabic text that he had not heard since he was a little boy. It was a poem, and it was being sung in a round in perfect harmony from each of the eight major churches and mosques of the village. The song built and echoed around the pretty valley he was looking upon. He puzzled how such calming yet inspiring music could be welcoming him to his new life and the adventure to come. As he looked about the town where the dawn was becoming morning, he noticed one more thing. None of the churches any longer bore crosses, and none of the mosques bore crescents atop their minarets. Suske had never seen a town like this, and he had visited Rableh many times before. The valley stood as one with such music to calm every heart, every soul. He pulled out his phone and was surprised to see 30 percent battery charge still there. He was also surprised to see such a strong signal without any obvious telecommunications towers that could be seen. He was hoping she would answer, she picked up. He would see her today.

Suske packed up his few belongings and his tent, skirted the town as the harmonies burnt into each other and finally faded with the softest of peals of the bells of the town. He found his way back onto the potholed and shelled highway and within 10 minutes he was across the border at which he was greeted by not a soul, and he was into Lebanon. As he slowed and paused to take in the numerous memories that he had from his times in this country, he noted the abandoned refugee camp to his left. A sea of tents without a single occupant. The cool morning breeze felt good against his bare face, and he let the bike have its way. To the sounds of Led Zeppelin blaring, the abandoned border simply reinforced his sense of purpose and freedom.

They had agreed to meet in Baalbek. Zoe, the Christian girl that he had fallen for all those years ago. She, who had ridden upon his conscience and who he had never forgotten in all the time he had been radicalised. The woman who had first shown him what true tenderness and compassion looked like within the intricacy of two people getting to know each other so overwhelmingly in such a short space of time. The person he could never abandon in his heart even though she could not journey with him before. He asked himself could it be different this time, his heart swelled with hope as he dodged the worst of the crevasses and obstacles on the road. Ten years before they had spent a day at the vast Roman ruins, marvelling at the reach and the sheer physical presence of that great civilisation at Baalbek. The columns seemingly reaching up to the sky, imposing their stature on all that might view them. Originally Baalbek was a site developed by the Greeks. Under the Romans, who built a temple here to Jupiter, it came to represent how magnificent Rome could be away from the swampy edge of the Tiber itself. Some of the stones here weighed over 3000 tonnes and were over 60 feet in length. To see them was to be able to shut out any extraneous thoughts as the magnitude of the buildings themselves and their construction consumed you. Suske parked his bike at the base of a steep rise of ancient stone steps; he knew that there was something atop them that would be able to override the mesmerizing effect that the place itself engendered within him.

There she was. Standing, facing away from him, her long, straight hair shifting gently in the soft breeze, wearing a flowery summer dress that almost showed her knees, simple flat shoes, she turned to him, on that ancient temple forum and her smile consumed him. A smile that included her big brown eyes that lit up the space between them. They quietly came together, hugged each other with all their being, finally releasing to find a place to be together, to talk, to understand. Their hands naturally came together, and they wandered about the complex and found a shady spot produced by a column that had been erected some 18 centuries before. Sitting on a pedestal they sat side by side, knees touching and gazes exploring. They spoke quietly and animatedly; they knew that they were home together. Their voices touching ancient sentiments between them, their hands exploring the touch that they had begun to explore when they had first met. His hand was drawn to her hair, and he stroked her neck and back as finally their physical meeting could pull together all the emotions and desires that they felt.

She melted under his touch, and it was as if the years had never come between them. They were drawn to each other like the moon to the earth. She was the brightest light in his universe, and he was her poet and muse in one. Their kiss was inevitable, it was soft, exploratory, dazzling, delicious. It was to seal their love that now made so much sense where once it had confused and divided them. Now, it was clear that their love really did conquer all other factors. Time and space had been drawn in their favour once again after all these years. In this ancient place, they reignited their commitment to love each other. There were no more places to hide or cultural nuances to be defied. Now it was just them, Suske and Zoe and their love.

They spent the morning walking the entire temple complex and remembering their days together, trying to make sense of all these years apart and how the world had torn them so. Zoe had trained as a journalist and had seen too much of the horror in her neighbouring countries and the pain it had brought to hers. She was overjoyed at the events of the last few days and had almost thought it expected somehow that Suske would come for her at that point. This was the perfect place and time for that. She invited him back to finally meet her parents and family and this time he was not afraid or anxious. This time it would be his family too. When they had first met, Suske had been visiting university friends in Lebanon and they had found instant chemistry. Just those two weeks together of chaste conversation and stolen kisses had cemented a love and a friendship. When it came to the practicality of being together however, there were so many barriers. They could not and did not dare to declare their love for each other publicly. Two nations, two religions, two cultures that were so similar and yet so far apart in expectations. Suske had just started getting more interested in the Egyptian scholars, and the radical paths of Islam and Zoe was coming out of a generation of Christian Lebanese once so strong in practical faith but becoming increasingly secularised. She was, however, deeply spiritual and embraced her nation's tolerance and its progress toward peace for all in the region. Falling in love with a Muslim man was one step too far for her family and even for her. The years and the events of their lives had often been a source of great pain to both of them. She knew in her heart that she would always love him but couldn't see how she could get past his radicalism and intolerance. It did not take more than 30 seconds in the shade of that high column to realise that Suske had reverted to the man she had fallen in love with all those years ago. He too was surprised and satisfied with himself. He had lived with years of doubts and anguish about the path he had taken and the cruelty that his comrades had imposed on the people they controlled. He told her about the meeting with his brother, and they both cried and cried for the joy that this embodied for all of them.

He followed her cute little Renault out of the dusty outskirts of Baalbek and onto the straight highway to her hometown. They passed through the small villages and well-ordered and fertile farmlands in a reverie both with enormous smiles on their faces. They pulled into the cafe overlooking the river where they had first met on the outskirts of Zahle and shared a small mezze plate of delicacies. The man in the fez hat kept their coffee coming just adding to their buzz. They decided to stop at the lookout of Our Lady of Zahle where they could take in the whole town and plan their evening. By the time they had chatted to the owners of the restaurant on their way out and made their way to the car and the bike and kissed for a half-hour on the bonnet of Zoe's little blue car the cooling breeze of the late afternoon was settling upon them. They headed, this time slowly up to the famed tower that again elicited memories of the time that they first fell in love. Before rising in the ageing lift to the summit, they spent a moment in the chapel on the ground level. Suske stood at the back whilst Zoe made her way to the candles at the front of the little chapel. He watched her intently lighting a candle, wondering and knowing what she was thinking. At that moment, Suske knew he would love her forever. They caught the lift up to the top with an old Lebanese looking man who had a kindly face. Also, in the lift, was a middle-aged man who had a bemused look on his face as he recognised the new love that was so strong between the two young people. They noticed the old man's right hand and arm were very swollen and wondered what had happened to him. The old man noticed they were watching his arm and spoke to them in English.

"Bloody surgeons, stuffed me up."

As they all got out on to the lookout platform, they each remembered how they had felt the last time this view was presented to them. The old man was thinking of his wife, who was now departed. The middle-aged man lost in his recollections of his first time in this timeless country. The couple lost in each other and doing their best to make up for all the years lost to their love.

Their eyes were drawn to the North and the East. To a line of great mountains with a mantle of white across their summit lines. The young couple drifting in the entire beauty of the moment. As the sun set, casting interesting shadows over that mountain chain that divided this strange and ancient country they talked of how to present themselves to Zoe's family.

It was a short ride from the tower to Zoe's family home and Suske really did not know what to expect. When Suske walked a little sheepishly into the enormous house that belonged to Zoe's father he was surprised to be immediately embraced by an older woman of generous proportion who hugged him as if he were a long-returned member of their tribe. The genuine warmth of her hug was almost overwhelming as she showered him also with three firm kisses on alternate cheeks. He blushed but felt immediately embraced as the rest of the family came forward to welcome him with hugs and kisses. Somehow, someway they sensed that Zoe was happy at last. That her long-held sadness had lifted, and it was this man that had brought back her beautiful smile.

Zoe got to introduce everyone and especially hugged her loving grandmother.

"Suske, this is my Nanna, you may call her Nanna, but her real name is Nazia. She is the most loving woman in the world and the best cook."

He noticed she studied him well with eyes that had loved all her life. There was compassion, intelligence, softness and clarity in those eyes. He realised they were the same eyes as Zoe's. It felt like there were 30 people there at least and before he knew it a plate had been put in his hands and he was ushered into the dining room where a feast awaited them all on the large round table in the centre of the room.

The table had eight thick and ornately carved round wooden legs, the top laid with a delicate lace tablecloth and the dishes arrived every few seconds from the kitchen. A procession of aunts and cousins bearing food that smelled otherworldly good. On a side table, Suske was encouraged to try the Kibbe Nayeh. Zoe showed him how to do it even though she was sure she had eaten this with him before. A thick slice of white bread, generous amount of salted butter, the meat and some mint and onion dolloped onto the bread and then drizzled over with olive oil. He barely got his mouth around it all but was astounded by the subtlety and textures of the food. More reasons to love this family on the tips of his taste buds. Before he could take a second bite, Zoe lead him out of the room as more dishes arrived from down the hall. She had him by the elbow and took him into the large and well-lit kitchen. People were coming in and out of the large pantry, little kids eating on metal tray tables and looking very well dressed and happy in the corner and Zoe's mum, apron on, sweat pouring from her as she supervised the huge gas stovetop and the remaining five or six pots full with delicious smells. She was the keeper of the delicious smells, but she turned to her daughter with an enormous smile. She wiped her hands on her apron, pulled it off and embraced Suske with a ferocity that outdid her own mother. She held his face in her hands and searched his eyes and expression and said.

"This is a good one Zoe. Let him eat."

"You think he is ok Mama?"

"Let us see if he can take some dishes in without spilling them?" Rania said.

Zoe organised a tea towel and Rania pointed Suske to the correct pot. It was an enormous vessel and was full to the brim with stuffed zucchinis and cabbage rolls in a rich tomato broth. His mouth watered as he took the steaming pot down the hallway to the dining room. He couldn't see his feet or anyone ahead of him, and he narrowly avoided messing up the ten pin bowling tournament that was taking place along the hall. As he turned into the room, he was greeted with hungry and welcoming eyes and even a gentle pat on the back from a tiny, wizened old woman who Zoe would later introduce as her unusual and feisty great aunt. The grandfather clock chimed in the lobby as he placed the pot full of flavour and skill and love down upon the heavy table.

As the last of the dishes arrived, a slim, gentle and tall old man emerged from the corner of the room from a single, large lounge chair. He had a generous glass of whisky on ice, which clinked as he arose, and almost as a unit the room quietened and turned to this man. The kids came in from the hall and the other men playing backgammon abandoned their game and stood about the round table attentively. Finally, Zoe's mother and grandmother entered from the kitchen with the Okra and Tabouleh. Zoe's grandfather raised his glass, the ice cubes announcing his words.

"Blessed are we with this food, this family. Blessed are we to welcome friends today. Eat with joy, my beautiful family. Eat with joy."

The group became a swirling whirlpool of devouring food devotees. They dipped and collected, they took in the wafts of broth and steaming dishes full with love. It was almost impossible to choose a combination and a second and often a third visit to the great table was necessary to satiate the curiosity and the desire to taste everything offered. To choose from the cooked kibbe, the okra in its tomato broth that hinted of coriander and garlic. There was Lebanese rice flecked with the longer, darker strands of noodles that gave it that certain texture, topped with cinnamon for an extra dimension to its flavour. There was the traditional struggle to push the chicken and lamb and onion and capsicum off the enormous skewers. The meat was tender and succulent, melting in everybody's imagination and soon their reality. The enormous bowl of Tabbouleh, with the freshest of tomato and parsley, chopped finely with plenty of onion, the grit of the cracked wheat, the taste of the salt, olive oil and the lemon juice. The large pot full of the cabbage rolls and kousa was popular and the chops and broth negotiated to find an intact stuffed zucchini that could be enjoyed from the beckoning opening to its base. So many hours put into coring the zucchini, cooking the meat and rice and tomato mix and stuffing the vegetables. Eventually, people settled in various spots within the dining and adjoining lounge rooms, chatting animatedly as they literally stuffed their faces. There was the nod to Western cuisine, the roast chicken and beef, roasted vegetables and crisp, simple tomato salad. The grandkids were drawn to their Jiddo and their Nanna, and they both relished the family that they had brought up to be so loving and appreciative of each other. The adult group who got to sit at the table often got to some level of heated discussion about a political decision or other, but today they sat quietly discussing things of the world in a completely respectful and rational way.

Suske had grown up in a smaller, more austere family. They too were devout and loving, caring and encouraging. He had been given everything that he needed to go on to become a doctor and succeed. Yet here he found himself crying, having seemingly found himself entirely at home, completely surrounded by love and nurturing. The food and the laughter, the joy that these people found in each other, he found stunning. He now understood better how he had come to love Zoe so quickly and without reservation, how her kindness and huge heart had formed. As he sat there, he imagined not very much had changed in this family after the strange events of the week before. The only thing that was definitely different was how he, coming from a Muslim Syrian background had been accepted unconditionally into their arms. He could not have been happier, in the bosom of this large and splendid family, this neighbouring and once rival culture that now seemed such an alien way of thinking about it. There was only one religion here, and that religion was simply love.

Chapter 12

Israel 12 months after I Day

They had lived in Gaza for nearly 12 months now. Just as happy as the day they were married 10 months previously at their enormous wedding which had taken place outdoors on the hills of Rableh. It had seemed as if the entire town, as well as all of their relatives, had come to celebrate their love. The border town rang out with ancient Syrian and Arabic love songs and they enjoyed the endless feast of Lebanese food that was prepared out in the open, where the women's scarves had played in the breeze, and the open flames beckoned trouble. The alcohol flowed, a little more heavily on the Lebanese family's side. For the Syrians, it had been only a couple of months since the restrictions had been lifted, they especially enjoyed the lovely French wines that had been ordered for the feast. The buildings that had once been mosques and churches peeled their bells and called from their towers in such a harmony as he had imagined from his dream such a short time before. From the very spot that he had awoken on the day he was to meet up again with the love of his life, he vowed to love her forever, and Zoe did the same for him.

The dancing continued on into the morning, and while Suske's family had been more familiar and better at the Dabkeh than Zoe's, it had allowed for much showing off and shenanigans as the families got to know each other. It seemed that romance was in the air that night and that more than one connection across the ancient border was made on this happiest of nights. Suske and Zoe remembered their guests demonstrated little coordination, the dancers were shaking and dropping on a knee and holding hands, circling slowly about a centre that no one could locate. The music was repetitive, exciting, percussive and mesmerising. It was a night that no one would forget. On the sidelines, the groups had formed, and it wasn't all about family cliques and old connections but new ones. Somehow everyone was now wired to accept, discuss and network. The formation of friendship, acceptance of cultural differences and an interest to understand them had become the new norm.

When they thought back to their wedding they were so happy that they had witnessed a curiosity not just about personality but about profession, of hobbies and ways people could reinvent themselves. A large gathering like that would produce a future hub of friends, colleagues and co-workers and borders meant nothing now because effectively they did not exist. The small conversation that happened over a beer or a wine then was not so easily forgotten now. The ability of people to focus and remember, to integrate and plan was so much better. Not only that, there was action. People actually did what they said they would do and so every day was one of building on the past in an intelligent and coordinated fashion. Things were said, but they were now also done. As the first rays of sun lit up the hills surrounding Rableh, the last of the conversations and revelling was had, and people returned to their homes. Suske and Zoe had felt much loved, and the blessing and well wishes of their friends and family meant everything to them.

Suske and Zoe very much enjoyed the new subterranean fast transport system that had been built quite rapidly over the last six months. It still had about 100 km to go before it reached directly to Zahle, but it could get them from Gaza to Tel Aviv in just under 10 minutes in their own car and into Lebanon in just under an hour. Utilising the very latest hybrid magnetic and vacuum technologies they drove to their transport dock outside Shifa Hospital and within 30 seconds they were carried down to the magnetic route and on their way. As they merged onto the main track, they felt the thrust as the capsule pressurised their vehicle and swept them north. Today they were going to visit Jerusalem, they checked their destination into the car's computer and were soon being lifted up into the main car park outside the walls of the old city.

Since coming to live in Gaza, they had often taken the transport system to have a coffee in the old city or to wander the streets with the eclectic mix of locals, tourists and out-of-towners. They entered through the ancient gates and were always immediately drawn to the extensive archaeological parks that had been dug up within the old city. The original Jerusalem was around 20 metres below the current surface, and as the historical data gave the ability to successfully integrate the two levels of life, more of the city had been opened to its past. Within ancient houses, a mixture of museum artefacts could be explored along with modern art from the city. In the old plazas and forums, they could relax with a coffee or a beer knowing that they were on cobblestones that had been placed more than 2000 years ago. Much of the 'modern' Jerusalem was still very much available to explore. It was easy now for anyone to wander off the old tourist trails and explore the neighbourhoods which were such an exciting mix of all the ethnic groups that had found Jerusalem as their solace and sanctuary, prison and playground.

Zoe, as a journalist especially loved to visit professionally to document the integration of the schools over the last six months. There was little to nil scepticism, and much enthusiasm as the obvious answer to tolerance, understanding, peace and love in the Middle East was to integrate all of the ethnic and past religious groups through the entire school experience and beyond into university. Zoe enjoyed being accompanied by her favourite photographer Simeon, who managed to capture so accurately the kids playing in the schoolyards. His photographs managed to showcase the slight differences in racial appearances, the subtle nuances of clothing styles and yet the easy and genuine affection that early friendship brings to the face. She had done countless interviews with the teachers, principals and the kids themselves. Zoe was able to draw them out on their experiences of learning the different types of foods, their approach to the new positive spiritual syllabus that had been introduced. She was interested in the patterns of cross-city population movements as fear, suspicion and hatred had died away to become curiosity, tolerance and love.

Today, after they bought some gorgeous ceramics in the subterranean part of Jerusalem from a very jolly and skilled man of Armenian background and after enjoying a wine from a rooftop bar that overlooked the Wailing Wall they wandered down and paid their respect to the ancient edifice as they had done many times before. Said to be a remnant of the Temple of Solomon, it still commanded a central place in the hearts of all who lived and visited the ancient site. It remained a place of silence and contemplation and respect. No longer segregated by gender, nor was there the compulsion to wear a yamaka. Yet somehow, there was more feeling and more respect than at any other time in the past as the thoughts in the form of a love letter to the universe were gently placed in the grooves of the ancient rock wall. Still, grown men wept as memories and cruelties, regrets and joys swept through their contemplation in front of this old and sacred thing. People owned the ironies of their own and their culture's triumphs were wrapped up somewhere deep within this stone.

Suske remembered how as a student that it had been so hard to stand in that plaza without feeling very judged, surveyed and unwelcome. Now, there was no security and the only thing limiting access was the number of people wandering through, he felt home. Finally, this was a part of the world that everyone could share with joy. A cradle for the birth of civilisation, of structured thought and enterprise and now a place of much celebration.

Since the subterranean Jerusalem had been discovered, Zoe and Suske would regularly take the spiral staircase at the base of the wall, and walk under it and up the corresponding spiral stairs on the other side, to visit the old site of the Al-Aqsa Mosque which had become Jerusalem's largest place for spontaneous learning. They had a moment underground in the cool tunnels where the ancient limestone arches and old abandoned water supply to the Temple Mount were to be found. Today, it was a moment to adjust the eyes and imagine the city as it was long ago. They emerged to the bright sunshine, the olive gardens and paved pathways leading them between the two striking buildings; within what was still considered around the world to be one of the most significant spiritual sites in existence.

Zoe and Suske always had high expectations coming here. They had been intellectually and spiritually nourished every time they had visited; they never came away disappointed from a visit to this unique place. This site like so many other former religious buildings had become a place where people could come and learn at random. Amidst all the glory and beauty of the structure one could come and learn from some of the most esteemed teachers in the world. Within what had been a site of veneration for the Islamic faith; now subjects of all variety were taught here. Interaction and innovation became expected in these places of learning. Like the Wailing Wall, it was openly accessible to all who came to this complex city.

Today, they had a Greek man, his enormous beard intact and reminiscent of an Orthodox priest. This, in fact, had been his prior profession. He spoke of the history of the Mediterranean and the way the explorer priests of the Byzantine empire would not only hide religious affiliations but also knowledge to stay alive. He used three screens, a holographic map and constantly involved his audience in philosophical banter as he explored that knowledge for an hour. The buzz as they all left ensured much enthusiasm for further visiting the ideas and places that were mentioned during the talk. The obsession of the Byzantines around the notion of the purpose and creation of the universe impressed Zoe. Of how the universe is being created continuously and the imagination of how and why that was taking place took up much Byzantine thinking.

The two of them then wandered the roofs of the old city, and as the sun set over the golden dome, they sat. Suske cradled Zoe in his arms, and they watched the last rays of sun glide across the stunning yellow mosaic that stood out so starkly from the Jerusalem stone of the rest of the city. That ordinary, common stone that they saw, the limestone that has seen out centuries, reflected the harsh sun, holding its people in their hopes and fears. Now it was just the start of a perfect evening in their young lives. Within 15 minutes they were back in their new and well-appointed apartment in Gaza. Suske had the barbecue going, and Zoe had a nap. Tomorrow they were going to Nablus to visit some friends.

The rapid transport system to Nablus was only just finished, and Suske still couldn't get over being in one of his favourite places within 15 minutes when it used to take him over 10 hours to negotiate border crossings and security posts. Their car was delivered to a subterranean car park directly under the old markets of the town. As they came up to ground level, Suske felt the chill of the past briefly as he pushed past the throng of people in and around the thousands of market stalls. The ease and the smiles and the mixing of modern and ancient such a contrast to times he remembered of abandoned market streets, fires and smoke in the middle of the night. He remembered too well the pop-pop of tear gas guns and the sharper sound of live ammunition scattering the boys in gangs here just a few years before. He had seen people beaten and shot, had seen the courage and stupidity and remembered deep in his consciousness the anger that had seen him radicalised. He also felt the soft and loving touch of Zoe holding his hand in this now vibrant market, and he knew how far he and this town had come in such a short time.

It was almost instinctive, and his expectations still sometimes worked on the perception that virtually every sector of this city was divided by barbed wire fences and security posts. Now, as he walked with Zoe, the market was busy and the faces happy. The main streets around the market were widened and landscaped with palms and street art. There were areas for sitting and watching, cafes galore with people of many origins pouring onto the European style footpaths. You could walk anywhere in the city and the mix of modern architecture, mostly Spanish influenced amid the older Arab buildings were quite intoxicating. Zoe bought some fresh coriander, tomatoes and parsley and Suske brought some peonies and wine. The couple walked the streets happily to their friends' smart apartment in the centre of town.

They loved to visit Daniel and Nariman, both for their company and their location. Their balcony was the perfect people-watching place to have a drink and talk. They were friends from university days, and as the afternoon slipped by they spoke of how different things had been, how it would have been impossible for Daniel to live here before, coming from a Jewish background and how good it was to see the end of hatred in this place. Where there had been watchtowers and walls going up between settlers and Palestinians, it was now a continuous bustling and well-landscaped metropolis. Daniel almost couldn't conceive of the time he had served in the Israeli Defence Forces and what he had seen. The fears and paranoia that he and his fellow soldiers felt patrolling these very streets below them. Often crouching behind a tank that afforded them some protection from the curses and stones that were hurled at them from boys as young as eight. The brutality he had seen inflicted on a daily basis at checkpoints where sudden movements alone could be interpreted as a terrorist act and the innocent perpetrator beaten or shot. The random arrests he was forced to make of the young men of families he had gotten to know and how now they were his friends and business colleagues. He recalled in shame the 'shit trucks' that would enter a troublesome neighbourhood in the evenings and with high-pressure water cannons squirt the foulest rotting liquid over people and their houses to teach them a lesson. Daniel told them how he had later found out that he had been responsible for monitoring his now spouses' family and their activist movements in and around this very city. Suske and Daniel had become very close friends again when the country united, and the borders came down. When the people of this land became one, it made their once brief close ties as university mates so deep in the context of all that had happened since. They were brothers in celebrating the end of the religious, cultural and tribal wars. They both possessed a depth of humanity and compassion that enabled them to see how very far everything had come both for them and their people.

Suske recalled his brief time in an Israeli prison, picked up in Nablus at a checkpoint, his papers taken, and his freedom deprived for 2 weeks.

His student and travel visas were up to date, he was not a known protester. He had kept a low profile but still they detained him. They hadn't beaten him, but simply isolated and fed him nothing but silence with a boiled egg, some rice and water in the evenings. He was released without apology or acknowledgement but in those two quiet weeks had developed a hatred of the oppressor and was on his road to radicalisation. He sat quietly with his friend now, and they contemplated before them a bustling city and happy faces, a town with not one prison, not one wall and no tanks or any men with any guns. It was impossible to be radicalised here apart from with a sense of purpose that there was freedom to pursue any idea that could contribute to the benefit of man.

Trying to make sense of it all the two recalled how they had been thinking before I Day. Suske had joined in some of the demonstrations after his jailing and he read the texts of the fundamentalists. He knew it was only a matter of time before he would be deported back to Syria, but he was now overcome with the desire to make it clear that it wasn't always going to be the Israeli Army that would dictate the agenda. He found like-minded people to try to publicise just how suppressed the outsiders were in this country hell-bent on security for an ethnic tribe.

From Daniel's perspective, there had been an increasing sense of paranoia created by the state. The vast majority of 'the animals' as some referred to them as were basically friendly, ordinary people keen to go about their business and live life safely, fully and with some fun. It was odd for him to come back from his Army postings and to have conversations with people far from any interaction with 'the animals'. He would try to give some sense of how they were exactly like 'us', but many people refused to acknowledge this and swallowed the propaganda of a state based on the fear of what outsiders would bring to their society.

Of course, the paranoia went both ways, and Daniel and Suske went over the rift that had happened at that time between them. Daniel found Suske couldn't distinguish the soldier of the state from the true friend that he had made. They also recalled the immense sense of relief when they had been reunited after I Day. The same sense of connection and love and forgiveness and understanding that Suske had felt with his brother. They sat, drinking an ice-cold beer on that terrace almost having difficulty recalling how things had ever been so awful. How it had been that hatred had ruled a land that now embraced love and learning and peace. Imagining the dreadful past was only possible in the context of learning a positive lesson going forward. So many lessons were learned from the mistakes of the past here.

They were four very different people from very different backgrounds. Lebanese, Jewish, Syrian and Palestinian and yet they were no longer labelled as such. Mixed marriages had blossomed in the past 12 months. There was no distinction by passport or papers between religious background or nationality as these now did not exist. There were free movement of goods, ideas and people; there was freedom to love whoever your passion, intimacy and commitment led you to. There was no such thing as orthodox or ultra-orthodox, Sunni or Shia. There was no Maronite or Roman. People were just people now, and in their personality and circumstances, met and enjoyed those who fulfilled them and who they ended up loving. There was much love on this balcony, on this fine evening as the bustle of the markets turned to the sophistication of the Nablus streets whispering the joy of freedom and the low hubbub of people enjoying life in peace.

Zoe shared her photos from the schools with Nariman, both delighting in the many faces of joy that she had captured in classrooms and playgrounds. Nariman had such a beautiful, welcoming face herself. She was the most intelligent woman that Zoe knew. Her eyes of such depth and her expressions at once slightly sad and understanding. It was as if she took in every emotion that had been captured in Zoe's photographs and took it directly into her own heart. After looking at the photos for some time Nariman stared up across the city, then looked intensely into Zoe's eyes.

Nariman said. "These are the most insightful photos I have ever seen, they make me cry. To see the kids playing like this together. When I was their age, I wasn't even allowed to talk to any Jewish kids. We stood on rocky hilltops and flung rocks with slings at young men like Daniel, yelling insults into the wind. We never got to play with little kids from the fancy Settlements and on the rare times we went into Israel proper we were told not to even look at, let alone talk to any other children. These photos remind me of the youth I did not have, of the innocence that was stolen when I saw my cousin shot at close range with a rubber bullet and die in agony a few hours later. More than anything, they fill me with hope for a future for our kids. Thank you so much Zoe, you have filled my heart to the brim with joy."

Chapter 13

Alabama 12 years after I Day

Mia lay on the sofa with her legs up watching television. Her husband Gary lay on the other lounge reading a car magazine. Mia found herself admiring Gary's calves, their shape reminded her of affection and devotion, the very hairs swept this way and that and there was his bald knee. They had been so close to leaving each other until I Day. Mia had been overwhelmed before that day by the burden of being mum to four little children under five and the way she had thrown herself into her own real estate business. Once I Day had come and gone, everything had changed. The real estate boom had signalled the commission of entirely new ways to plan the housing for people. No longer was it the hard sell; It wasn't the charm of the agent that helped win the sale and fee but rather those with knowledge of the market and its needs. After I Day Mia became integral to planning the great influx of migrants, architects, town planners and educators that flooded into Alabama overnight. The opportunities to lift the community were felt by the whole nation. Alabama became a magnet for intellectuals as the local community welcomed decision by consensus and integration.

"Gar, cut the light."

"Bless you Mi. I'm a readin', feel free to fixing to come right on over here won't you."

Mia got up and turned the light out, came over to her husband and kissed him passionately just under his left ear. Gary gave out a low moan and reached for Mia who had already disappeared into the kitchen. She came back, turned the light back on and resumed her position on the sofa and her admiration of Gary's calves with only a little attention to her television show which was describing all the new medicines that were being discovered in the roots and swamps of her own state.

"Mi, I'm 'bout to pop."

"Gar, I'm not bout to take you to the bathroom. Ya get yourself out there."

"Ya know I'm not talkin about my bladder. I'm fixin' to come over yonder and give you a southern kiss."

"Lordy Gary, you're all talk."

Just then their youngest walked in. Ryan was now 14, and he acted as if he hadn't heard his parents' conversation as they did also. Ryan was incredibly intelligent, and he found it hard to disguise his broad smirk. He loved that his parents played and toyed with each other and loved each other so passionately. He had grown up seeing their cheesy love for each other and adored both of them.

Mia especially loved Ryan and was incredibly proud of him. There was something very special about the way he would hug her. As if he somehow remembered the pain she had when he was little and the disenchantment that she had in her life. She had felt a disconnection from duty and a hankering for adventure; now she saw in Ryan that quest for adventure. She loved that he looked at the whole world with such curiosity, that he wanted to explore beyond his family, his house and school. He was always ready to help, and his gentle ways made his mother swoon for his future. Ryan seemed to take everything in stride. Strong and constant was how he felt, and everyone could see that in him.

They were a close family and truly loved each other's company. There were plenty of smiles goin' around as Beau, the eldest, walked in. Beau, was the most stubborn but so handsome that he made a room stop and stare almost every time he walked in. Beau knew that he was a good-looking young man, but he was also humble. By his side, almost constantly, was his partner, Sherrilyn, who complimented his presence with her grace and beauty. Mia found her darkness extraordinarily attractive. She loved to sit by her on the sofa, their arms side by side. The pale shade of Mia's forearm by the rich darkness of Sherrilyn's.

Mia loved to hear Sherrilyn talk about her grandmother, Vivian, who in the 1960s had with another young black friend almost single-handedly desegregated Universities in the state. The legal proceedings to enter the University of Alabama took two years after Vivian had completed her initial degree in Marketing at a completely black campus. Mia particularly loved the story of how Vivian walked up to the Registration Auditorium of the all-white University of Alabama only to be greeted by a very incensed and determined Governor of the State blocking her way. She was fortunately accompanied by the Federal Attorney General's deputy who tried to persuade the Governor to step aside. Sherrilyn described in detail what her grandmother was wearing that day, proud of every moment. Vivian, herself, loved to mention how she had been saved by President Kennedy himself that day as he had ordered the state's Army National Guards to be directly under his command. The Governor stood aside, and Sherrilyn's grandmother was enrolled. As she sat in the dining room on that first day, she was deeply comforted by the group of white students who sat down and ate with her. Her grandmother graduated two years later and despite her two degrees and a brilliant academic record was never able to get a job in Alabama. She married a kind doctor and raised brilliant children and even more brilliant grandchildren according to Sherrilyn, one of whom had returned to Alabama and had fallen in love with Mia's son.

It was almost laughable now that the state had been segregated at all. It wasn't in the mindset of anyone anymore. All neighbourhoods throughout the state now had an even mix of black and white. The ghetto areas transformed and all the historical houses restored with care, heritage and much skill. Many of the white people that now lived in these towns and streets had been drawn by the amazing food that was available and the exciting feeling, especially in the first years, of the rediscovery of African and slave era culture. The arts in dance, painting and writing flourished as thousands discovered their roots and the richness of their own cultures. Almost every third marriage in Alabama now was mixed, and this drew and inspired social and artistic collaboration and innovation. Love was not blinded by town, religion or skin colour. It was absolutely normal to see kids of every shade in schools these days, and the mix was beautiful. People understood that there had been discrimination and economic slavery and hatred, but no one could really understand it anymore. The transformation had been incredibly smooth. Strangely, it had been the influx of Asian and Northern immigrants shortly after I Day to Alabama that had created most of the friction. They had to adjust to the drawl and the spicy food and craved pizza and sashimi. It didn't take long however, for the talented southern restaurateurs to adapt, becoming more creative, adding to an already delicious cuisine.

Mia had always been a loving person, but she had loved her country, her state, her way of life and her beliefs to the exclusion of the idea that everyone was entitled to opportunity free of oppression and prejudice. She was an adorable deplorable who had taken herself up from difficult circumstances to build a life by selling real estate on the beach to affluent white investors. Her charm was indubitable, she knew which buzzwords to touch and drew upon the emotion in a buyer and her true love for her hometown drove her to success.

On the day I Day arrived; Mia was in the middle of a sale. She had a gorgeous oceanfront house in Orange Beach, and she was about to clinch the deal with a wealthy Caterpillar Executive from Texas who had flown in on his own chartered plane. Desmond was a short man, with a Pilgrim style beard, a very rotund midriff and thick glasses and even Mia struggled to stay with his accent. His belly jutted out between the buttons on his flannel top over an enormous elliptical belt buckle that held up his very baggy jeans. Mia couldn't help staring at the buckle as it had "Cowboy Butts drive me Nuts" emblazoned upon it. He was asking her where he could get a good burger with fries, but she was determined to settle the account that day, so she took him in her large SUV to The Gulf and watched him order and begin to eat two Gulf beef burgers and the two lots of fries that came with them along with copious ketchup and two cokes. Just as he was signing the contract, the harmonics were switched on, and Mia immediately bid her new friend goodbye and got back into her car.

Desmond was stunned for a few minutes. He poured his Cokes into the sink at the side alley of the Restaurant and threw away his second Gulf Burger and fries. He ordered an avocado and sourdough with salad and he sold all his shares within 15 minutes of Mia leaving. He booked himself into a 7-week retreat in Nepal that focused on self-discovery and colonic cleansing. He then walked the five kms back to the airport and his plane. Within 48 hours the proceeds from his share sale were redistributed to Eritrean water and sewer works, but he had enough cash left for the fuel to take him to Nepal. Desmond would go on to become an artisan barrel maker in the old style and settled into life selling them in the marketplaces in the foothills below Darjeeling in India. He lost 78 pounds in three months, did his first marathon at age 62 and was fluent in Sanskrit within a few months of I Day. He became somewhat of a guru on the ancient textual interpretation of *The Birth of Kumara,* the great love poem by Kalidasa and despite the enlightenment of his family back in Texas since I Day he still shocked them with his analysis of the lovemaking of the gods. He became a favourite around the world of spontaneous video education as he appeared with his long beard and balding pate, sitting cross-legged in the busy market square espousing the inevitability of love between Shiva And Parvati and the sensual birth of the universe. His white linen garments loose about him and his expressions of calm and excitement coming through his subtle hand movements. Fifty-five million people tuned into his live teaching sessions.

"Shiva and Parvati
Lord of watching
Goddess of feeling
He takes her energy
So seen and felt
Then becoming one
Accepting

Lover and beloved
Mountain and cave
He uncouth, tall as a horse
As beautiful as life can be
They could not help but worship him.
She, a princess
Daughter of the mountain
As beautiful as darkness itself
Turning to light"

He would pause between lines so people could take in and understand the tale of creation from the mountains that needed retelling in this modern world. People needed to be reminded of myth and metaphor in a world that had turned to such trivial distraction. Despite I Day and the thirst for knowledge that it created; there was still 100 years of growing emptiness in a population ruled by a media that was designed to constantly distract. In the 20 years before I Day, people had become slaves to mobile devices, and human presence had deteriorated further and further. Part of Desmond's search and mission was not just to save himself from the emptiness that had been his life but to recognise the depths of self-discovery and the value in ancient knowledge that could be brought from that. His mission once he had found himself was to use the modern techniques of connection to bring to a vast new audience the ancient wisdom to be found in this special part of the world.

He only once returned to Texas, but his family frequently visited him in India becoming fans of tea and Thukpa, aloo and roti. They would trek up the foothills every third or fourth Christmas for the colours and music and food and of course the mysterious cloudy Himalayas.

By the time Desmond had eaten his sourdough and avocado, sold his shares and finished his double espresso Mia was a long way out of town and heading up the I29 toward Selma. She texted her husband to make sure he would be home soon for the kids; told him she would be away for a few days and added a pulsing love heart emoji for the first time that she could remember in years. She shocked herself as she saw it on the phone screen, even more surprised at the emotion behind it. Suddenly she remembered why she had fallen in love with Gary in the first place and went over and over in her mind those very moments that made her love him so much.

As she was driving, almost on autopilot, drawn by her reading, immersed in her consciousness of what was and what needed to happen, she turned up the volume on the music. It was Immigrant Song by Zeppelin, and the lyrics washed over her as the bass and the drums touched her soul. She opened her sunroof and both windows and blasted the sound. Her body bouncing with the rhythm and excited to finally be on the road she was meant to be on. She noticed the other people in their cars. Mia saw that no one was honking their horns, most people had a smile and a wave for her, and she wasn't the only one blaring music. Motivation was never Mia's problem; she was infused with purpose as well as an innate drive and she knew her job now was to organise and motivate and reconnect people. It really didn't require much additional thought. She had been thinking about this for years and had no solution, but in the space of a few minutes, her confidence that she was destined to make a difference had gone way over the point where she could even question it anymore. She knew Desmond would be ok, she looked forward to finding out how he would go in the future and smiled to herself as she thought of him finally as a human being rather than a sale. She understood he would change, but she was focussed on what she needed to do this day. From the moment she set out she made phone call after phone call to organize what had crystallised for her. She knew how to put pressure on and who would be helpful. She was set after those 12 important calls. After a couple of hours of driving, Mia decided she had to go visit Boykin and buy herself some quilts. It was to be a last act of selfishness on her path of reconstruction. She knew Gary and her boys would always appreciate this drive to pick up the purples, yellows and oranges of the bright rectangles sewn together with such love, skill and extraordinary heritage. She emptied her purse of almost all the cash she had and bought three exquisite pieces that were folded and wrapped with great aplomb by some of the quilters themselves. She gave them all an enormous hug and headed back north to Selma.

Mia knew in her bones exactly what she was meant to do. She drove over the Edmund Pettus bridge just to get a feel for the 50 years of history that she had tried to ignore. She hadn't even really tried; it was just part of her culture to get on with things and leave any other matters of opportunity and equity to nature. There wasn't a feeling sorry for anyone because everyone was given two eyes and two arms and a brain. Before I Day Mia believed everyone should have been able to achieve as she had if they just had the willpower. If people chose poverty and poor education, well, that was their choice. This day, everything had altered, she suddenly saw with a new light the immense changes that were coming, and she knew she had to be part of it from the very first hours. It all clicked, and as she did a U-turn in front of the National Voting Rights Museum, she pulled in for a coffee in one of the tourist shops on Broad Street and picked up the local newspaper. She knew what she was looking for and flicked through the paper. As she was reading intently, she looked up to the early evening news on the tv in the diner.

"All drugs in the United States of America will be decriminalised from 6:00 pm this evening. The President has resigned stating that better forms of government will be in place by the morning. All military personnel are to report to quarters for dismissal or reassignment within the following seven days."

Reform after reform was announced. International news was also stunning and followed a logic that saw the abandonment of military solutions and the advent of true democracy across the globe. Finally, the people were about to run the administration for the people. Ideas for developing systems of communication and the ways to get the best people and ideas into action was the biggest early focus. Mia turned back to her paper impressed and totally understanding what was happening on the outside with even more clarity on what she was doing here.

Mia was standing out the front at 988 Sellafield at 7:00 pm. This was the moment that they let out 95 percent of the prisoners from Selma County Jail. Five per cent were retained as they needed to be transferred to a secure mental facility to deal with a psychosis or sociopathic condition that hadn't yet been able to be adequately assessed post I Day harmonics.

There was a buzz around her as Mia waited which was somehow reflected in the evening sky as the prisoners came out one by one from the front gate. Every single one of them beaming and with eyes that spoke of a joy many of them had not felt for many years. The look of freedom but more than that, the look of hope and determination. There was a purpose to their walk. Mia was there to greet every single one of them, small white guys with terrible leather jackets, enormous black guys whose smiles often demonstrated a need for dental intervention. She was there to hug every one of them. She had a quick word with every single man who came through and gave out her card with her mobile number. Somehow in a very brief moment, she had been able to convey that she was here to help and would be in their lives if they needed her. There were other people there as well. People who had long been involved in calls for prison reform and transitional programs to the communities. They soon realised that Mia was someone that had immediately recognised the crisis that the new laws would bring and how she and they would be crucial to a smooth transition.

Small groups of ex-prisoners gathered to chat and say their goodbyes, to exchange contacts and to try to figure out where they were going. After a few minutes, most of the prisoners had made their way out from the compound, but there was still a considerable crowd left there, and this was when

Mia acted.

"I'm here to help guys, I have organised the medical and funding to sort out your methadone and other drug rehabilitation needs, I have the money organised to start our work first thing tomorrow morning. Come back with me, and I'll show you where we are going and what we are going to do."

The men looked at the diminutive and very gorgeous woman who was making more sense than anyone else had in the last few miserable years of their existence. The words, brief, somehow made absolute sense. They all fell in trust with this person, her determination and vision. They organised transport and Mia led a convoy of vehicles into the most rundown part of Selma.

Inside the half burnt-out cottage and in the four cottages immediately surrounding they set up camp. The first thing Mia did was send three of the guys around the neighbourhood to collect all the guns. These were happily handed over after explanations were made and then the guns were turned over to the Safety Committee compound that had been set up in the old prison complex for the dismantling of weapons and recycling of raw materials.

It was clear that the addicts amongst the guys were in nowhere as much need of their drugs of dependence than was anticipated and the medical team was able to administer a few days of treatment and the men allocated officers to supervise the transition to drug freedom and withdrawal. It was astounding as they developed personal and familial connections and had their minds stimulated by the work Mia had initiated them into, that their desire for drugs dropped off sharply within a few days. Occupied with catching up with family, stimulating work, becoming aware of the larger world around them and the opportunities it was about to afford them was intoxicating enough. Almost all the men were drug free by week two.

Mia was a dynamo on that first morning. She had already mobilised the medical people she needed, but now she had summoned the craftsmen and architects and engineers and micro financiers to meet her workforce. All were allocated to one specialist or another to help plan, decide and build. Their first jobs were the four cottages they were living in, but they had the entire street in mind, the whole city. This was just the start. One of the architects said he had found an abandoned old mansion on the outskirts of town. This was where the group had their lunch meeting. By the afternoon, they had gathered all the useful materials, including the handmade colonial bricks that would form the theme for their renewal. Old verandahs of the cottage that were leaning into the ground were dismantled, rooms were stripped back and cleaned to prepare for the new layouts and interiors. Publicity was drawn, the newspapers and tv crews all over it extolling the ideas and action as a role model for reconstruction across the land and within 72 hours Mia was back with her family. As soon as Mia caught Gary's eye they knew what was next. The trip they had dreamt about for a decade. They finally sat down, planned and booked their vacation to Australia, and Mia penned in her next visit to Selma shortly after their return to Alabama.

Mia was proud of her innovation and got the very best people she knew to support it. She became recognised nationally and internationally for her initiatives and went on to become an ambassador for renewal projects initially across the southern United States but eventually globally. Her favourite thing to do was return to Selma on the hyperloop and wander the back streets and take in the myriad of styles and architecture that had blossomed and returned. The community was a mixture of artisans and writers, and the cultural history of America was writ large in this laid back but intellectual centre. She loved to go to the old prison site and wander through the gate where she had greeted those men as they had been delivered to freedom and trust that night. It was now an art gallery for the region. Mia could almost never resist buying another quilt on these visits and her smile was always a welcome sight in her adopted town. She couldn't leave the beach. Her children adored the summer days growing up on the sand, but she relished her revisiting of Selma.

The rebuilding took nearly a year. Everyone contributed when they could. People flew in from all over the country to learn how to organise the build. The coordination of design, materials and labour was crucial, but the efficiencies that were initiated in those first few months after I Day were responsible for the coordination. Capital wasn't a problem because the redistribution of investment and decision-making meant places that needed renewal were a high priority. Logistics were at the core of this revolution, and the success at Selma begged the question, where to from here? The answer lay in reproducing its success across the South and went hand in hand with the elimination of racism and discrimination. Opportunity was seized, educational needs were met, and the integration of cultures was smooth.

The City of Selma then had to work out what was next. The culture flourished, the movement of ideas and expertise was fluid, and the town was a beacon for progress. Selma found herself with a little help from her friends. No more gangs, no more jails, no more addiction issues, no more poverty, no more hatred. Selma and Mia were mates for life.

Chapter 14

Australia on I Day

"I just felt drawn here. I woke up, and I dragged the comb across my head, got up and just had to come here."

"Yeah, same mate. 'Xactly. Sure, I had the weirdest dream ever. I was standing on a clifftop looking out over a perfect beach, just like this one but there wasn't a person on it. A huge sea bird swooped down and picked me up and flew me along the length of the beach and set me down on the opposite headland. When I looked down the beach, it was full of people splashing and playing in the water, sunbathing and jogging along the shore. Then I woke up and I just had to come here. Have no clue why I told you that. What's your name mate? I'm Dave."

"G'day Dave, I'm Rajiv. Strange, that you mention it. I also had a dream last night. In my dream, I was taken up in the air by a giant bird as well. We crossed many thousands of miles of flat country with almost no visibility. The bird seemed to know where it was going, but the land below us was empty of any sign of life. There were no mountains, no rivers, no animals or people. And then I woke up and just had to hop on my motorbike and get down here."

"Mate, this is weird. It's just breaking dawn and I'm seeing hundreds of people arriving. The car park is almost full, people are swarming down from the station. The rest just wandering in on foot. I've never seen anything like it. No one is rushing, there's no honking of horns, just everyone seems to be 'round. Weirdest thing I ever saw down here."

They noticed people gathering and having as intense conversations as they were. The sun was gripping the horizon and the clouds were splitting the rays into interesting courses through the sky. The colours shifting through purple into pinks and lighter blues. The natural amphitheatre of the park behind the beach now swollen with people telling their own stories of their extraordinary night and the stories of their dreams which remained so vivid in their minds. People just spoke to whoever was next to them. Somehow, they were meant to be there, and the dreams were exchanged and explained as the sun rose over the ocean.

It was a murmuring that spread across the little beachside village. Kids, adults, the elderly, people of all backgrounds; Italians, Greeks, Vietnamese, Indians and Chinese, every race that graced the wide brown land. The grandpas with white socks and sandals, even the guy who slept in the park every night; animated, willing and able to talk and try to understand the magnet that had pulled them all here. Not one person was looking at their smartphone, the focus was personal and real. Not a screen to be seen and people noticed the nuances of people's faces, their faraway gazes and intense stares as they told their story. People listened with a natural ferocity and somehow fully digested what the other person was trying to convey. There were a million styles, a thousand accents, but understanding somehow was what was underlying the buzz. People were convinced that they were being heard and that was making the difference. Some people expressed themselves in dance, some with music but it all centred around what they had experienced in their sleep and how they needed to be in this place, on this land, on this day. Rajiv and Dave remained sitting higher on the bluff and noticed the surfers really taking their time between waves, clustered in twos and threes, obviously also in deep conversation.

When the perfect wave came through, Mitch and Shane took off but were quick to paddle back to rejoin their chat.

"Shane, how was that last wave?"

"Mate, that was a near-perfect wave. What do you make of all the people on the beach and in the park today?"

"Mate, I dunno, but I'm just glad to be out here, away from all of that for a day. Did you see the way the sun rose this morning? Shano, never seen anything quite like it."

"There were people here before dawn, as I was heading for the water there was all this talk of dreams. Everyone wanted to talk about it to me."

"Yeah, same thing happened to me Shane, and the surfers at the point were on about it as well. Come to think of it I had some pretty wild dreams myself last night."

"Really? Hang on. Oh shit, look at that wave."

"Fuck, it's perfect. You go right, I'll take left."

The wave curled in at the slightest of angles to the beach, about seven foot, it was shaped as a perfect crescent, the base was made of the softest foam and the lip pulled back in anticipation as the slight breeze held it up well. They launched themselves at it as both their hands swept the back of the waves on opposite sides as they glided up and down the front surface at pace.

"Maaaaate, how'd you go? That curled about me, glassy as."

"Man, that was hot. I was tempted to go in but I just had to tell you about last night."

"Tell me Mitcho. Then I will tell you."

"Ok mate, just ignore this wave, it's a ripper. So, last night I slept amazingly well, but I had this vivid dream just like all those clowns on the beach. I was blind mate, not drunk, I couldn't see a damn thing. It was terrifying at first and then I'm not sure how, but I was healed. I felt a warmth being placed on my eyes, like two palms that were warmed by a fire and placed onto my face. After that, I could see, but my healer wasn't there. When I woke up, I could see perfectly normally, but everything was a little more vivid than usual. I felt the things I was looking at; I could concentrate and take in all that was about me, and this is the best goddam surf I've had in years. It's amazing mate."

They took off for another perfect wave, this time one after the other cutting right and across the wall of water that seemed to go on forever. They took it into shore and sat on the sand dripping wet and just shook their heads at each other. Sometimes, nothing is said after a ride like that. You just sit and take in the ocean, the sun warming your face, the saltwater dripping from your hair, your board by your side and experience it. The presence of someone that has witnessed and felt the thrill by your side just makes it all that much better. After catching their breath, Shane couldn't help telling Mitch what had happened to him late last night as well.

"I didn't get to bed till really late last night. I've been overthinking and working evenings and sitting up late watching telly. I was texting this chick in Melbourne, and it was clear she was just mucking me around talking about her new hot date on the weekend and then suddenly the conversation really didn't matter. It was about 2 am, I was totally exhausted but real quick, like over a minute, a bit like you were saying, everything became a whole lot clearer. I knew I had to get to the beach in the morning and the telly was weird as well. All the reality show reruns and analysis that I had been watching were just not on anymore. Most of the stations were taken over by various music genres as if the producers just couldn't bring themselves to keep showing the same old shit. There were no ads anymore, and I suddenly had the urge to get to bed and get some rest. I went to sleep looking forward to today, knowing something had just completely changed."

"And what about this morning? How did you feel?"

"Yeah, Mitch, just incredible. I'd only had three hours sleep, made myself a coffee, grabbed some fruit and came down here. The rest is history, best freakin' ride of my life. So good to share it with you mate. Just the best. And how's this beach? Let's get back out there."

The cafe was humming with people sharing stories. The coffee was savoured, and the avocado and sourdough were being tasted like they had never been made with love before. It was a connection to the people around that was almost universal. People took in more than words, they took in the aspirations and meanings of what was being told to them. They were relating it and interweaving it with their own experiences of that strange morning. Then someone turned the television on in the corner, and all eyes turned for a moment to the Prime Minister addressing the nation for what appeared to be the last time.

"My fellow Australians, today we are returning to the land. This is my last hour as your leader, but I have taken steps to have the meetings arranged to end this government and to adopt a learning phase where we seek wisdom from every elder of this land. We must listen to this country from now on, we must become one with the land and relinquish our notion that we own our little space. Rather, we will move towards the notion that the land owns us. This was my dream, and this will become this nation's dream. I am taking advice from the wise, those with the best dreams, those who understand our balance with the land, those who understand how to connect us.

"This, my good friends, is a revolution of ideas and action, do not be afraid. This will be the age of kinship, sharing, equity, health as a priority, and the disarming of our military. We have heard this morning that many of the world governments have followed a similar trajectory. We look forward to working with the world to offer the very best of our inventiveness and resources, and we expect to gain much from opening our nation up to sustainable development and to lead the charge into ideas that can make our world a better and better place. I will take my place as an elder, I hope. I am prepared to be judged for the knowledge, ideas and compassion I have to offer. I open the concept of being an elder to the entire population, but it is time, especially, to listen to those who have belonged to this land for the longest time. It is time to be humble and listen to the dreams that matter."

People in the cafe went back to chatting as if this had been the most natural and logical thing for the PM to say. There was discussion around who they imagined would be involved in the future governance of the nation, but a kind of relaxed yet interested notion of a better future hung upon the discussion. People simply accepted that things had dramatically and logically changed, there was not even any great discussion of why things had changed. It just all made sense and gave them the notion that finally, logic and dreams had met and that there was a future that could be molded and influenced by them and other ordinary people. A sense that not only the person next to them was listening but that they could be heard by a wider audience if they had something original and constructive to offer. They were empowered by the very idea of true democracy before it had even started. They imagined this was the week that the land that had been called Australia was restored to itself and that they, the people, were now merely again its custodians.

In the very centre of Australia, the people started to gather as well. Just as on the beaches and headlands, some were drawn to the centre of the land. On the Sturt Highway from Adelaide and Darwin, every 4-wheel track and overland trail were heavy with people returning to the heart of their land. As if they had awoken to a call for Corroboree but that it was for all. As the sun set on Uluru, there were maybe 500,000 people ringing the great rock. The shadows as the sun fell across and behind the rock assailing the imaginations of a people close to the red-orange dust. Some had travelled hundreds of kilometres, but there were enough to hold hands and encircle the monolith in the desert, it was as if the land had taken its rightful place as prime mover again. People had come to learn from the earth, and the next few days were ones of intense learning about what the land really means to its people.

There was much dancing, and there were many discussions. Groups began to form talking through areas of various interests, the demise of politics, the end of religion, and the new economy. Others gathered just to learn about the legends and the art of the centre of the land. Many dreams were passed on from person to person, elder to child. In that place where the orange of the dirt, the green of the trees and shrubs, and the lightest blue of the clear desert sky drew together so too did the people and their ideas. Everyone learnt how to make damper, and Billy tea was trending as every night the sun bade unforgettable farewells to both the rock itself and the people witnessing its metamorphosis. Eyes turned upwards in the evenings as the Milky Way imposed itself on the discussion and imagination.

On the seventh night, it rained and the sea of tents and iron roofs thrummed to the steady beat of water falling. As they awoke to a steamy and wet morning the great rock was awash with waterfalls across its wrinkled ancient surface. The pools at the base of the rock were filled by water streaming in bright white lines across the red face of the rock, dripping and pouring through gullies and sheer cliff and spraying into calm ponds fringed by grasses and shrubs at the base. There was a sense that the rock was evolving and changing as were the people gazing upon it. It was time to return to their homes and communities and to pass on the dreams, the ethics and laws, the songs and traditions, and the spirit of what the land had given them.

The road trains they passed on their way back to Adelaide, Darwin, Perth and Sydney were among the last to be seen on the straight black tarmacs of the desert country. Within six months the centre of Australia had become such a focus of the nature of the country that hyperloops had been installed and the 14-hour road trip was reduced to an hour and a half from every direction. The red centre had become the beating heart of Australia, and the landscape was preserved for 100 km around the great rock.

Elsewhere huge areas of the desert began to bloom, ancient forests started creeping in from the coastal fringes, and pasture lands went from arid and desperate to lush and sustainable as water management and land care was coordinated across the country. Vast underground pipes brought water and life to marginal areas that had never been able to be lived in before and only rarely admired by the adventurous tourist or indigenous group for its own stark beauty. There was still much of the Australian outback that was desert, deliberately kept as the local people wanted it but millions of acres that had been the dead heart of a dry country had been resuscitated and reinvigorated. Transport became quick and non-polluting, there was no mad development and in fact, the entire ecosystem was taken into consideration. Small indigenous communities opened their 'doors' to the wider community as trust and understanding grew. People were strongly drawn to the lifestyle, wisdom and art that the first peoples offered. The indigenous that were so in touch with their land and now so willing and confident to teach people about it. The marriage of reusable water sources and solar technologies allowed these communities to flourish as did the land.

People brought with themselves their hope, knowledge and personality. The mix of urban Australians, Aboriginal people and tourists with open minds brought a heady junction of new and ancient ideas. Incorporation of traditions into new technology and respecting everyone's way of life and the land itself so few outside had previously ever had the opportunity to develop. Desert towns became the trendy places to raise your kids and young families started flocking there when education became universally accessible in the home environment. The opportunities for sport and social interaction, the chance to learn multiple cultures and languages, the very breathtaking nature of the night sky drove people to seek a more integrated and wholesome life.

Once the water and transport logistic problems were solved the cities themselves became transformed as more people moved inland. The franchises in the cities were bulldozed, and the parking lots became parks. You could get from your desert home to the beach in less than three hours. So Australia shrunk, but still, the wide brown land as the vast greening land held its share of wonder and mystery that would fascinate the visitor and the native for generations.

The enormous cattle stations like Nulla Nulla were transformed as well and attracted the local people in to manage the great changes that were necessary. As more water arrived diversity and ingenuity in farming returned to match it. Carob and oak trees were planted, saltbush and a mixture of farm animals were introduced all over the vast holdings in well designed and rotating pastures.There were beehives and gardens of every type and the chooks were free to roam. Huge stands of new forest were planted with the Sydney gums and other eucalyptus species introduced for the first time in a hundred years. Compost became king as the hard work of the soil became reinforced to create the best conditions for the fruit and olive crops. The arid stations became a colourful panoply of peach and plum, apricot and nectarine cherry and mandarin, mulberry and fig. The great farms diversified into nuts and woods, cheeses and yoghurts, honey and eggs as well as the much more efficient management of their previous main business of the cattle runs. Water consumption actually fell for the cattle as they ate more of their nutrients and fluids in the rich grasses of the fields dedicated to them. It was true there were more cows together in one area but they fertilised their own fields, grazing on the natural grasses and not requiring any antibiotics or steroids or feed to progress.

It overjoyed the people to transform their land. Day by day, they could see the changes and the benefits. The return of the fantastic wildlife, the green and other colours of the crops and pastures and the healthy animals and people looking after them. It took months of earth moving to create the terraces, to redesign the pastures and fencing and to plant the trees that would bind the soil and provide some shade on those faraway fields over the years to come.

Suddenly, the world was bound to one another, transport made it easy for people to come stay awhile in these once remote places and the community welcomed advisors, workers and tourists year-round. It was exciting to see the station become a farm. One of the happiest guests that came to Nulla Nulla Station was Alan Savory. He helped design the pastoral movement of the cattle in large herds that mimicked nature, working on the logistics of how the animals would get from one area to another, peeing on, pooing on and trampling on the grasslands to create a microclimate where water and nutrients could be trapped for regrowth. The dusty gully and eroded bases of trees were transformed quickly into rich grasslands that brought a diversity of native animals back to the land. The Koalas were always favourites with the visitors, swaying high in a gum, in a fork of the tree, perfectly balanced and chewing away on some delicious green eucalyptus leaves, seemingly very, very relaxed about life. The evenings saw the kangaroos and wallabies emerge and the red wine and canapés would be consumed between quietly spoken people there to watch the grazing and hopping as the light faded and the stars emerged. Nulla Nulla had returned to something its soil had only dreamed of in the dry dusty, cracked and eroded heart of the country.

As the weeks and months emerged after I Day and consensus was being reached on the best way forward for this unique island deep in the South Pacific it was clear that people had more leisure time as the efficiencies of production and the actual needs of the people changed. Having 95 percent of the cars off the surface roads in cities like Melbourne and Sydney completely changed the urban environment. Much of the land that had been offered up to worship that inefficient transportation system was now being returned to better uses. Regreening and the design of parklands had become a busy affair for the architects, town planners and biologists of the big towns and even of the smaller seaside villages. Vast areas of the most boring urban developments were bulldozed and a clean slate of interesting urban design and corridors for the rapid return of nature were established. It was now not uncommon to see kangaroos, echidnas, koalas and emus in the urban environment. They were no longer threatened by cruelty or fast-moving motor vehicles that had left them in the past knocked to the sides of country roads. The number of cats and the control of domestic animals were crucial to this, but for the average person, the joy of having the true nature of Australia returning in their daily encounters was more than the sensible sacrifices they had to make. It wasn't unusual to see platypus again in the local creeks that had been reestablished to replace the now unused stormwater drains. All of the storm and rainwater was now gathered very early into separate coastal and urban piping that would be sent out to the dry centre. Every new rooftop was a designer solar panel, disguised into the individual preferences of the architect and owner. Gardens were eclectic and varied, many styles and traditions encompassed into a streetscape that held together as a statement. There was not a paling fence to be found nor a wall to be seen. Subtle hedging and flower beds the only hint of a property line. Every suburb and town were somewhat different but smart and intriguing without any building being an eyesore. The buildings became part of the land again, the gardens part of the greater urban renewal. Kids were out on their bikes in the afternoon sun in the quiet streets playing chasings; every sport was played on what were left of the roads which were now mostly new parks for the people to enjoy.

People rarely used their own vehicles unless they needed them at the other end of a countrywide hyperloop. Mostly, people got around the vastly quieter cities with public transport systems that could get them anywhere in the larger metropolises within an hour. Every house was completely energy self-sustained. There was only a rudimentary electricity grid because everyone's energy needs were supplied by themselves. The grid was for the needs of large energy users for commercial purposes, but all of this was from renewables via hydroelectricity, solar plants, wind and wave energy generators.

The average person in the land that had been called Australia now worked 18 hours a week, but most spent around another 20 hours in either places of learning or creative environments. Art, writing and cultural enrichment flourished; there was a generosity of presence that the artists felt which encouraged them to reach deeper into themselves for expression. There was so much more to explore as the intelligence of people and their desire to be challenged culturally had altered dramatically. Australians already had a rich mix of culture, science and art, and now it seemed there were no bounds to the gifts this land would bring to the world. People had more time to eat and to savour food. The chefs and cooks became even more famous and sought after as people abandoned all of the commercially prepared foods. As the farm lands became more productive, vegetables and organic products were cheap and readily available; with the better education around nutritious foods, chefs became icons of creativity and deliciousness. People demanded originality and freshness in their diets, and this resulted in a massive drop off in obesity, diabetes, cancers and cardiac disease.

The cost of providing health care dropped dramatically but it remained a field of intense research as the puzzle of human health and disease was a complex one. Billions of dollars that had been poured into dealing with the consequences of lifestyle-related disease were now able to be utilised in basic science research, targeting diseases that befell people randomly and through no fault of their own. Providing the best support for disabled people and the quest for remobilising people who had lost limbs or the use of them became intense. The illnesses that had affected people chronically for years that had not been solved or understood were also targeted and the scourge of conditions like Rheumatoid arthritis and Motor Neurone disease became a particular focus of researchers in the land down under. Research across the globe was now coordinated and designed to support and build on found facts. Much of the task was the integration of the knowledge that had already been and was being discovered. Putting the facts together was crucial to solving so much of what previously had been seemingly insoluble. The elimination of commercial interests, the establishment of communal interest; now combined with the furious determination of academics to cooperate lead to innumerable breakthroughs in medicine, science and industry.

The beach returned to normal, but the village around it changed quickly over the first two years. The people sat in a Cafe that was not set back behind a row of ugly flats that cast shadows over the early afternoon sand but rather cleverly designed to sit within and resemble a dune. The sound of the ocean flooded the room where people enjoyed their coffees discussing everything under the sun. They ate from a menu that changed every day as the cook invented and sought the freshest seasonal foods from the land and the sea. They watched the surfers riding perfect breaks with an inventiveness that was stunning and amusing. Eventually, the cafe goers wandered back through the rainforest to their own homes that peaked out over the vast ocean. Kookaburras laughed raucously into the evening sky.

As the summer turns to winter, as it slowly does in this place, the crowds packed inside the seaside cafe and not the patio, where the lonely seagull stalked the rain-soaked tables, the scavenging proved difficult. Talk inside turned to the way the country felt now about itself and how far it had to go. The word 'respect' was on everybody's lips. It was as if the country was physically smaller, but it was still actually mysterious and vast. The conversation was about learning. How we could learn what we could from the myriad cultures that had entered upon this land to dwell. How all of us are migrants, even the first inhabitants. Now there was a sense of value in listening and of how to appreciate the broad perspectives, cuisines, know-how about the land and about how to look after each other.

The big, red dry country had much to tell us about survival, about caring for the land and each other. The land of drought and fire, flooding rains, ocean and beach became more loved as every man and woman came to appreciate her in light of other's perspectives. The drizzle hit the cool glass as the ocean stretched beyond the yellow strip of the long beach. The coffee was delicious and the smiles warm. It felt good to understand each other in the land down under.

Chapter 15

Old Mexican Border 6 months after I Day

The flow of Chryslers, Fords and Chevys south was relentless. Now that Mexico was a safe destination millions of Americans were trekking down across the Rio Grande and through the Californian border towns to commence their exploration of Central and often South America. Vacation time for Americans had been increased to six weeks per year in the week after I Day with a proposal to enable consensus legislation to extend it to three months if productivity targets were reached. The way the world economy was humming it was almost certain that this would occur. The push for complex and wandering holidays into those lands accessible by road was enormous. Within months the electrical grid infrastructure was installed all the way through to Quito in Ecuador and beyond. The illicit drugs that had been the backbone of criminality and tax avoidance in Mexico and Colombia were legalised worldwide the following week. The economies built on the narcotics trade had quickly collapsed as demand plummeted due to personal use minimisation and the lack of push from criminals. As the money from drugs dried up, there was a swift change to income from the service industries and tourism. More novel micro businesses were started in Colombia in the month after I Day than in the previous 40 years.

The flow north was very much as per usual.

Half of the people who had been illegal migrants in the States returned home as news of the new economies opening up in their homelands became known. The other half instantly became legalised migrants to their communities. Passports were no longer necessary worldwide, and so citizenry became a concept around the local community and of the world rather than on a national basis. Immigration and travel became quite common as professions, trades and skills were globally recognised. If you were an appropriately trained neurosurgeon or apple picker, you could do that in any part of the world. Testing of skills became relatively simple, and confidence in worldwide referencing for skills and knowledge became a whole new field for data scientists and academics. Not unexpectedly, it was shown there was little difference in knowledge and skills across the world in any particular field and that deficiencies could be addressed efficiently and promptly to allow easy fluidity of movement for people.

Demand for the knowledge, entrepreneurial and technical skills of Americans was high and the new-found freedom they had to explore the mysteries and cultures of their southern cousins often resulted in them finding communities and towns that they felt comfortable making a home in.

Translational technology continued to advance rapidly and while people were more adept at learning languages and exploring the nuances of their own cultural language heritage, the ability to easily communicate with someone who could not speak your language was simpler than having an interpreter present. Now there was access to developing natural-sounding audio translation in the speaker's own voice and this was rapidly evolving and improving. Of course, the charm and slight frustration of attempting to speak in someone's native tongue was still favoured and appreciated by many. Never had the learning of other languages been more popular and this was driven entirely by the mass migrations that were happening. There was hope that these cross-cultural skills would bear fruit in the migrants that returned to their home communities.

It took about two weeks to bulldoze the entire 800 miles of barbed wire and concrete wall that Baldwin had built. The zeal that people took to rip the ugly symbol of separation and racism down was marked. Even Baldwin, as he offered all of his corporate network and commercial property to facilitate the transition to logical governance and democracy admitted in his resignation speech that the wall had been a very silly idea in retrospect. It was Baldwin who flew down to Texas the day after I Day and put the first sledgehammer blow to the ugly icon. Soon, just as the Berlin Wall had fallen, pieces of the horrid border structure were placed upon thousands of mantlepieces north and south of the border to remind people of the stupidity of separation. Baldwin was to disappear quickly and quietly with the embarrassing realisation of all the hateful things he had provoked. His self-awareness and intelligence allowed him to analyse, in light of all the progress that happened after I Day of how very wrong he had been to try to make his own country great in his perspective at the expense of the rest of the world and how ultimately that had been so counterproductive. Baldwin was, however, secretly proud that a Californian research lab and University had launched the technology for I Day under his watch. He did realise he could not take credit for the enormous positive changes that had gripped the world since the day he had left public office and made way for the governance of the people by logic and compassion.

On the day after I Day, the entire Mexican government and opposition resigned as did 75 percent of the civil administration. Anyone who had been involved in corruption at any level of government realised that they had to leave for now and let the country be led by those not tainted by greed. Within a week however, those with excellent skills to offer their communities were rehired with a completely different ethical and practical emphasis. No longer did anyone accept that bribery could lead to a significant difference in the outcome of an enterprise. Mass migrations quickly brought other cultures and other ways of doing business to the community. Inventiveness and entrepreneurship were the key factors in the progress of a community or business project. Within minutes of an idea forming it could be assessed and acted upon according to logical and democratic decision pathways that were totally transparent. The Anti-Corruption Body was disbanded immediately as it was clear that it was no longer needed; more than a tenth of the Mexican economy had been wasted in bribes and once it was eliminated there was an immediate and compounding boost to the economy. Ideas were the new economy and profit was not the prime mover, rather achievement, equity and implementation. Productivity soared as projects that had been stymied for years were now given appropriated funding and backing. People noticed something else about their country in those first few weeks. It was a return to the culture of meticulousness and execution. The idea of cutting corners and getting things done in a slapdash way was abandoned. There was a national upsurge in the inheritance of the indigenous culture; of what the Aztec and Mayan people had achieved, and what there was to learn from them. Entire cities and innumerable artefacts of great national importance were exposed in the first few months as people rediscovered the scientific and social constructs these ancient people held. Of course, some aspects of the culture were horrendous to modern sensibility and the new attitudes of equality that I Day brought but there was much of value to be gained in the exploration and the understanding of their ancient societies.

In some contradistinction to the Aztec and Mayan culture that was being discovered, there was one change that swept the country overnight that did take some getting used to. Murder and violence that had accompanied the bribing of officials in the days of the narcotics economy were now no longer seen. Like everywhere on the planet, the mass gun returns and their destruction was the norm. It wasn't so much an amnesty as an awakening to the sensible course forward. Having guns to defend anything was pointless because, with honesty and respect widespread, there was no need for defence. With peace on the streets, people walked without sideways glance, they happily greeted their friends and neighbours in the street, and the suspicion and fear was gone as teenage boys were no longer recruited to hold their families and friends as ransom to allow the cartels to function with impunity.

With the violence and drugs behind them, there was to be a revolution in education in the community that had been Mexico.

This passion for change spread throughout South America as the youth, who had been starved of time and proper methods for learning, embraced the rapid changes of the first few weeks. What became clear was that those nations with the very best systems of education had an opportunity to travel and explain how best to deliver the learning tools. Countries like Finland, Estonia and Sweden were called upon to export their knowledge and people to improve the delivery of education in other places. The first thing that was eliminated was school over the first three traditional years. Daycare which involved songs, play, games and conversation replaced formal schooling up to age seven. At school during every hour, there was a 15-minute period of physical play outside, an immersion in nature and breathing fresh air. Exams were immediately abolished and replaced with daily quizzes, assessments and direct observation. Even in the classroom, the best tool of learning was to let children be children and to allow play to drive the learning environment. The teachers all were immediately embarking on degrees beyond their primary one, and Master's and Doctorates became the norm for this all-important profession. A culture of nurturing the love of learning, the joy in knowledge, and the fun to be had throughout life as one learnt about the world, was instilled through the teachers. There was little in the way of homework, but kids read more than ever, and there was no doubt a new generation of brilliant engineers, doctors, painters, writers and actors were emerging from the new education system. The Estonian and Finnish teachers benefited from the rich cultural heritage that history afforded Mexico and Mexico inherited the best tools for learning that the world could offer. Happiness became known as the key to learning.

The greatest change in Mexico was income redistribution. Just as in the United States, the poor suddenly were getting a fair share of the national income. There was a lot of debate as to how this would play out. What would the poor do with that level of wealth and would it be put to good use? What would happen to the sudden influx of discriminate income where decisions apart from what cheap food to buy had to be made? The interesting discovery was that because they had spent so much time in abject poverty, the extra income that they now had was actually invested incredibly carefully and wisely. Micro-projects to help their communities were the priorities but also money was used in getting the best people from all over the world to educate them. For the first time, many of these poorer people were able to consider travel, to try other cuisines and cultures, and thus the fire was lit. Many brilliant minds that had hitherto been unable to find expression suddenly were found in abundance. Of the poorest indigenous people, their knowledge of culture suddenly found importance in the wider society, and many were invited to teach and share. Rich people in Mexico gradually gave up the excesses of their lifestyles and found ways to sustain their place in society. Many were talented professionals with children already well educated or had unique talents that helped them remain in high demand. The pleasure of giving was already well established in their hearts. The monetary remuneration for these talents was now not 1000 times that of their poorer folk but maximally set at five times, which, when income was fairly distributed still represented a good lifestyle and excellent reward for initiative and hard work. There was incentive, but there was no ability to be greedy as this had essentially been outlawed worldwide in the first few days after I Day. It was seen to be a fundamental tenet of compassion in the newly democratised world that excessive wealth and excessive poverty were beyond the intelligent dignity of man.

In San Cristobal de las Casas the mountain streams provided the local Tzotzil peoples traditionally with pure water for drinking for many centuries. Until the day that the Bubbly Cola factory set up in the town 50 years ago the soaking rains on the carefully manicured agricultural plots had given the people the organic sustenance that had kept them healthy and active on the high mountain tracks. On I Day, about three quarters of the adults and a third of the children were obese, and a half of these had diabetes. The town had many people dying in their forties and fifties of heart disease and the slower death of nerves and eyes and kidneys from rampant diabetes in the community. On I Day the Bubbly Cola factory that had been established in the town just those 50 years prior was razed to the ground by the entire community. There was no violence to the workers or anger, there was just a final recognition of the destruction that had been wrought by the presence of that enterprise within their midst.

An enterprise that had, in fact, taken their precious mountain streams and secured for them routes of getting processed foods that ultimately became even part of their sacred ceremonies. Bubbly Cola had entered the hearts and minds and bodies of the good people of San Cristobal and made them very, very sick indeed. Such was the addiction created that people actually believed the soda could heal people and prayers over cans of cola became blended with the Catholic and Mayan culture establishing legitimacy for the sugar that would ultimately cut them down in sickness and early death.

Within two months little Jose Martinez lost eight kilos and was off the medications to lower his cholesterol and sugar. His attention span in school was now normalised. He loved that his physical abilities and strength was returning . His previous diet of two cans of cola a day with his doughnuts and cakes was just a horrid aberration of the last few years and he was loving the traditional plant based and organic food his family now carefully prepared.

It took a little longer for the adults to normalise their blood sugars and obesity. The sugar addiction was strong and despite their best efforts and new knowledge about how dangerous their lifestyle had been the lure of the red can was still there for a while. They too were soon empowered by knowledge, and as they started to restore their water supply and their gardens, they also began to see the need for sugar to wane and their waistlines come in. Gradually, San Cristobal de la Casas and its people returned to the wiry, clever and hardy people that the mountain had known for centuries before.

Lucia took Juan's hand, and they took off early morning along the cobbled streets of the town where the gorgeous, colourful buildings every day made them feel at home and happy. They had their blackest of black coffees in their favourite cafe. Sunlight filtered across the intricate woodwork of the tables, chairs and stucco walls and the scent of delicious coffee filled every corner of the shop. The pair trailed off toward the farm smiling about the day and their love. They had known each other for many years now and romance had not entered their heads until the day they found themselves smashing the factory down together. Somehow, the fun, determination and joy in reclaiming their town had taken hold within their own hearts, and from that day they would be seen hand in hand, inseparable and very much in love. Since I Day, they had been involved in the restoration of the colonial buildings and the renovation of the slum areas. They were now so proud to walk to the edges of their town without seeing shanty houses. Everywhere people were out in the early morning going about their business, some exercising and some just taking in the town for the first time as the waves of Americans and Europeans came to enjoy the mountain air, the waterfalls, the gorges, the sinkholes and the ruins of old Mexican civilisations deeply camouflaged by dense and lush forest.

It filled Lucia and Juan with joy to witness so many now free of illness and lethargy. Energy had returned to San Cristobal. It was with enthusiasm they left the outskirts of the town and headed for the stables. The stable boys had already prepared the equipment for the day, and the pair simply supervised the boys placing the colourful saddlery upon their gorgeous horses. They took their time to love every one of the horses with whispers, treats and water. Soon the first of the riders arrived, and there was the greeting and safety talk and assessment of experience to be done. The horses neighed their approval of their upcoming trek.

They savoured meeting people that had come from all over the world to trek with them. There was something so embracing about the cool mountain air and the horses taking a group of strangers up into the mountain tracks. There was a sense of camaraderie, as you figured out how experienced a rider was, or if it was someone new to riding, you knew that they would fall in love with his or her horse by the end of the ride. Today, the morning was crisp, and the group before them were full of positive energy. Lucia and Juan were intrigued by the short, handsome dark man from Afghanistan who introduced himself as Gholam. He was a very curious and interesting man. He found himself talking to not only the horses but also a beautiful redheaded American girl whose name they later found out was Amanda. It would take them years to realise how much that morning in San Cristobal would mean to them all in years to come.

They mounted their very friendly horses and headed out on the dirt trail that took them up steeply along a ridge. Very quickly, they were into the morning mist as they were getting to know their horses and vice versa. Gholam and his mount Margarita somehow naturally went to the front of the pack despite Juan and Lucia supposedly leading the group and following in the rear. It was clear that Gholam was very comfortable on Margarita and Juan had no concerns. It made for an interesting ride, and all Juan worried about was tiring the horses which were now trotting and galloping after Gholam.

They settled their horses under a group of large trees, dismounted and gave them water as the Mexican sun lifted the mist from the mountainside. The group had a chance to sit down and compare notes from their ride. There was an Aussie surfer and his attractive Peruvian girlfriend who couldn't wait to tell everyone about the connections they had discovered between the Mexican indigenous practices and the newly found love they had developed about their own countries' aboriginal peoples and ways. There was the black physician from Chicago who was thoughtful and worldly. He spoke of the welcome that he had received in Mexico and how he was thinking of going to Africa from here to teach and learn.

Between Amanda and Gholam, there was little physical space. There was something immediately intense between them. Amanda normally wouldn't be charmed by a show-off horseman but in Gholam as she sat quietly listening to him talk about his homeland, she just knew there was something exceptional about him. If Juan and Lucia had not brought the local brew to them and interrupted their chat, the fire of their togetherness would have been a little uncomfortable for everyone else very soon. The mint tea and Juan refocusing on the ride and Gholam's evident proficiency on his horse settled the situation.

"Ah, Juan I love it. I have always ridden. Almost born with a saddle beneath me. I love all sports and getting out and about but riding a horse is just so magnificent. That perspective from just above and a little faster than we can normally see things. The communication between the rider and his horse. A little give and take like all things in life that are very good."

"Gholam, how did you come to be in Mexico right now?"

"Juan, I have always dreamt of travelling. I have read about the outside world now for these last 20 difficult years in my country. I have lost so many members of my family, and my country has been torn apart. As soon as the border opened, and I had citizenship of the planet, I knew that I needed to start seeing everything. It was the colour and rich history of this land that has drawn me here first but I intend to keep travelling until I am sated with interesting places and amazing people and then I will return to my land with my joy and my memories, and I will show people the true face of my beautiful country as well. I have much hope for this world and my poor battered homeland."

Off to the side was an unusual couple sitting in the now very warm Mexican morning sun. One dressed in a little too much bling for a sensible horse ride and the other in Camo gear from head to toe. The one dressed in khaki gear appeared to have a set of medals pinned to the outside of his jacket but had a completely blissed out and bewildered look to him. His friend, considerably younger, did nothing but attend to the older man's needs much as a loving family member would do.

Lucia tried to break the ice.

"General Horowitz, how are you enjoying the countryside?"

The General looked vacantly about and asked Lucia if he was in Nova Scotia.

"No General, this is Mexico, and it is soon time to see some more. Is he ok Mr Falinski?" Lucia asked.

"Oh darling, he is fine, trust me. He's never been better. He's not been so used to the sunshine. The tea will perk him up. Thank you for asking darling."

The group was rounded out by two very average looking guys in their 30s that looked like completely lovely nerds. They never stopped talking and asking everyone else how they were feeling, and they never stopped watching how everyone was interacting and behaving. It was as if everyone was a lab rat out in the Mexican countryside. There was no way you couldn't like them though. Every sentence they uttered was positive or probing or affirming or inquisitive. A couple of Cali mates with the sunburnt faces. A surfie-looking tall guy and his shorter darker friend. Vacationing forever they said. Their work was done.

"Pete, check this out!"

Mike signalled for Pete to come to the edge of the mountain ridge and they both peered off down the enormous canyon. The aqua ribbon of water far below them having cut through the mountains for millions of years was almost as impressive as the Grand Canyon. It wound about the sheer walls in a lazy S and disappeared in a funnel of rock and a horizon of endless trees.

"What you seeing Mike?"

"What are you seeing Pete? Remember last time we were here? What you said about that river."

"I said it was dirty and disgusting and couldn't believe that no one had cleaned it up. I was furious and said that something ought to be done."

"Well, look again crusader."

They both remembered the speed boat having to swiftly manoeuvre to avoid vast flotillas of plastic coke bottles and plastic bags and all kinds of waste. It had seriously spoiled Pete's enjoyment of the river.

"Hey man, you are right. It's pristine. Even the colour of the water is several shades bluer than algae green. That's really cool man. I guess somebody did do something about it."

Juan and Lucia came to join them. They never tired of that view, and there was always a languid conversation to have at this point in the ride as they overlooked such beauty and contemplated where the day would take them. Who they would meet and what they would learn? Every day brought new wonders and new people, and their horses and this country endlessly allowed them unforgettable moments that they anticipated sharing forever. The colourful cafes, the rich, strong coffee, the holding hands in their walk to the stables and this moment by the gorge. In the sunlight, they were blessed.

The guys returned to the third man in their group. He was engrossed, fixated on the General, staring at the man who was staring vacantly in turn upon the gentle hillside and the impressive vegetation they were sitting amongst. How could he have ended up on a horse ride in the middle of Mexico with the man who nearly single-handedly brought down I Day? Lorenz couldn't help himself, the scientist in him was still very strong. The last 18 months had been incredibly successful but also incredibly stressful, and in so many ways this trip down to Mexico had centred him more fully. They had listened to the entire Beatles collection a couple of times on the winding road down to the mountains, and it had been a peaceful adventure, but he had to learn more about Horowitz.

Lorenz recognised the man from the hundreds of television minutes and newspaper print that had been given to the sentinel moment of his otherwise entirely successful introduction of the technology. The one fly in the ointment, the loyal and somewhat crazy General in the bunker.

"Sir, can I ask you with all due respect, are you the famous General Horowitz of Area 51 fame?" asked Lorenz.

The general looked somewhat puzzled.

"That is classified information, young man."

Falinski butted in.

"I just love your Polo. The General has had a tough couple of months. He thinks he is to be taken to Nova Scotia for a court martial, but there is no case for him to answer. He has already been assessed as harmless, and I will be taking him to Waikiki for his retirement party next month. May I ask who you are? My name is Falinski, and I am his carer."

"I'm James Lorenz. Just a curious person."

Lorenz took hold of the General's hands and told him that everything was going to be alright now.

Chapter 16

South Africa 2 years after I Day

She sat on the beach looking out onto the Indian Ocean with her baby playing in the sand beside her. The umbrella shaded them, and Onkwaye was so happy every time he felt his mother's fingertips wriggling toward his as they played sand tunnels. The warm sand and the happy smile of her boy made her feel complete. The wet sand covered her hands and lingered under her nails, but she didn't care. Olivia knew that she would be back in the warm ocean in a moment and loved the thought of taking her little man into the shore breakers. Olivia imagined her boy surfing in the years to come and admired the young surfers and the odd old one taking on the big waves coming in that day. How she had longed for this child. How much it meant to be a mother finally and in a way she had never expected.

As they entered the sea, she showed no signs of fear and Onkwaye picked up on that. The waves quickly enveloped them both, and Olivia simply dived through them with the confidence that she never had as a young woman but now wholly embraced. As they came up, there was utter joy between the two of them as they caught their breath and felt the tang of the breeze. A quick dip and Lungelo emerged from the ocean with his classic Malibu board and a huge smile on his face as well. He kissed Olivia passionately as he passed, the water swirling around their hips and hugged his son.

"I'm going in. That was some ride. I'll see you at the cafe in a minute."

Olivia grabbed him by his biceps and pulled him into her and Onkwaye again. She hugged his broad back and made him kiss her again. The salt on their lips adding to the sensation. Onkwaye wanted some more waves and pushed his Dad away. The two, tight together slipped under another of the shore break waves that still carried a lot of the energy of the monsters from out the back.

Onkwaye simply loved the sea, immersed in and surprised to come up from the water even as it tossed the two of them about in the turbulence and gasped at the shoreline's air full with salt and seaspray. Olivia could tell how much he loved it by his insistence on staying out for one more wave. He held on to her neck firmly, but the two of them would never forget this joy.

For Olivia, he was the baby that she thought that she would never be able to have. Her first marriage was drab and listless, and they had not even thought of children. When I Day came, everything changed for her. She had always had a nagging feeling that she really needed to be a mamma and after I Day it crystallised. She had a frank discussion with her husband, and left, that very day. He just wasn't ready after all these years to adapt. Olivia quit her marriage, house and job all on the same day and volunteered to help the transitional government in any way that she could. While she longed ultimately to live back in Europe where her roots were deep, she felt she owed it to her adopted country to help with all she could. Already a sensitive soul before I Day, she only became more pragmatic in her idealism and actions after that day and had been ready to help change so much that she saw was wrong in her country.

Her skills were in people and knowing how to organise and motivate them; so much of that was easier after I Day. Everybody was seeking ways to actively improve things and the large projects around the world had everyone very excited. In the first weeks after I Day the world-wide democracy had become like a single brain for the planet's best interests. This worldwide system for decision making became active in redressing inequality and poverty; really the first priority of the new world. The massive redistribution of wealth was generous, logical and forthcoming. Military budgets were abandoned and directed to those economies that had desperate numbers living in poverty and without sanitation and health care. The task of organising that redistribution, how it was to be efficiently spent and how the monies were to be monitored for their efficient use fell to those who with the vision and energy to carry that out. These pioneers were seen by their peers as the custodians of this monumental task. Olivia had been and was still at the very heart of this moment in Southern Africa and brought with her the organisational skills and resource distribution skills she possessed.

Clinging on to her precious baby, all of these thoughts swept through her as they plunged once more under the powerful wall of water and then emerged triumphantly to head back to the shore. With the sun on her back and her sweet child in her arms, she had so much to be thankful for these past two years. All that responsibility and all that was achieved and how she had blossomed herself, a mother, madly in love with a man who she was about to have coffee with.

When Lungelo saw her, his eyes lit up as they always did when he saw her. Since she had their baby, his love for her had deepened even further, he appreciated her mind and the way she had been by his side in everything these past two years.

He, who had been such a klutz and an academic and who owed so much to Olivia for bringing him out and into the world. She introduced him to the beach, to poetry and to passion. He could barely remember the dry, arcane, and awkward man that he was prior to meeting her. Now he was a father and seen by many as a father to his city. One who had engineered the changes that mobilised the funding into reality for hundreds of thousands of his countrymen. He was a quiet man, but everywhere he went, he would be taken aside, and advice and praise would be metered out to him equally. People were surprised to see The Professor out on the beach, his Malibu board in his long arms but then they would think to themselves. 'No, this is him.'

Lungelo greeted his two loved ones and ordered a couple of espressos to see them through the early afternoon. He loved this cafe as it overlooked the promenade and ocean. He could watch the world go past and the ocean rolling relentlessly in to the shore.

"Olivia, what will we do for dinner tonight?"

"Awey, Lungelo. It's your turn to cook, you promised your famous Okra dish."

"Ooooh ya, no problemo. I put my apron on first thing we get home."

"Excellente Lungelo, I'll look forward."

"Lungy, you remember the night we met?"

The clouds scattered across the blue sky and a happy crowd of people sauntered by on the promenade. The afternoon closed about them, and as usual, they got to talking business.

Often their serious discussions would start with that memory. The euphoria that they had both felt as the world changed below their very feet on that same sultry Durban night.

"Yes Livy, I do remember it well."

"We were in the street dancing, freedom rang out, and we knew something incredible was about to be."

"And there you were dancing beside me my love."

"Ah, you were too beautiful for me. I couldn't resist. We talked and talked and talked all night. We didn't kiss for a week."

"We had a lot to talk about. You knew what we had to do, and I knew how to do it. Apart from falling in love, we had to move the earth. Lungelo, what will we have to work with this year now that the housing and schools, roads and hospitals are sorted?"

"In Africa alone, we spent the US military budget reallocation of $500 billion a year, and we are finally seeing the last of the informal settlements razed these last two months. So now we tackle adult education on a massive scale. This is our year for that."

They packed Onkwaye up into his pram and headed out along the promenade toward their home. It wasn't a long walk, but there was always so much colour and activity as they chatted.

"This year it will be steady. Although our urgent needs are less, the productivity of the world has gone up more than 40 percent so we can all benefit. Beyond the universities and colleges, nature will be getting more of a slice of the pie this year. The continent will be cleaned up, rivers, lakes, all the water sources will be looked at. This is the year we make our animals happy again."

They got home to their large apartment a block back from the sea and greeted their house guests. For two years Ayanda and Uluthando and their three kids had lived with them. In the week after I Day, the family were moved like so many other families from the informal settlements into people's established homes. Most of the sites had been razed and new homes built and about 80 percent of people were now in their own comfortable homes with all of the infrastructure needed to sustain them with dignity. Electricity, sanitation, schools, shops, manufacturing plants in dedicated areas had all been thoroughly thought through and delivered. Ayanda and Uluthando had been offered a place twice now but chose to stay with Livy and Lungelo a little longer for the sheer joy and friendship that their coming together had brought them. They knew that soon they would be departing again, but it wouldn't be far. So mixed now were the cultures that there was no distinguishing by race or ethnic background; people lived where they pleased. Ayanda dreamed of her own place by the sea, and soon they would be able to realise that dream as their studies were coming to an end. The prospects of a good job were excellent. One of the most surprising consequences of moving the disenfranchised, the drug dealers, the poverty-stricken and hopeless into the comfortable homes and generous empty bedrooms of the rich in Durban was the instant and intimate understanding that was brought into those homes. Olivia and Lungelo had been instrumental in engineering this massive physical shift and then it was up to the brilliance of the town planners to level the shanty towns and to begin the architectural revolution that was to then grip the rest of the country.

Lungelo was always worried that the integration would destroy cultures, but his fears were allayed as the months after I Day passed. The collective wisdom that was brought to the problems of integration dealt with his concerns. There was a melting pot of Indian, African,

Coloured, Boer and English culture where every element was encouraged to be shared not abandoned. People were not afraid any more to learn about the other cultures and to embrace the cooking styles, dances, fashions and speech. Fear was no longer a factor for anyone and learning was the main agenda. People spent time being present for the important ceremonies of others and trying to see how life was lived from other perspectives. Some elements were less popular. In general, western fashions gave way to a more rustic and authentic South African dress. Music was no longer a barrier, and a unique African style emerged that was loved right around the world.

Once fear was removed from the entire equation that was South Africa, the peace of mind, the quality of life, the spirituality and progress of the people was secured. Tourists flocked to the wonderful shorelines, the inland gift of Kruger Park and its fascinating inhabitants. Southern Africa was touched by all cultures and in turn, left an indelible mark on everyone who visited.

There was a time when walking the streets of Durban, Cape Town, or Joburg after dark was unthinkable as a visitor to the country. Streets that were full of colour and relatively safe and interesting during the day became no go zones when the sun went down. Locals also knew exactly which streets with the right lighting and right people were safe to traverse of an evening. Now, there was a sense of festival, adventure, and mixed experience that everyone craved and sought out of an evening. The weather called people out, and tourists felt very safe on the streets full of colour and fun, music and interesting cooking smells. Artisans were everywhere with authentic crafts from their own hands.

Security firms were amongst the first to be put out of business, and some of the men involved were amongst the more challenging to retrain but retrain they did into innumerable productive and creative roles.

The catchword that Olivia and Lungelo had instilled into the early days of the local democracy that was to include the whole of Southern Africa deciding which way forward on every social and structural decision was Equality. That word became the basis for everything. There was no longer the need for affirmative action in any sphere because all decisions were based around the notion of giving everyone in society an equal opportunity. There was equal education, and that accompanied recognising differing talents and gifts. There was the chance to go on endlessly with education or exploration of such a gift. All had the opportunity to go to the best universities and the numbers at university. Accelerated programs for those brilliant students who had had to leave school and college because of social circumstances were readily available and widely used. The poorest lapped up the opportunities for education and entered the market economy with glee both as consumers and with their own innovations.

Apart from the peace of mind from just being able to walk the streets without fear of being assaulted or robbed the other thing that Olivia revelled in was the absence of corruption. One of the first things that was done in the territory that had formerly been South Africa was the return to the people of all stolen money and goods that had been won through corruption. Through tears and humility, sometimes loudly and sometimes quietly, the spoils of corruption were returned. This initially did not include vast land reforms, but over the first 18 months of the new government, as people became trained in the most modern of agricultural techniques, the old white farmers became integrated as supervisors and managers and were well rewarded for their work. With the threat of violence gone and a willing and educated workforce, the farmland of this fertile country became ever more sustainable and productive.

Ayanda hugged Olivia every time she returned to the house. She loved her with every fibre of her being. Never had she met a woman with such a ferocity for change and such unconditional love for strangers. She loved her generosity and her smile. She loved her physical presence, and Olivia felt the same way about her friend. Ayanda brought joy and songs that Olivia had only a vague familiarity with. She taught her authentic African cooking the likes of which even Ayanda couldn't believe tasted so wonderful once she had access to fresh vegetables and meat. She would hug Olivia and recall the night that they had taken them in. She regularly reminded Olivia of how lucky she had been to be allocated to the house of such a generous and kind person. Ayanda would well up with tears as she described where they had come from and how they had buried two children in the hell that had been their home.

"Ahh Olivia, you and Lungelo are angels you know this? And now you have a baby angel. We lived not so far from here but another world away. My brother and my father, both dead too young. Drugs and diabetes. My dear brother cut down in what you could call our street at age 14, not even a courier for the gangs. Just caught in the crossfire between gangs. I have never really gotten over seeing him like that in the mud, and we had to drag him back into our tin shed to clean him up and prepare him for burial. How everyone had to put in to have Esilusizi transported and buried in our sacred grounds in the East.

"My father impoverished and depressed, unemployed for 20 years and not motivated to move from the burning furnace that was our hut during the summer lived on soda drinks and processed food; dying with no toes or vision before he was 40, smoking on his deathbed. And now my children are full of hope as we are. You have welcomed us as sister and family. We will always, always be grateful."

The extended families loved to get away in the two big electric cars they had between them and spend a few days in Kruger. With the hyperloop in place, it only took half an hour to get up to the Park and now that the national borders were gone the park was three times bigger than it had ever been; It now extended well into what had been Mozambique and Swaziland. Farmland that was marginal and broke up the natural corridors between habitats were bought and returned to nature. Wildlife experts delighted in the chance to design an African range that resembled the very original Savannah and rain forest and hill country that was suited to the animals native to this broad area. There was much debate as to how humans could best be integrated into the new park. The first thing that was done was to remove all the unsightly 'man-made' installations within the park. From a perspective of 100 metres, the presence of a human structure was made indiscernible from the natural surroundings. Brilliant architecture and camouflage did, however, allow for every type of accommodation from six stars to camping without an impact on the animals or the environment. Livvy and Ayanda almost always persuaded their families to stay in one of the newer lodges. It was a little more expensive, but the interaction with the animals was extraordinary and especially at night where guests could walk out deep into the forests via tunnels and emerge in low round glassed-in burrow outlets to see what they could see. The big cats slept a lot, but they could be seen walking across the treeline as dusk settled and the burnt oranges were giving way to the vast canopy of stars above. To watch a leopard turn and gracefully set itself down, the spots on its muscular chest so gorgeous, eyes so alert and actions so feline was a sight to behold in the evening.

All the children, including Onkwaye, loved to sit with their parents all bundled and cuddled up in the cool night air to see which animals would wander by and which ones they could hear. The look on Onkwaye's face when a jackal howled, or an owl hooted was priceless. Livvy always remembered the herd of elephants that simply walked straight over them. It was a group of around 40, and they ripped into the trees as they wandered across the undulating hills and had a feed and the odd argument between themselves. One stood literally on top of the 'burrow', and the thick steel of the shelter groaned a little but was nothing compared to the trumpeting from the tribe above. Civets and genets, zebras and the odd lost warthog or bokkie occasionally wandered through, and the air was filled with the sounds of their wonderful continent at night. They came back time and again to experience such magnificence and were never disappointed.

The return to nature they found to be very grounding and humbling. It brought back a sense of the wildness of the universe to their daily lives in Durban. They developed a sense of respect for the natural world and for the care of each other's natures. A week out there in the Park brought them moments that they all would carry for the rest of their lives. A sense of the vast patterns of nature and how they needed to fit into that across their own world interacting with the creatures they came across. A sense of the depth and wonder of Africa that cannot help but touch everyone who has had the privilege of experiencing her.

Chapter 17

China 5 days before I Day

Alim faintly heard the knock on the door. He asked Aynur to answer it and didn't hear a response.

"Aynur, did you hear me? Answer the door!"

He wondered who it could be so early in the morning. It was an ordinary workday, and he was just about to get into the shower.

Aynur came up quietly to the bathroom and whispered to Alim that she thought the men waiting outside were trouble. She had not the courage to open the door. The knocking and shouting became ever more insistent and louder. Alim quickly changed into his work gear without showering and came down to the door. Two enormous men in the uniform of a force that Alim did not recognise bustled themselves through the entranceway.

"Alim Tekin?"

"Yes, that is me."

Not only did they bustle into Alim's house, but they physically imposed themselves around the diminutive and gentle man. One of their children walked into the scene and started screaming when they saw the fear in their father's eyes which just launched a tirade from the two uniformed men to remove the child from the room. Aynur picked up 5-year-old Hala and took her into the small kitchen at the back and hugged her tight, telling her all was ok. She hoped Adina would stay asleep but heard the baby starting to cry and with Hala in her arms ascended the stairs. She hugged both her children and wondered what Alim was saying to the two angry men.

At that moment throughout the home, every Huawei AI Cube started with the piercing and insistent call to prayers. It had been many years since the prayers were called from the neighbourhood mosques. It couldn't have come at a worse time. Aynur quickly let go of her children and rushed through the bedrooms and study upstairs to turn the speakers off. Alim went to do the same but was pushed onto the dining room table as the officers dashed the speaker against the wall. A further call could be heard infuriating the men even more, and they slunk through to the kitchen and smashed the other speaker on the floor. All that could be heard now were the cries and sobbing of the children upstairs.

Alim almost knew what to expect from these men, but it was a surprise to have them come in and be so aggressive as he had always been a respectful citizen and had not attempted to push his own privately held political and religious views. So many of his friends and relatives by now had 'disappeared' with few returning to their communities and those who did had nothing to do with their old friends and communities. Even close family members who had survived detention had come back like ghosts, never to speak of their experiences. They returned to work with silence, a vacant look on their face, sullen and defeated. They knew that in the months after 'reeducation' they must not appear on the state's radar. Secretly, they dreamed of escaping the nightmare that their lives had become, and they mourned their old selves and the days where their culture was not reviled in this land.

Alim thought about all the families that had been affected as he stood before these bullies and he knew exactly what he was in for. His best friend Yusup was the only one who would speak to him after he returned from reeducation. In just one stolen moment, Alim learned of a bitterness so deep he almost couldn't recognise the eyes of his brother. They had grown up just as brothers, they'd had the happiest of childhoods, and now he caught the hatred in Yusup's eyes. After a bitter description of the loneliness that he had felt he started to cry uncontrollably but quickly brought himself back to his absent, lost stare with Alim left in no doubt his friend was lost to him for now.

The men identified themselves as State reform officers and told him that he and his wife had been selected for observation and China heroism reorientation.

"We have no one below us, and we only have the highest command above us. Our task is to examine your lives in detail and support you into the correct understanding of the purpose and direction of our State. We ask that you pretend that we are not in your home. You will go to work as usual, and we will observe your wife and children. They will be safe in our hands, and we can start on their reeducation today." Barked one of the officials.

Alim asked "Why is this happening to us? We are a quiet and non-offensive family. We love our country and support the supreme leader. We have his photo on the wall over there. I am a simple worker, I have caused no trouble, I seek no trouble."

"Do not quarrel man. This is a deep offence in itself. Define yourself by your silence and compliance. You will do as we say."

Aynur came downstairs leaving the children in their bedroom and pleaded with the men to leave them alone.

"Alim is a good man, a loving man. We have two little children. Please, let us go on with our lives as we have been. We are a quiet and peaceful family."

She started to cry but was quickly silenced as one of the men struck her across the face with a baton that he produced from his belt. Aynur crashed to the ground and did not move. Alim went straight toward her, but his path was blocked by the other large man. It was more than a minute before Aynur moved; she at first crawled before she stood and slowly made her way to Alim. They hugged whilst the two men started rifling through all of the drawers and cupboards downstairs.

Within minutes the house was a complete mess, and the children could once again be heard screaming uncontrollably as they were disturbed by all the noise of crashing items downstairs. Alim and Aynur stood together, hugging each other, frozen for now as they silently watched their home being trashed. They looked into each other's eyes, and each saw the strength of the other. Alim whispered to Aynur to make sure she was ok. She was lucky to have only been struck a glancing blow but the bruise on her forehead was obvious and they moved to the kitchen to get some ice before heading back upstairs to reassure the children.

As they were climbing the stairs, the realisation struck them that they had been chosen, how their luck had finally run out. Always, always they had hoped for change, for a chance to leave this country that they had loved so much all their lives. They had hoped that the oil and gas would run out and the persecution of their people, religious and economic that had robbed them of their own resources and land would somehow, sometime end. Now it was visited upon them, and while they had half expected it, the terror of sliding into this nightmare was only too real. How were they supposed to fight, resist, or even survive this? Their eyes searched each other again and the love and determination to get through together was their paramount thought. Somehow, someway they would see this through.

They were able to quickly soothe the children, but the kids knew that something was terribly wrong and Hala kept putting the bag of ice back onto the bruise that was forming on her mummy's brow and telling her that everything would be ok.

Downstairs the banging and destruction didn't stop. Alim and Aynur had absolutely nothing to hide. They were practising Muslims with Uyghur ancestry that they could trace for over 300 years. Their family was held in high esteem in their community, and they were peace-loving and had not a radical thought in their lives. Yet such was the paranoia and strategy of their Chinese masters that simply because of their ethnicity and religion, they had two strange men ruining every room of their simple but proud house. Alim, Aynur, Hala and baby Nur stayed upstairs for a long time and comforted each other with hugs. Alim told Aynur that she was to remain steadfast and strong, but to do as she was told no matter what happened to him; she nodded and hugged him again. The children started laughing and playing together which made them smile until finally, they heard the heavy snap of solid boots upon their wooden stairwell.

The slightly overweight one of the two men addressed them. "Alim, we have found nothing offensive in your house so far. You are free as planned to go to work. We have some paperwork for you to sign when you come down and one of our officers will very kindly take you to your workplace. Of course, while you are at work, we will be doing an extensive search of the rest of the house. Are you ready to go?"

Before Alim had a chance to kiss his wife goodbye, he was bundled roughly to the stairwell by the burly officer. They reached the table in the dining room, and the other officer picked up a chair that had been dashed on its side and sat Alim down to sign the papers.

Alim asked "What is this? What am I signing?"

"This is simply permission for us to examine and reeducate your family here at home. It is an agreement that you can be supervised by the state and that you consent."

"And if I do not sign?"

"Do you want another quarrel silly man?"

Alim signed the papers, collected his briefcase, suit, and his jacket, and was led from the house by one of the men to an unmarked car parked a little way up the street and on the other side. He noticed that as they left another officer entered the house immediately. They drove quickly to the University where Alim was due to give a lecture on physiology that morning to the first-year medical students. When they got to a small side street near the University, Alim's cell phone was confiscated, and he was presented with another set of papers to sign. He told them that he needed his phone to talk to his wife and they did not reply.

"What are these papers now?" Alim quietly asked.

"These are our government arrangements and agreements. You sign here and here. It is simply stating that you are happy to have your beard shaved and for you to undergo appropriate reeducation as deemed fit by your supervisor."

As Alim signed the papers, the men firmly grabbed his arms, roughly pulled them back and handcuffed him behind his back. They then produced an enormous blade and Alim thought that his life was about to end. He felt the blade come at his neck and braced himself and the other man sprayed foam onto his hands and rubbed it into Alim's neat and small beard. Before he knew it, his beard was gone, and his hands were free. They issued him with a jacket that identified him as a Muslim for reeducation and accompanied him to the door of his classroom. Both the men then entered the back of the hall and watched him intently as he gave his talk.

His students were a mix of Han and Uyghur, and while he tried to hold back the tears, his humiliation was near to complete as some openly wept at his situation and some had no emotion at all. The reactions did not seem to be limited to ethnic origin with some of the Chinese-background students distraught at their teacher's situation.

Alim was one of the most loved, brilliant, and fun teachers in the medical course which was highly prized across many regions and states. Those who graduated from the course did so with a degree that conferred the best of practicality and academia. So, to see one of their finest subjected to this degradation was too much for some of the sensitive souls. Others were well aware of the presence of the police in the theatre and held back any outward sign of emotion for their own and Alim's sake. Sadly, they had seen this scenario over and over again, and it had always ended the same. With the disappearance of another teacher with little pattern to understand who went and who stayed. It made the mourning and understanding of what it all meant utterly impossible.

Alim had sad, expressive enormous eyes. Eyes that could reach across a whole lecture theatre and engage and entrance. What everyone could not fail to see was the absolute sadness and anxiety in them today. He delivered his words, his explanations brilliantly as always, but the presence of the police at the back was spine-tingling and terrifying for everyone in the hall. His jacket was recognisable as belonging to someone condemned, his beard was gone and these men were here. All of this designed to advertise what was happening to Alim and his family. The notion that he had been caught, that he had been found out and that he needed to be weeded out but not before it was publicly announced in his workplace. As the final words of his lecture were delivered, he felt nothing but the impending catastrophe that was his fate. He just hoped that he could survive somehow and get back to his treasured little family one day. The reality was very few of his friends and work colleagues that had been sent for reeducation had actually been able to come back. His hope was forlorn, but his determination keen for survival. Some of the other teachers, good friends and colleagues stood outside his lecture room as he was bundled outside. No one dared to say a thing as the price of questioning the government's actions became steeper every month that passed. There were eyes everywhere willing to give good people up in order to ensure some safety for themselves. Trust had eroded substantially in society, and yet the very measure of acting as a witness as Alim was hustled away, was appreciated by the young Associate Professor. His eyes, so expressive, not filled with fear but with fellowship and friendship for those he was being taken away from so roughly. A few of the Freshmen on the library lawn jeered him as he was paraded out of the school as the security police remained expressionless throughout.

At home, when Alim failed to come back in the afternoon Aynur started to fear the worst. Her day had been a nightmare with every cupboard, every drawer pulled out, and the contents strewn across the floor below. They didn't find or take anything but confiscated every book of Arabic script and every memento of their life together. Not a family photo, not a picture drawn by the children, no toys were allowed. All of this was gathered up by the mid-afternoon and thrown into garbage bags and taken to the van outside. They also took nearly all the phones, televisions, computers and of course their car. Aynur was left with two screaming children who were severely traumatised. Her house a terrible, chaotic and sad place. She was missing the person who gave meaning to her life, her heart completely broken. For a while all she could do was rock her children into some kind of reassurance. She hugged them with all the love and peace that she could find within her being as she knew that she would have to be strong to get them all through this.

She wondered where Alim was, and she had flashes of black thoughts that she had lost him. That he had been killed or taken to a place where he could never return from. Soon she put those thoughts away and wondered how she could go about helping him or finding out where he was, although she had no means of communicating with anyone, and she was terrified that anything she might do could compromise him. She felt that the safest thing was to get away from here and get to her family in the South. She couldn't see how they could get through the weeks and hard months ahead without the help of her large and loving family. She packed the kids up and dressed them in the warmest clothes they had and gathered everything she thought she could carry for the journey and left her once happy home behind her. The air was bracing, and the baby started crying again as they stepped down the street. Aynur thought that she was being watched by a car she didn't recognise at the end of the street, but they walked on in the cold toward the central train station.

The little family waited on the miserable, dark platform watching the rats race about on the train tracks; Aynur was wary of every person that appeared on the station with a large overcoat. She just wanted to get onto that uncomfortable train carriage that would take her 16 hours away from the nightmare of this day. She felt that at any moment, she would have her papers searched, and they would be dragged back into the town and to a situation where she may never see her little babies again. So many families had been destroyed in the past three years. Aynur huddled close to her children, kept them under the wings of her loving arms, holding back tears as she worried what was happening to her husband. She smiled through gritted teeth at the station attendants, and her children were calm and reassured by her. She felt that once she was on her way that somehow everything would be ok. She knew from experience that there was no point in appealing or making a fuss when a family member was disappeared. All she could do now was to try and make the rest of her family as safe as possible.

Just before midnight, the train slowly rolled in. The three of them were shivering from the cold and she was worried about her kid's fingers and toes. They clambered on to the second-class carriage and sat in the back of the car, not a lot warmer but finally with hope that they were safe. A few times the train lurched forward a foot or two, made some tremendous noises and then halted at the station. From nowhere Aynur spotted what looked to be an official party entering each carriage one by one. Three or four burly men with peaked caps and grey coats were hustling quickly through the train. Aynur almost panicked but it was too late anyway. She sat there as they came up the carriage toward her, hugging her children and with her papers ready to be inspected. She was calmer than at any time she had been today. The men briefly looked at her photo and rushed off to the next carriage. Ten minutes later, the train jerked into motion and took them far, far away from that troubled day.

Alim was beaten severely once he was in the secure reeducation facility. He was thrown into a room that was painted entirely white with bright neon lights in the ceiling that flickered annoyingly on and off every few seconds while other spotlights remained focussed continuously on the prisoner chained behind a simple white laminated desk. There was a bed crammed into the corner of the room, but he was not able to get to it. His feet and wrists were shackled by chains to the floor, and the sheer exhaustion of staying upright was starting to get to him. Every time he slumped forward on to the desk as sleep and fatigue got the better of him a reeducation officer would storm into the room and smash him in the thighs, the back or the face with a baton and shocked him with an electric cattle prodder. He was able to resist the urge to lay his head down for hours at a time, but eventually, he would be woken by the brutal reminders. It was impossibly awful to stare at the white walls of this place as his mind tried to find ways of staying awake. He prayed, the words shuttered away in his mind, he tried to imagine his family safe, but he was tremendously anxious for them. Despite his best efforts, his face fell toward the white desk more than 10 times and each time he was rewarded with a brutal beating. He could not make out the faces of his tormentors. They said nothing to him apart from warning him to stay awake. He started shouting at the walls and was beaten for that also. He began hallucinating, he couldn't focus or understand what was happening to him. After two days they unshackled him and gave him some stale bread and some broth that tasted like salt water. He collapsed onto the tiny bed and was granted four hours of sleep. For the next three days, he was re-educated by being alternately shackled at his desk and subject to beatings for in any way failing to focus and being allowed to come to his bed. His spirit was broken quickly in terms of any tendency to disobedience, but deep within him he retained his purpose and dignity.

On the fourth day, Alim was let out of the white room to the freezing courtyard. Surrounding him was an enormous concrete wall and he stood with about 19 other men in the large rectangular space. All of them had the same look of utter sadness and dejection, most had visible facial bruises, and many walked with a limp. In every corner of the rectangular space was a guard tower. Four guards with machine guns stared from under their black-rimmed caps over them from each corner. A similarly dressed man came before them and started bellowing instructions to them. Despite their injuries, they were drilled toward military precision. Being taught the specifics of standing at attention, to turn, and to salute in unison. As one, like a dance. Whatever the commander barked out, there was an expectation of immediate obedience and manoeuvre. Despite the exhaustion and punishment for getting things wrong, they were surprised at how quickly they could marshall themselves and shocked to find themselves pleased as a group when they got it right. Alim found it very hard to salute the commandant, but he never gave away his feelings about this as he became one with his tribe of prisoners. They hardly looked at each other, but despite the commandant feeling that he had the complete acquiescence of his charges, there was no doubt that between them the bonds of humanity, the compassion of fellow sufferers, the solidarity of their ethnicity and history were the principal feelings they had.

For days now, they had been isolated, and it felt so good to have the acknowledgement by someone other than one in an official uniform that they were alive and in their own ways defiant. There was no talking allowed as they did their drills, to show respect to the Party and the commandant. Soon they were returned to their white-walled cells, chained again by the ankles to the floor and made to stay awake as utter exhaustion crept upon them. Little did they know that their group of 20 or so men was replicated for hundreds of complexes around them. Thousands just in this facility were at various stages of reeducation and resignation.

The system was designed to break every last measure of their identity as Muslims and Uyghur people. They would return as either non-practising, non-provocative, lower-class working units with no claimed social identity and no social status credits or they would not return to society at all.

On the 5th Day, Alim noticed a considerable amount of commotion in the hollow metal hallway on the other side of his prison door. The scratchy ethnic Han music that was pumped non-stop through the audio system stopped and was replaced by a song he had last heard as a young man at University sitting under a Cherry Blossom tree with his friends in the quadrangle. Despite his exhaustion, it made him smile broadly as *A Hard Day's Night* rang out just as scratchily through the cheap speakers tucked into the corners of the roof space as had the patriotic songs. Soon after this, a guard who had discarded his greatcoat and tie, his cap no longer present and his weapons nowhere to be seen, opened the door to his cell and released all his chains. They embraced heartily without explanation, and the guard finally pulled away telling him that he must release all the other prisoners in this block. Alim wandered out into the cold hallway and saw some of his fellow inmates as lost and bewildered as he was. Some were crying but for joy as they all embraced each other and chatted loudly. Some of the guards had joined them and brought them some quality broth and fruits. They also shared the wines that they had, and no one really knew what was going on.

There were extraordinary scenes outside of the vast gated and razor wire protected precinct as ex guards and families of the prisoners hugged and the now casually dressed inmates came out through the main gates in the thousands. Rather than rushing straight home, people sat in circles, groups of ex-officials and prisoners, reporters and the curious, families and friends. Nobody quite knew what was happening apart from the feeling that something disastrous had now come to a peaceful and loving ending. It was time to reflect and in the middle of most groups was someone brewing up the most delicious and precious tea that they could lay their hands upon. Cups steaming in the cool afternoon air carried wonderful scents that brought everyone a sense of unity and warmth as people found their loved ones and began discussing their way forward in this new and ancient land. It was the quietest revolution that had ever swept through this place, with respect and whisperings of relief and hope carried between sips of the steaming brews.

Little did they know that this was happening across the entire globe, not just in Xinjiang. People were gathering, quietly, peacefully and intelligently talking their way forward to an entirely new day. Alim did not see his family as he came through those massive metal gates, but he expected this, and he knew that his wife would have kept his children safe and that soon they would be together. For now, he celebrated with his new friends, getting to know the story of quite a few. He had only briefly connected with them through their eyes on the drill ground but he felt drawn to some of those he had encountered, and they would go on to become lifelong friends. He too was not afraid to talk with the guards that had so brutalised him, and he spent the evening becoming human to them and they to him. No longer were they officials but simply men like him and somehow their brains only recognised these facts from this day.

Alim's body was still weak and battered from his days at the facility, but his mind was now full of hope and ideas, and he couldn't wait to start again with his family. There were no official orders and no announcements apart from the fact that within 48 hours the Chinese government had agreed to worldwide democracy and would participate in the mass democratic systems that had begun to be set up. Some kind people were about giving the ex-prisoners some money to get started again and Alim was extremely grateful. People seemed to just know what to do, and Alim's focus was first on his family and then what he could do for them and his world. He was able to get a lift back to his home in the evening and was pleased to see that it was unchanged and safe following him being taken away. He was soon able to replace all the drawers and their contents and he threw out a few broken pieces of furniture. He was home but unable to contact his family for now. He had a feeling why and he knew what he must do in the morning, but for now, it was a long, long warm shower and the comfort of his bed. Tomorrow he would journey.

As the sun rose, Alim awoke and got dressed. He was very excited and happy and tried to reconcile everything that had happened to him in the last few days including his bizarre exit from the reeducation council. He turned on the bedroom TV which the officials had missed. He noticed that now he had a choice of over 300 channels including all the major Western channels as well as a few new Chinese channels. They reported on events in a style that Alim couldn't remember seeing apart from the short trip he had taken to Europe as a young man. There was clearly no censorship in place now at all. Every subject was broached in detail and without bias, and if he didn't have important places to travel today, he would have stayed glued to the fascinating events gripping the world.

Alim walked briskly towards the train station with a spring in his step. It was just a few kilometres away, and as the sun pulled up in the eastern sky, the indigo turned to pink and the clouds played with his imagination quite like they had never before. People were out in numbers, looking purposeful and cheerful, they smiled and acknowledged him as he did when he passed them by. He bought a ticket South and bought the cheapest mobile phone he could buy. He waited on the platform and watched the workers start their day cleaning up the rubbish and food scraps that had been thrown on to the track area for years past.

As he sat there, somehow full of hope and optimism even after all the humiliation, degradation, pain and anxiety that he had felt for the last few days. He looked about him and breathed the early morning air in and watched. He could not help but feel a buzz within. Not just for himself but for the people he saw around him. There was something about their very movement and facial expression. A purpose in their stride, a genuineness of their smiles. There were fewer greys and blacks and more colour in the clothing, a sense somehow of rebirth and renewal.

As if yesterday was the first day of a new Dynasty and of course it was. It was the day that saw China finally join the world as a brother, not as some other, some strange place that must conquer or be conquered. The People's Army came home, 2 million skilled men and women. Returned to their communities with their talents and determination focussed on making their homes and lives peaceful and innovative. No longer was there a dictatorship or an Emperor. The Chinese Government and Premier resigned that very day and quickly the democratic process took root in a million different ways.

Originality and innovation became the region's number one focus and China was to provide the Artificial Intelligence that could sensibly put together the brilliant ideas that were coming forward to take the world to a fairer, safer and more pleasant place to live in. Chinese scientists in the first few months from I Day were at the forefront of handheld technology that would feed from individuals into focus groups and then into action. The beauty of the system was in how transparent it was taking ideas forward through the local, regional and continental solutions. Ideas that were rejected were not lost in some random accidental way, and the documentation around debate and outcomes could be easily tracked.

Alim put the spare Sim card that he had hidden at home into his small little phone and stared at the screen as it came to life. There was only one message on the phone, and he started to well up as he pushed the buttons to open the message.

The train pulled into the station, and he boarded. He felt the great machine leap forward, lurching, screeching, onward, he heard the wheels gain their rhythm and watched his town disappear in a blur of abandoned shacks and tall skyscrapers and a backdrop of raw, enormous mountains with snow-filled crevasses and peaks.

Of course, the message was from Aynur, and it simply said:

"I will be waiting for you by the Apricot blossom tree."

A huge smile drew across his entire face. He knew exactly what she meant the moment he read it, and his heart leapt out of his chest. He was in exactly the right place, and he knew that his family were safe. On the edge of the city, he alighted the train, made his way to the highway and started thumbing a ride to the West. It wasn't long before a truck pulled over and offered to take him.

The driver was an enormous man who wouldn't stop talking about golf, but nothing could faze Alim now. He enjoyed the man's banter and was lucky enough to have some golf stories of his own that he could share. The large man would laugh from his belly, and his whole body would shake when he did. Somehow the hours went by, and the mountain valleys grew steeper and more picturesque. After the large man had finished talking about golf, he suddenly became quite serious and explained how he too was looking forward to seeing his family again having been on the road almost constantly these last three months. He told Alim he was always happy to take on someone for a ride to break the monotony of the road, but he had realised just yesterday exactly how much he was missing his children and wife and golf. Alim could see a tear on the large man's cheek that he quickly brushed aside, and they sat quietly for the next half an hour feeling each other's emotion in an easy silence. At the end of this period, the fat man asked Alim where his final destination was. Where was he to see his wife again?

"My friend, it is at the end of the road, far to the north of Kuytun."

"I will take you there my friend."

It was Alim's turn to weep. They spent the next six hours talking of everything. Their childhoods, their parents and the things they dreamt of as kids. The stuff they still dreamed about.

When it came time for Alim to leave his new friend and reach for his final destination, the large man got out of the cab and came around to Alim and gave him an enormous hug. The big chap was sweaty, and his body moulded itself around Alim's slim, sore frame, but somehow it felt entirely right. They exchanged numbers and wished each other the very best.

It was a short walk and he knew exactly where he was going. The fat man had dropped him on a quiet road in the foothills that were barely visible in the fading light. His feet knew the way and the trees and small huts of the valley guided him home. On the porch of a small wooden cabin beside a wild Apricot tree, there stood a beautiful woman with their two children. To the place that they had come to when their love was young, they had returned, the house where they had started their married life together, in this valley of wonders. He was home.

Chapter 18

Russia 2 hours before I Day

Valdis Outski sat staring out of the large glass window to the manicured lawns and gardens below and the small white-topped waves across the windblown Black Sea in the distance. He loved to stay at his seaside palace. His knees were far from each other, and their knobbly nature was evident as the white socks and black Nikes accentuated his small calves and considerable thighs. He was undoubtedly a handsome man thought Mitya Lomonosov as he walked into the large room. Valdis, of course, was not wearing a shirt, he was sitting doing one-arm curls with a five kg weight and apart from loudly calling out his name as he entered, he did not acknowledge the other man by even looking at him until he was within touching distance. He suddenly put down the weight and embraced his friend. His hairless chest glistening with sweat and his body odour imminent and pronounced. Mitya looked into his eyes and finally caught the recognition he ever sought in those fleeting glimpses. They embraced for quite some time as Mitya took in the manliness of Valdis's grip and Outski finally had someone he could trust within his grasp again.

Mitya was pristine as always, his hair perfect, his suit resplendent in deep blue which somehow set off the soft brown darkness of his eyes and the subtle tan that he always seemed able to sport.

"Mitya, my friend!" The sweaty man boomed into the ear of the Prime Minister.

"Vald, so good to see you." The highly coiffed, sophisticated man in the suit whispered back.

Mitya had to look up and rocked onto his toes to whisper his greetings to his hero. Outski was a short man, but Lomonosov was even shorter, and the President felt good embracing his friend and searching for any hair loss at the same time. None was to be found so he roughed the perfectly placed locks into a wildness he could smile at.

Once their embrace had finished, Valdis rocked from one foot to another repeatedly, animated clearly by the presence of his protege.

"Vodka?" asked the President.

"Da, of course."

"We will go shooting deer in the forest but first a little Ice Hockey my friend."

The vodka was gone in three seconds followed by a further two shots, and the men made their way to the basement Ice Hockey arena down the golden spiral staircase as Mitya took in the opulent taste of his friend. There were a couple of new Impressionist paintings on the stairwell.

Mitya mumbled.

"Monet."

"Da"

Mitya stripped in the icy conditions and Valdis watched him the entire time as he put on every pad and protector, the thickest gloves he could find and a sturdy face shield. Valdis, of course, kept himself shirtless and with little protection apart from some knee guards and they went out on to the ice with just the one Federal Security Service of the Russian Federation agent in attendance.

"Be gentle Vald, Pozhaluysta!"

Mitya had come away from this traditional fun activity with his friend usually with very firm and bruising memories and injuries. In the past, he had suffered a haematoma to his buttocks and thigh that both needed surgical drainage. He had also had an elbow fracture from a stick injury that he had no way of explaining to anyone outside. It was their little secret.

Within five minutes, Outski was winning four goals to nil and was starting to look bored. As Lomonosov let him go past for the 5th Outski circled back, stick erect and headed for his friend's torso. Mitya caught this move with eyes in the back of his head and swerved just at the moment his friend thrust the stick forward, and this sent the President sprawling headfirst into the sidewall. Outski quickly got up, swept the ice from his bare chest and proceeded with the game as if nothing had happened. It was the first time that the Prime Minister had escaped without injury.

"Shooting?"

"Da."

The forest was surprisingly thick as they made their way to the coastal pathway and looked out across the enormous expanse of water before them. In the far distance were a few Navy and cargo ships and the beach at the base of the cliff was a brilliant yellow-orange with the sand imported from Brazil in the last six months. Wildlife ducked briefly off and on the trail and Lomonosov expertly bagged a slow-moving rock wallaby with an early shot. Not to be outdone Outski bashed through the thick brush and found himself a nook from which to spot his prey. Lomonosov knew to quickly rally behind the boss as he had seen others nearly caught in the crossfire as Valdis's enthusiasm for the hunt had got the better of him. The semi-automatic with the large scope rarely failed to bag a deer or two within a few minutes as the headland was a mere 400 hectares and the animals introduced regularly. The gun fired repeatedly and a fawn and her mother were laid low. Outski produced his hip flask and asked his friend if he would like a swig.

"Da"

"Chess?"

"Da"

Lomonosov had never beaten Outski at chess and he never would. He could see through every clumsy move and strategy of his master but always had a worse one to respond to it. Valdis loved playing his number two man. It was where all the great decisions of state were made.

"Lomonosov..."

"Da, Valdis ?"

"Have you dealt with Malkin yet? He is gathering too much power to himself, he is not quiet in the right ways anymore, and his little bank needs to be shared with a few of our Ukrainian friends."

"Done, Valdis."

"Speaking of Ukraine. Why is it not annexed yet Mitya? What on earth is the hold-up? There are good Russian men and women inside that are suffering the freedoms of European dreams. They must be liberated and liberated soon from this silliness."

"Da, Valdis. Our agents are infiltrating government and the army as we speak. The coup backed by our Navy is mere weeks away. Do not worry, you will be holidaying in Odesa and dining in Kyiv before the year is out."

"This is good Mitya. I hope you are right. Otherwise, I might need to find a new hunting partner."

Mitya looked at his friend across the chessboard while Outski fiddled with his pawn, his gaze back out through the high glass windows and across the darkening sea.

"I'm just joking Mitya, checkmate."

"Valdis, you are just too good for me. Rematch?"

"Da."

"Valdis, you will be pleased with what we have done with the cocaine trade in South America."

"Oh, you finally sorted it?"

"Da. We have some of our finest bankers join with our best Bratva to sort out the runways and airdrops in New Mexico. Our Colombian growers are now very much more cooperative after our little intervention last year."

"I want to meet our friend from Cali in the next few weeks. My boys have been telling me he has been syphoning off a few billion to pay for his football team. No Mitya. He needs a little Russky welcome and education. Can you arrange that?"

"Da, Valdis. He will arrive with the Cuban cigars next week."

"Mitya..."

"Da, Valdis?"

"Why do you always lose your Queen to me, in the same way, every match?"

"President, I have no alternative."

"Checkmate."

The great grandfather clock struck 9.00 PM. It was said to have been owned by Czar Nicholas and was taken from the very room where the Czar's family were shot. Outski prized it above all his other trinkets as its chime reminded him of the gruesome passage of time and the enormous responsibility that power in his country demanded. Once the chimes had struck, something magical started to happen.

One by one, the men in black suits came into the lounge room and laid their Kalashnikovs on the dining room table. As each one arrived Outski and Lomonosov hugged them with tears streaming down their faces and said their goodbyes. They could see that the gates to the property were thrown open and that a cavalcade of animals of all sorts were quietly making their way up the front paths to the exits. Some simply came out and played on the lawns of the palace, finding the manicured grass and flowers to their liking. Lomonosov turned to Outski and punched him square across the chin sending the little fellow tumbling on to his backside. Mitya hauled him up, and they laughed and laughed and laughed and hugged, only this time Outski meant it and wasn't trying to find a bald spot in his friend's hair.

"I've been such a bastard to you, Mitya, all these years. I very much had that coming. Thank you."

Little did they know it, but millions were dancing in the streets of Moscow, St Petersburg, Vladivostok and thousands of other Russian cities and towns. It was as if a great weight had been lifted after centuries of oppression and corruption. All the people wanted to do was to dance.

Valdis started to receive calls from his Ministers of state and army staff tending resignations, and he accepted them all with grace explaining that he would be stepping down and dissolving the Russian government in a televised statement that would be organised this evening. Even before the announcement, hostilities in the Crimea and Eastern Ukraine had ceased, and thousands of soldiers had handed in their weaponry, and many were heading home. It was a process that seemed to roll from the very nature of the change of thinking around the globe. The world had changed as the grandfather clock struck its hour.

"Mitya..."

"Da Valdis?"

"What have we been doing all these years? For what?"

"Aghhh Valdis, you and I are both very, very smart men. We both have known for a very long time that this was all about money and power and keeping all of that for ourselves and our friends."

"Da."

"But why did it keep going on? Why Mitya?"

"We had a small opportunity for success, my friend, we were ruthless, we were clever. We have eliminated many, many of our enemies and we have stayed resolute."

"It was madness Mitya."

"Da, Valdis. Complete and utter madness. We have held back the whole world, we have not made our country great, we have people addicted to useless substances all over the world in their millions, we have covert wars to sell arms that kill and maim thousands every day. But Valdis, we had money, fine clothes, fine lovers and houses that were warm in the dead of winter. We had people fawning on us. And yes, it was madness, and we are sad human beings and it's good to finally admit it."

"Da, Mitya. We have failed our very humanity, our very intelligence. Did you ever feel guilty for the other things we did my friend?"

"Valdis, always. Always. There was nothing to do however other than to enjoy the madness, the power, and to go along with what we were doing. It was like a festival of guilt and regret amidst a sea of glitter that couldn't be resisted. What about you?"

"No. I wanted every minute of this madness. I equated it with a world view of our people discriminated and destroyed in their millions for century after century. We had the brains and the muscle to infiltrate and subtly derail our enemies. For me, it was payback for our demise. A lifting of the yolk without giving up our fierceness. I know I was ruthless, cold, selfish. I see that now all too clearly. Such stupidity Mitya. Can you see all of the possibilities we missed to become a truly great nation among friends, and we blew it every single time? We moulded ourselves as enemies and ingrates. We were deeply foolish for our people, complete failures. A handful of people we benefited. Millions we made to suffer many years beyond what they needed to. Get the TV people in. It is time to talk to the world for the first time."

Outski put on a plain t-shirt and some jeans and sat down in front of the crew about to broadcast his message to the world.

"My fellow Russians, people of the world. Today is perhaps the most momentous day in the history of the world. I greet you tonight not as the President of Russia but as an ordinary citizen of the world working to dismantle all the mistakes of our past. It is with much joy, seeing you dancing in the streets of our cities that I come to you to resign my office, but much more to offer anything I can to help to understand where we have gone wrong and how we may rectify that.

"It is time to confess, despite my intention to simply advance the cause of my own nation that I have made countless selfish and stupid mistakes. As you are aware from 9 pm tonight, I received the signed departures of my Prime Minister and very good friend Mr Lomonosov and all the army and navy chiefs.

"In the morning the Kremlin will be opened to the best people from our lands and from across the entire globe to use its facilities to help to arrange the measures to take us through to our new governance. I have been on the phone tonight to my dear friend ex-President Baldwin, and he too has opened up his personal empire and the Pentagon to take us through this process. There will be over 400 Russians of the highest technological and enterprise skills leaving to work in the former territories of the United States tonight and another 1200 travelling worldwide to give the unique competencies that our people have to the processes of democratisation. Every Army and Navy personnel, and every Bureaucrat in the Kremlin without appropriate skills will be decommissioned in the morning and given a role in a more suitable area. This will occur in every regime in their equivalent institutions throughout the world as a priority. Our intelligence services have been terminated from their spying and surveillance roles and from an hour ago have been specifically working on facilitating the open communication lines that urgently need to be established to progress a world working together at last.

"All wages will be reset in the morning to reflect the skill set, entrepreneurial ability, technical knowledge and training performed along international norms. As an ex-President and depending on my future contributions to society, in general, I will be eligible for 2-2.5 times the basic wage, which I agree is very generous. It has been agreed that the maximum that anyone will earn in this country or any other will be five times the basic living global salary. It is expected that with improvements in productivity and elimination of trade and immigration barriers alone that the basic wage will be equivalent to $150,000 per annum within six months and much higher in the years to come.

"This is an exciting time for our land and our world. It is with shame and contrition that we put behind us the years of isolation, corruption, illegal activities across the globe. When I say I will be eligible for 2-2.5x the basic wage, this, of course, will be subject to not only the intelligence and organisational skills I can bring but also is dependent on the acceptance of my contrition for the deeds I have perpetrated in my previous roles. As head of the KGB, I was responsible for the silencing of more than 200 of my countrymen and more than 100 foreigners. Since becoming President, I have personally ordered the elimination of more than 40 people. I have placed more than 40000 people in prison purely to manipulate the political opposition. My government has illegally annexed the Crimea and been involved in countless destabilising military exercises to remove or antagonise our opponents' interests on almost every continent. I have banned memes that criticised me personally and French cheese.

"The short-sightedness, the brutality, the selfishness, the stupidity of all of this is now so very apparent to me and of course to you as well. The people of Russia, partly through your own innate dislike of change and the hankering for a golden age that in fact had never existed prompted many of our mistakes together. We have held ourselves back through our ultimate conservatism, our lack of natural justice, our lack of openness and our corruption. We can all see now where we have gone wrong, and I talk to you here and beg your forgiveness. Fear has been banished, and I beg you to accept me for the very flawed man that I am. One who is capable and strong but who now only wants to be a humble servant to the greater good of the entire world not just our ancient and tortured lands."

Lomonosov, at this point, wandered into the camera shot and embraced his old friend. Together they turned one further time to the people, excited looks upon their faces as if a world of pain had been lifted from them. They were handcuffed and lead away peaceably as the camera followed them out to the van. Their smiles did not abandon them and even at their trials in the Hague where their crimes were laid bare some month or so later their optimism remained.

The trial continued for less than four days as every crime, every admission, every corruption was well documented in the open paper and email trail that followed them. Every drug deal, every election manipulation, every war crime. Their sentence was two months in prison each, a reversion to basic wage entitlement only after release for a minimum of five years and a promise to add their considerable intellectual and organisational ability to the world's governing system. Already it was patent that the men were truly contrite and contributing positively to society. All agreed the punishment rational and forward-thinking and indeed the pair did contribute extensively to the formation of the governing systems in the very early days. They were not able to attend the inaugural council of world governance conferences but in their later years were experienced and brilliant contributors to the new world taking shape.

For Russia, everything changed. Vodka was still quite popular, but the rates of alcoholism, seasonal depression and cirrhosis dropped dramatically. The entire globe wanted to experience a Russian winter and Russians couldn't wait to experience the whole world. That certain accent and dress sense could be seen and experienced at Bondi Beach on a warm summer day or away helping with medical technology in South American rain forests. Many of the oligarchs did continue to thrive. They were rewarded with wages near four or even five times the basic global salary and despite having to give up all of their personal assets in the millions and even billions they were happy to see their children well educated but more so the children of all of their workers equally well educated in schools of quality both at home and abroad. They saw the specifics of where and how their assets were redistributed to quality programs in health, education and environmental protection. Much of the excess money found in Swiss Bank accounts were redistributed for investment in sustainable energy sources. The brilliance of the minds directing capital was only enhanced by the free availability of knowledge around inventions and production techniques. Rather than hoarding ideas and creating rules through their government to maintain a monopoly the goal was to create systems to export for the productivity benefit, safety and progress of the entire global community.

People loved to come to the lands that used to be called Russia. The native Russians were generous and warm. The cities were full of history and the words of the great Russian authors now echoed strongly in the hearts of those travelling those great plains, those marvellous cities and frozen mountain ranges. People would come intending to stay for a year to study and end up staying a decade such was the charm of this part of the world. Every church became a place of sacred learning, whilst the priestly garbs were abandoned. Each offering a portal for the study of meaning, leaving aside ritual for meditation and conversation.

The poorest of Russians now were often not the peasants of Siberia or the peoples of the Eastern provinces but rather the backpackers that came from Scandinavia and Oceania and the Celtic Isles to pick the fruits in the summer and to ski and wait tables in the winter. The face of Russia had changed entirely, and it was very much one that smiled with a joy that came from somewhere very deep, a heartfelt smile born from the release of ancient anxiety.

Chapter 19

Rio de Janeiro and Bangalore 3 months after I Day

The beach swam with activity. The sun bearing down upon children frolicking in the small waves at the water's edge. Hundreds of kids doggedly chasing and challenging the shore, screaming with delight and fright as every so often a larger white-topped turbulent body of water would swallow a dozen of them and then they would all madly dash back to get their feet solidly on the sand. Further out the body surfers and board riders soared through the incoming breakers. The water so clear, crystalline at the edge of the wave and you could see the colour and shape of their swimsuits before they survived a crest or got swallowed in the dumping wave. On the sand, it looked like there were a million smiling people, each below a red, purple, green or blue umbrella, clumped in groups by colour each controlled by the sand holders, the drink and snack providers, and the sunscreen sellers. The blue snacks said to be slightly better than the purple ones. The beer colder and more real, the limao cocktails more luscious. The taste of life was a little richer further up the beach. On the crazy patterned pavement, the people in their bikinis, t-shirts, and fancy clothes weaved upon and around each other in a swirl of dancing feet. There was music everywhere, and while no one was actually dancing if you took it all in, everyone was dancing.

In Bangalore, there was colour everywhere. Each street, every cow, every schoolchild, and building were ablaze with all the colours that could be imagined. From the first day when it was announced that

Rio and Bangalore were to be the sites of the first World Democratic Congress meetings, the Indian city had painted itself and secured every colourful Sari, scarf and hat to celebrate. The flower sellers were so busy distributing and arranging all the beautiful plants and flowers that had been sent from all over Southern Asia. Each street corner and windowsill were overflowing with growth and beauty. On the opening day of the Congress, balloons were filled and hung on the outside of every house, the dyes and paints of Holi applied to almost the entire population. There were smiles on everyone's faces as they took in the riot of fun and feelings of celebration that had taken over the city. The people knew how important this date and place was. Every rational and thoughtful energy of the entire world was applied to getting this right. To start this process in the very best way, with generosity, fun and attention to detail. Bangalore had risen to the occasion, and Rio lived and breathed joy as it had always done.

Amanda had decided to come to Rio. She had been chosen by her city, Carmel, and its hinterland and ultimately by what had been known as California to represent the people following a series of brilliant and practical ideas that she had proposed in the days following I Day. It became logical that if a single person's electronic proposal for major change became a democratically agreed-upon course of action in multiple and progressive steps, then that person deserved the right to go forward in person to discuss how that future integrated with the entire world. Amanda found herself at the forefront of many ideas and multiple progressions as lead proposer and she was to be honoured with the First Congress position. This was replicated all over the world as communities recognised each other, responded to needs and found the champion ideas and the champions who could take them forward. Once selected they could choose Rio or Bangalore, and such was the enthusiasm and grace and fire that Bangalore had produced that the numbers to each city were about the same. Some of the simplest ideas led to the most complex final answers, and it took courage, foresight, and determination to see an idea through. In every media that was available ideas were expressed and debated, projected, costed, weighed and understood ethically. So often it was the gentle, considered, and loving voice that finally won through. A personality that could bring to bear fruits for others, that created notions that people became excited and passionate about. For Amanda, by the time she had thought through and then articulated her ideas almost immediately she was encouraged and hailed to press on and come up with more detailed and radical plans that would not only positively change her part of what was America but the entire world. She never faltered in believing that she could add in meaningful ways to progress and that is what drove her. A brain that refused to rest upon its laurels, a mind bent to solving the most basic of human problems. There was just so much to do, so many horrid, backward, selfish, and wasteful practices had been tolerated. Amanda was all about identifying the worst of these and finding the easiest and most practical way forward with them.

She never expected the passion she would find in Rio.

Amanda sat in the sun-soaked semi-enclosed plaza on the edge of the Atlantic and looked out across the blues of the sky and the ocean. She'd been participating in the 4th round plebiscites for her proposals to eliminate plastic production around the world within the following six months and was intensely researching her fellow champions' thought processes and plans. Somehow, in these moments, she frequently was able to come up with the synthesis of all of the best ways forward. Her ideas and propositions were often adopted; this was why she was in Rio as a champion of ideas which would dramatically be able to change the world in the most efficient and productive way. Amanda always considered the wider implications of her ideas, and it was very difficult to find fault in her thinking and her way forward. She loved the democracy that she was now such an important part of and finally felt that her years of study in environment, philosophy, and psychology were being utilised to the best of her abilities. She was relaxed and radiant, and the waiters were especially attendant because she was so attractive in almost every way. Her physical beauty, her personal charm, her very demeanour.

And then the massive seagull struck.

Amanda wasn't aware at first what had hit her with such surprise and ferocity as she felt her chair lurch backwards and she almost fell onto the pavement. Somehow, as she was falling, she was cushioned and lifted up by some magical force. As she righted herself and turned around, she found herself for more than a moment or two staring into the eyes of a man of such style and composure that it took her a good while to focus on his bemusing smile and to hear him introduce himself.

"That was some kind of hungry seagull, Bella. My name is Giovanni."

"Thank you, kind sir, I believe you saved me from a cracked skull. I'm Amanda"

Amanda found herself blushing as she took her enormous sunglasses off for a better look at this remarkable lifesaver. As she removed them, the look on Giovanni's face transformed as he took in the whole of her face as if he had seen a ghost or an angel.

"Do I know you?" she asked.

"Bella Amanda, I think you do from now." He said in his soft, serene Italian accent.

"May I join you for a cappuccino?"

Amanda simply said yes with her eyes and Giovanni swung his chair around, and before long they both knew that something quite remarkable had happened between them.

Gholam wandered the streets of the Indian city his eyes full of wonderment at the tall modern buildings and raised highways and sleek railways. The colours of Bangalore filled his heart and reminded him of the kites he knew from his hometown of Kabul. The swooping, dancing, flirting, fighting kites of his entire childhood. The colours reverberated in his mind and made him contemplate how far he had come in such a short time. He was genuinely excited about the peace that he had finally witnessed at home and couldn't wait to begin the process of letting the world know exactly what Afghanistan could teach them and of course to acquire the means and help his country needed now to rebuild. He was such an avid reader that the act of walking down the streets of a modern city translated into a thousand processes and permutations of the way he understood the world. Gholam saw beyond and this was his gift. He yearned for the brighter future for which he had unique abilities to envision and facilitate.

He imagined, as he walked past a thousand shrines and temples of every old religion, how they might look in a world without religion or distinction by country or ethnicity. These principles had been established earlier in the democratic process, but there was much debate about what was to become of houses of religion and belief systems. Gholam had spent his childhood, youth and early adulthood seeing the destructive forces of these three elements in disrupting his own life and family. Death, maiming, and terror had struck almost every part of his broader family and friends. Gholam led the gentler side of the debate and was gaining worldwide acceptance for his ideas particularly about the meticulous preservation of the houses of worship and how they should be used for the most in-depth and scientific and logical analysis of the history and meaning of spirituality. Others argued that these places needed to be abandoned and forgotten. Gholam needed to convince the world of exactly why these places were perfect for exploring knowledge at the same time being open to the spirit. How could he do it? And then he realised. He smelled the insane scent of a million flowers overflowing from the windowsills and pavements of the street. He recalled the stories of the people walking back into their homes in Syria just a few weeks ago with their white flowers in hand, and he had an idea.

Before too long Amanda and Giovanni found themselves walking the fascinating little streets of Rio, their bare arms touching as they laughed and came to know each other's stories. Amanda had never done this before in her life, but she found her hand in Giovanni's shortly after they stopped for another coffee in a quaint cafe on a cobblestoned street a few blocks away from the beach. Their hands never left each other's for the rest of the day, and it was the most natural act of love that either of them had ever experienced before. Somehow, they both knew that not only was there a strong physical attraction between them but that their hearts and minds seemed to be made for each other way before they had met. For hours, they wandered, up steep bustling streets and into the vast jungle-like parklands. Every pause in their happy conversation was disrupted by a wide smile or spontaneous laughter that had people around them turning to watch them. The observers in their turn would invariably smile at the wandering couple who had eyes only for each other and so oblivious to the world about them.

"Amanda, I think I have had the happiest day of my life so far today. I have fallen in love with a seagull."

"A seagull? pfffft. You have clearly fallen in love with me."

"Amanda, if it wasn't for that silly, crazy bird we would not have met. I love that bird."

"If you insist Giovanni, I think I need a wine, what do you suggest?"

"Let us go to the heavens. I know just the place."

After another half hour of walking they came to the base of their ride, the Trem do Corcovado, and Giovanni produced two tickets for 4:30 pm and showed them to Amanda.

"What? You have to line up for an hour to get that. Who were you going to go with?"

"It seems I was always going with you."

"I don't believe you, but I must. Let's go."

On the tram, as they looked out on glimpses of the city below and the dense vegetation crowding the carriage, they spoke of their childhood and what their dreams were. Giovanni was studying architecture and had always imagined designing a building that would be forever remembered. Amanda spoke of her vision, as the child of two University Professors, of escaping all modes of conventional thinking, yet she lived a conventional life. Her parents had taught her the value of lateral thinking, and she applied it in almost every situation. For the first time in her life, Amanda had found herself carried away by a day where she had little say in the narrative. She was living a dream with a gorgeous, sensitive and handsome man. As they reached the summit and climbed the stairs, they briefly took in the enormity of the stone edifice. Arms splayed in an embrace of the whole of the fabulous city below them, probably of the whole of the world. It was time to take a seat, and they found a spot out of the wind and in the sun where they ordered a bottle of pinot grigio and a bucket of prawns. The two of them took in a view of a city that was begging to be part of their romance.

When they found themselves drunk in love back at Amanda's apartment opposite Ipanema Beach, Giovanni wrapped his arms around her as they took in the twilight from the balcony. Hundreds of people walked along the pavement below them in a blur of activity but Amanda was consumed by passion and desire for this particular stranger. Her body melted at his touch as she slowly turned to face him and kissed him with wanton abandonment. She could feel the heat of his chest and pelvis and whispered to him that this was her first time.

He didn't stop kissing her neck, but rather her confession accelerated his evident desire to have her for himself. Handed over, lost to passion, enmeshed in a desire that was unstoppable on both sides. They literally tore each other's clothes off, and he worshipped her from toes to forehead and front to back with his lips and hands. Amanda opened herself to every feeling and every touch offering herself up selflessly and generously. She was an incendiary lover and had always known it, and she and he became as one in mind and body. When he entered her, gently and slowly, their eyes were locked on each other and then they warmed somehow even more furiously to climax after climax. Amanda became more and more adventurous as the night wore on. Demanding of Giovanni his eyes, his body, his mind. She was not spent until early into the morning. They slept deeply until the late morning sun and the bustle outside finally woke them.

There was no lovemaking in the morning. Something clicked in Amanda's mind, and she refocussed on her tasks in Rio and contemplated the day before, which was one of the more extraordinary of her life. As she woke and saw Giovanni by her side in the morning light, she knew that he would be but a fond and strange memory. He rolled over and gazed into her eyes, but she hopped out of bed and offered to make him a cup of coffee and some toast. He was struck by her form as she walked out of the room and a little surprised, she wasn't in his arms. When she returned with his coffee, he beamed at her, and she touched him gently on the back of his head and brought him to her chest. She put her other arm around his back and enveloped him, and they stayed that way for two or three minutes until Amanda sprung up and had her coffee on the balcony. Giovanni rolled over and went back to sleep, he felt he was falling in love.

When he awoke, Amanda suggested they have lunch back where they had met on the beachside plaza, and there they laughed about the seagull and their crazy day together. The weather was hot, and the wind still, the water called them.

In Bangalore, Gholam plotted his presentation. So many of the children of Bangalore were excited to be participating in the first Democratic Congress and were keen to be addressed by this charismatic, handsome stranger from Afghanistan. All he wanted from them was to collect from the streets, from the vendors and the people a half dozen white flowers of every kind that they could find. The following day they were to place a single flower on the seat of every delegate and hand all the observers a flower as they came through into the Congress Hall. 700 children immediately felt the sincerity and meaning behind this gesture, and after receiving some further instructions, they dispersed and headed enthusiastically to their task.

The two of them walked and walked along the shoreline, occasionally holding hands with Amanda invariably dropping Giovanni's grip and dancing into the small waves of the long golden beach. Amanda was acutely aware that this evening was the first time she would be presenting to the Congress in Rio and while these last two days had been quite the distraction she knew exactly where she would be taking her thoughts and ideas to the world at large. She found it odd that Giovanni really had nothing to say about her ideas and seemed to be focussed entirely on the moment, which she found attractive in its own way as well. Emotionally, however, she drifted and drifted away from him as they walked and talked.

They came to a high rocky outcrop at the end of the beach and sat together looking at the surfers taking their rides to within a few metres of the cliff face below them. Giovanni turned to Amanda, gave her a kiss on the cheek, stood up and dived straight over the cliff in front of them. It was a graceful, arms wide then forward dive toward the blue, blue sea. Amanda saw his feet trail his upper body in a blur as she scrambled quickly to the edge. And then she just saw the sea, waves smashing against the rocks below and no sign of Giovanni. She screamed in panicked horror, ran to the beach and to the first group of people she could find. None of them spoke English, but they could see she was distressed and some of them ran with her to the lifeguards that were about 100 metres further along the beach.

Very quickly, people understood what had happened.

A large crowd gathered on the cliff top as the rescue craft and lifeguards came to the place where Giovanni had dived. There were small and large craft gathered up and along the entire headland. Jet skis, sailing craft and rowboats were trying to help the lifesavers and scoured every inlet and right along the shores of the beach close to the rocks. The activity, shouting and movement were at once alarming and reassuring that something was being done. Amanda was hysterical with anxiety and panic with the vision of his last words to her and his graceful dive playing over and over in her mind. The surfers had abandoned their quest for the perfect wave and were sitting bolt upright on their boards looking about the area close to the shore. And there were no signs of Giovanni. Amanda spent over an hour with the police going over everything she knew about him and exactly what happened. As the hours dragged on, there were fewer and fewer people watching from the cliff top and less rescue craft and onlookers on the water before them. Amanda suddenly was left at dusk near to alone, bewildered and grief-stricken. She was due to go to the preliminary session of the congress that very night. She made it back to her apartment and sobbed looking out toward the sea.

Somehow Gholam had inspired the children of Bangalore to find enough white flowers to bedeck the congress hall lobby with enough beauty to stun every single delegate that came through the doors of the Conference Centre. And when they entered the Congress Hall, the scent of the flowers was overwhelmingly lovely. On every seat was a single white flower, and on the screens surrounding the Hall, on every wall were video replays from over 15 smartphones of the very moment when a Syrian motorbike rider encountered the young girl who gave him the white flower on his way to love and on her way to home. Somehow, this moment had been captured from every angle, and the faces of those about the pair lighting up were as beautiful as the words between the two that were said.

The delegates streamed in and were mesmerised by the scent and the vision. It was impossible not to wonder how this had been organised and by whom. It didn't take long for people to realise it was the quiet, respectable, funny and handsome man from Afghanistan with the outrageous curls. He would be a voice; there was no doubt.

Even Gholam didn't quite grasp what he had done. As half the screens in the hall switched to the Congress opening in Rio, he was met with an almost identical decor in the Rio Congress. There were white flowers upon every registration desk, on every wall and every seat. One of the children organisers came up to Gholam and whispered in his ear.

"Sir, we thought it would be good if we could follow through with your ideas in Rio as well, so we communicated with the group of children that were supporting the meeting there and they thought it was a great idea. It looks like everybody agrees. We love you sir."

Gholam was overwhelmed and took his seat in the Congress and watched the reactions of the people from all over the world to the events unfolding in these two continents. There were cameras everywhere capturing people's reactions and thoughts and wishing the delegates well. Gholam was very impressed with the video editing and sound as meaningful snippets and sights came through into the Hall. Somehow despite the cacophony of screens and images, it all made sense.

Amanda was exhausted. Emotionally, physically and spiritually exhausted. She sat on the balcony, legs up against the rail listening to some of her favourite songs and wondering what on earth had just happened. She had spoken with her sister and mother and had got her breath back. Finally, she took a deep breath, quickly put some casual clothes on and headed downstairs and hailed a cab. She knew that the conference had already started, but she could not help feeling absolutely drawn to this moment in history. She imagined walking to her seat in the Congress Hall and being over an hour late for the commencement, and she would be embarrassed, but it felt right that she should be there.

The entire world watched as Amanda entered the Congress Lobby and into the main hall. They could see her reddened eyes and scattered makeup, and yet everyone fell in love with her. There was something about her. A grace that could not be missed. She wondered as she walked down the main corridor of the hall why there was so much quiet about the place. She could smell the delicious fragrance of the flowers, and she knew that her place was quite close to the front and to the left. As she turned into her row, the entire Congress stood up and looked at her. She made her way to her seat which was entirely covered with white flowers and hundreds of notes of friendship and condolence. There was a movement in the crowd about her and people began coming up to her and hugging her. Initially, just a few, and then scores of people were there to greet and comfort her. Amanda was overwhelmed by the powerful message of love that she was receiving. She sat down and began her journey of ideas.

Gholam, of course, fell in love with the beautiful redheaded woman that he saw on the screens about him in Bangalore and imagined and maybe even knew that one day their connection would mean everything to both of them.

ACKNOWLEDGEMENTS and Bio

Sincere thanks go to the many friends and family that have helped me to bounce ideas around the world of John Lennon's wonderful song. To the man who wrote the song that has inspired many people to rethink their world I owe tremendous gratitude. I acknowledge that there has been no endorsement from John's family but I would welcome their comments at any time and my purpose was to simply honour his message in this book. To my industrious and brilliant beta readers Tim, Saadia, Amanda, Cath, Johanna, David, Laura and my superb editor Katherine Jones I owe many, many thanks. For help with proof reading I would like to acknowledge my grammatically wonderful father John Harris and also Louise Johnson who further contributed with her amazing Imagine artwork on the back cover.

Richard Harris is a Vascular Surgeon who loves words and has always written. He is richharris2 on twitter and has been amusing himself there for years. Richard set out to write two novels together about 4 years ago and this is the first. The second is a historical romance and will be available when Richard finds time and a small cottage by the sea to finish this lovely and tragic tale. He hopes you will enjoy Imagine and that it sparks a few thoughts.

www.ingramcontent.com/pod-product-compliance
Lightning Source LLC
Chambersburg PA
CBHW060558310726
48982CB00008B/1164/J
9780645079616